# ORPHAN TRAIN DISASTER

RACHEL WESSON

*To all the victims of the Triangle Shirtwaist Factory Fire. Those who died in the disaster, those who were injured and those who lost loved ones.*
*Many lost the sole means of support for their families which in turn led to orphaned children, both in America and abroad, having to find new homes and lives. May they never be forgotten.*

# CHAPTER 1

$\mathcal{F}$rieda Klunsberg walked through the hospital, rubbing her hands on the side of her skirt. Her heart fluttered as she grew closer to the office door. Was this about her application to the Obstetrics department? She had spent ages preparing the written document, even asking Lilian Wald, the nurse famous for setting up the Henry Street Settlement House, for a reference. Knocking, she waited for the command to enter. Nothing happened. She pushed the door open but Miss Waters, Dr. Guild's secretary, wasn't at her desk. The door to Dr. Guild's office was closed.

Frieda stood waiting, checking the clock as she did so. Dr. Guild didn't tolerate lateness; he didn't care if a patient seized just as you were about to leave for a meeting. She paced a little, wondering if she should knock on his office door. Where was Miss Waters?

Frieda waited, watching the minute hand on the clock as it ticked past eleven. She was now officially late. She moved closer to the door and knocked, jumping back as if it would attack her.

"Come."

Frieda opened the door.

"At last, Miss Klunsberg." Dr. Guild stared at the clock on his desk before looking back at his papers. He didn't suggest she take a seat, so Frieda stood waiting.

"Miss Waters, that's all for now, thank you. Perhaps you would close the door on your way out?"

"Yes, Doctor." Miss Waters didn't acknowledge Frieda as she walked past her and closed the door. The elderly secretary didn't approve of female doctors and never missed a chance to show it.

Dr. Guild shuffled some papers on his desk, leaving Frieda to stare at him for a few minutes. Had he forgotten she was here? She coughed, but he didn't react. Dr. Guild had a reputation for good reason. He was rude, intimidating, but he was also the most powerful doctor in the hospital. She had to remain polite.

"You asked to see me, Dr. Guild?"

"I can imagine you know why. Your latest test results are, shall we say, less than impressive. When I gave you the chance to study at this hospital, I made it clear it was on condition you keep up with your peers."

Frieda bit her lip, trying to stay silent. She'd passed

the exam but hadn't attained as high a grade as on previous papers. She had done better than some male students. They hadn't had a call to see Dr. Guild. He glanced up at her as if waiting for an explanation.

"I passed the exam, Dr. Guild. I spent a lot of additional hours getting practical experience, and it may have impacted the marks I achieved. It won't happen again."

"Excuses carry little weight with me, Miss Klunsberg. I believe the exam results prove that while you have some level of intelligence -- "

He ignored Frieda's gasp of outrage.

"You don't have the level of intelligence required to become a doctor. If women and men were equal, they would both have the right to vote."

Frieda opened her mouth, but he kept talking.

"I recommend you take some time off to reconsider your career choice, Miss Klunsberg. The field of medicine requires the highest standard, especially in Obstetrics. Women aren't suitable to be doctors."

Women got pregnant and had babies, most would prefer a female doctor look after them, but she didn't say this.

"Perhaps you might train as a midwife?" he added as he picked up a piece of correspondence and read it. "I certainly cannot make a recommendation you join the Obstetrics team, even as a student."

Frieda stood, staring. How dare he dismiss her just

like that? After all the extra hours she had put into the hospital, besides her home visits and extra duties.

"Dr. Guild, excuse me, but may I say something?"

"I doubt it has any relevance to my decision."

Frieda forged ahead. "You may not be aware, but I have spent a lot of time with Lillian Wald, working with her in her clinic. I believe this experience will help me in my chosen field. Miss Wald has given me a glowing reference."

She knew she was taking a risk. Not all doctors believed in the work Lillian Wald was doing, but the results spoke for themselves.

"Wald is a good example for you, Miss Klunsberg."

For the first time since she'd walked into his domain, her hopes rose.

"SHE MADE the correct decision to give up becoming a doctor. She quit medical school back before the turn of the century. I believe she serves some purpose as a nurse."

FRIEDA HAD to fight to keep her temper in check. To hear Lilian's achievements dismissed so casually after everything the woman had done for the poor of New York. "Excuse me for saying so, Dr. Guild, but many believe Lilian has made significant progress. For example, the Metropolitan Life Insurance company now offers a nursing service to all its policyholders."

Dr. Guild held her gaze. "Perhaps she can find you a job as a nurse."

Frieda scrunched her hands into fists. This wasn't fair.

"With respect, Dr. Guild, I don't wish to be a nurse or a midwife. I intend to qualify as a doctor. I may not have scored as high as some on the last test, but I was far from the bottom of my class."

He yawned as she spoke. She wasn't getting anywhere. What did Lily say all the time, you catch more flies with honey than vinegar? She forced herself to act more demure, as she supposed he expected women to be.

"Dr. Guild, may I please ask you something else?"

At her request, his eyes widened. At least she had surprised him.

"Will you stop me from qualifying as a doctor?"

He stared at her. She returned his gaze, noticing the patch of red spreading up his neck. She wasn't the only one struggling to contain her temper. At least she'd rattled him as much as he'd annoyed her.

"Miss Klunsberg, are you suggesting I will interfere with your exam results?"

"No, of course not." As if I would put that accusation into words, you old goat. "I just wanted confirmation that I can continue working at this hospital until I qualify."

"As a doctor? I made that commitment to Dr. Green. But you won't be joining the Obstetrics department. They have sufficient students at present."

Her nails hurt her palms. If she didn't get experience in Obstetrics, how would she qualify, never mind get a job, in that department?

She waited for him to finish.

"After you qualify, we will review the matter. We don't have any openings in a suitable department at the moment. That may change."

Not for her it wouldn't, but she'd deal with that in time.

"Thank you very much for being so direct, Dr. Guild, and for your time. Have a good day."

She turned and walked out the door, keeping her shoulders straight as she felt his gaze. Only once the door had closed did she let them slump. Why did it have to be so hard for a woman to become a doctor? Some of her male peers had scored lower than her in every exam, yet they had guaranteed positions once they qualified.

"Are you feeling ill, Miss Klunsberg?" Miss Waters asked as Frieda, lost in thought, forgot she was standing in the office.

"Not at all, Miss Waters. Just reviewing the excellent career recommendations Dr. Guild suggested. Thank you for your concern." You old bat, she muttered under her breath, but the woman didn't hear her.

# CHAPTER 2

*F*rieda rushed to the closest ladies' room. She didn't want any of her colleagues to see her cry. She was used to struggling to achieve her dreams, but the unfairness of Dr. Guild's attitude was too much. She realized no matter how hard she studied to get the highest grades possible, it would make no difference to her future. Not at this hospital, at least not while Dr. Guild was in charge. Why couldn't more doctors be like Richard Green? She thought having a man of his caliber on her side would be enough.

She stared at her reflection, a few drops of water wouldn't cure her red swollen eyes. She couldn't go back on the wards like this. She washed her face, thankful she'd planned for someone else to cover her afternoon shift. She hoped Dr. Guild had asked to see her to deliver the good news in person, that he'd approved her transfer. She wanted Lilian to be the first to know as she'd gone to so much trouble helping her find relevant experience. How stupid she'd been to think it would work out for her. She'd promised Lilian more help when she moved to Obstetrics, but now she'd have to go back on her word. Frieda wanted to kick or slap something in frustration. She needed to leave the hospital for fear of running into Dr. Guild or one of his cronies. She wasn't sure she'd be able to keep her feelings to herself.

She walked out the main door of the hospital meeting no one she knew. She kept walking, just as fast as her skirt would allow her. That was another thing. Why couldn't she wear pants? Whoever had invented skirts wider at the waist than the ankle didn't think women had to walk far.

Frieda wandered around Fifth Avenue, gazing at the store windows. She watched the women going shopping, hobbling along in their high heels, their legs constricted by narrow ankle-length skirts. She wondered if she should get her hair cut short like these women wore, it would be practical for work, but she wasn't buying a large hat no matter how fashionable they were.

Were these women happy with their lives? They didn't have the vote, couldn't decide for themselves how their life would work out, but they had plenty of money to spend on clothes and food and they lived in the best houses. Was that enough? Could she be happy living a life like that? Patrick would be wealthy one day. What was she doing thinking of him? He'd made his feelings clear. What had he said? She was like a member of the family.

She took a streetcar towards Henry Street, staring out the window at the streets and people. It was like stepping from one world into another. The almost care-free atmosphere on Fifth Avenue gave way to one with an underlying theme of desperation. Street hawkers did their best to outshout each other, highlighting the advantages of their stall.

Skinny kids dodged in and out of the horse bound carts. She thought the streetcar would hit them but at the last minute; they jumped out of the way. They were used to them. As she neared her destination, she got out to walk. Few automobiles took this route. Crowded streets filled with decades old tenements, washing lines full of clothes slung between balconies. She admired the women who lived here. They tried to clean their dwellings but no matter how well you washed the sheets, hanging them in a dirty space would not let them dry clean.

She was tempted to head home to the Sanctuary. There she could put her head on her pillow and wallow in her misery. But she'd promised to visit with Lilian. She owed her a report on her interview with Dr. Guild, especially after the glowing reference the lady had written for her.

Arriving on the Henry Street steps, she heard different people calling out her name in greeting. Some children ran up to give her a cuddle. She greeted the mothers who'd come for lessons on nutrition and cleanliness. Lilian understood more than most just how difficult it was to keep a tenement home clean. She gave practical help to these women, providing them with soap and other items. But even Lilian couldn't do anything about the dirty air.

"Frieda, what are you doing here so early? Or am I late?" Lilian looked up. The baby she was measuring was squalling, his little arms and legs kicking out in protest.

"He's got a decent set of lungs." Frieda commented as she took the baby in her arms. She never tired of holding babies. Lilian looked relieved. "Frieda, thank goodness. I can't speak German, and this lady doesn't understand English. Can you please tell her to stop feeding the baby sugared water?"

Frieda turned to the weary young mother and translated what Lilian had said. She barely needed to translate the mother's reply. The tone of her voice together with the movement of her arms and her facial expression told Lilian of her frustration.

"I know finding money for food is difficult, but it's imperative babies are breastfeed where possible or fed decent clean milk. Tell her to come back daily until he settles better. Otherwise, she will bury another child."

Frieda gaped at Lilian.

"Go on, tell her. She's buried two children already."

"But she only looks about fifteen."

"Married before she got on board the ship, brought two children with her on the boat. Both dead now. The one in her arms, she was pregnant with. Husband has disappeared."

Although Lillian rattled off the woman's life story, Frieda knew the nurse cared deeply for those in her care. She worked tirelessly for the poor not just here in Henry Street, but through her work with the government and whatever agencies would listen to her. She repeated Lilian's message to the mother who held her child to her breast, tears of rage and frustration flowing down her cheeks. Frieda wanted to offer the young woman hope, but she couldn't. She felt ashamed of how envious she had felt earlier when watching the women on Fifth Avenue. Frieda knew compared to this poor, unfortunate soul she was rich in every way that mattered.

The young mother left. Lilian gestured for Frieda to take a seat. "We've a few minutes before the next rush. So what's with the glum face? You look like you lost a twenty and found a penny."

Frieda looked over Lilian's head, squeezing her eyes shut to stop the tears. She had so much already. So what

13

if she couldn't stay at the hospital? If she qualified, she could find a job somewhere else.

"Frieda, what's wrong? I can't help if you don't tell me."

"I had my interview with Dr. Guild. Not only is he not transferring me to Obstetrics, but he believes I should reconsider my chosen career. He suggested I become a nurse or a midwife."

"Because you are female?"

"He believes Congress had the right idea in not allowing women the vote. We aren't as intelligent as men."

Lilian shook her head. "Stubborn old fool. He hasn't changed a bit in all these years."

"You know him?"

"Yes, I know Guild. He was one of my peers in medical school. Didn't tell you that, did he? He was just as stupid as he seems to be now. Had to retake several exams if memory serves me."

"How did he get to be in charge of the hospital then?"

"Money, my dear Frieda. His family comes from money, made it rich during the War, producing cannons and ammunition for the North. Not that they would admit that now. His mother liked to pretend they're descended from English royalty, her family having come from across the seas. The eldest brother inherited most of the family steel holdings, so Guild became a

14

doctor. Married an only child from a rich banking family."

Lilian made Frieda a coffee. "You can't let Guild or those like him put you off, Frieda. You were born to be a doctor."

"He suggested I follow your profession."

"He would. He believes nurses are little more than skivvies to run around after the doctors. Many share that view, but I'll change it, one person at a time. I aim to educate New York and the whole of this country on the benefits of employing nurses as professionals."

"I think you have achieved a lot already, Lilian."

"What I have or haven't achieved is neither here nor there. What will you do?" Lilian pierced her with a look.

"He's agreed to let me stay in the hospital until I qualify. But there aren't any suitable positions available for me at the hospital."

"That's their loss. So why do you look so stricken? It's not the news you wanted, but you can still qualify. Can't you?"

"I don't know how much impact not having experience in Obstetrics will hinder my qualification. How can I work with pregnant women without experience?"

"You can gain experience at any of the hospitals."

"They won't be willing to take me on without practical training experience, will they? It's hard enough to get them to accept a female doctor."

"Now Frieda, if life was easy it wouldn't be worth living would it? You need to dust yourself down, my dear, and get back in the fight. Until all men and women agree to equality between our sexes, the fight will never end."

Frieda didn't have the energy to agree or disagree. She was sick of fighting against the world. She was too tired.

"Go home, Frieda, and get some rest. You've been working too hard, here and at the hospital on top of your studying. Take some time to yourself. There is always another route to achieving your goals. You are not without friends, and I know they, like me, will do everything we can to help you achieve your dream. You were born to be a doctor, Frieda. Don't let anyone, especially that puffed up, self-important old goose, steal it away from you."

Frieda couldn't answer, her throat swollen with tears. She was lucky. She had the best friends in the entire world.

## CHAPTER 3

rieda did as Lilian suggested, and went home to rest and recover her fighting spirit. She opened the front door quietly, and escaped to her bedroom, meeting no one. There she had a little cry in private.

"Frieda, are you up there? Patrick came to visit."

Frieda heard Kathleen calling her and sat up. What was Patrick doing here? It was dark outside. How long had she been sleeping?

She'd fallen asleep fully clothed. Glancing in the mirror, she groaned. She looked a mess.

"Coming!" she shouted back as she pulled off her dress, changing into one that looked a little better. It could do with an iron, but she didn't have the luxury of time. She ran a brush through her hair and decided she would get it cut off. It was time to be more practical.

17

Picking up the shirt of her dress to free her ankles, she ran down the stairs, pausing on the last landing to slow her pace. She didn't want to look too eager to see him. She heard him laughing; he was in the sitting room with his mother. She could hear other voices, too, but couldn't tell who it was.

Pushing the door open, she walked inside and almost collided with Patrick.

"Frieda, I was worried when I found you'd left the hospital early. Are you feeling alright?"

"Fine, thank you. Evening everyone." Frieda glanced around, only spotting Richard Green as she did so. "Dr. Green, sorry I didn't expect you to be here."

"I met Guild. I figured he'd upset you. I thought we could come and offer a show of support."

"Why would he upset Frieda? What haven't you told me, Dad?" Patrick asked, but his gaze never left Frieda's face.

"Not my place to say anything, Patrick."

Frieda heard the slight note of censure in Dr. Green's voice. He rarely corrected anyone publicly. She looked up to find Kathleen staring at her, her eyes lit up with concern.

"Frieda, do you feel up to talking about what happened?" Dr. Green asked.

"Nothing much to say, really. Dr. Guild doesn't believe I have what it takes to be a doctor, nothing will change his mind, and he suggested I take a leaf out of Lilian's book and become a nurse."

Patrick turned on his father, "I thought you said the hospital had guaranteed Frieda would qualify as a doctor so long as she passed her exams. She kept her end of the bargain so why aren't they?"

Frieda quickly intervened, although it was nice to hear Patrick's support. "Patrick, it's not your dad's fault. He's done nothing but try to help me."

"It might be partially my fault, Frieda. Dr. Guild is no fan of mine and he may take his feelings out on you. I'm sorry if that's the case."

"Never be sorry, Dr. Green. You, Kathleen, and Lily helped me achieve more than I ever dreamed possible. I wouldn't be even partially qualified if not for you. I would be a seamstress working in a sweatshop some-where. Or married with five children."

"You want five children?" Patrick blurted out, as his cheeks burned crimson.

Frieda wished the ground would open under her feet as she stared at Patrick. Kathleen broke the awkward silence.

"Frieda, my poor girl. What a day you've had. Why didn't you come and find me? Lily has been home all day with a cold, but I've been here since lunch. I just assumed you were at the hospital or with Lilian."

"I went to see Lilian to tell her." At the hurt look on Kathleen's face, Frieda hurried to explain. "Lilian helped me get some experience in Obstetrics. I think she bullied some friends of hers to let me watch them as they assisted women give birth, including in one case, by section. She also wrote a long reference to support my application. So I felt obliged to tell her. She thought, and I agreed, I could help the Henry Street Clinic even more when I had some experience in Obstetrics."

"Guild is a silly old -- "

"Richard!" Kathleen intervened quickly.

"Pompous fool," Richard finished. "I will speak to the board. This is far from being over."

"Please don't do that. Dr. Guild is a formidable enemy, and I know you need more funding for your work in the burns unit. Dr. Green --"

"I wish you would call me Richard, Frieda. At least outside the hospital."

"Richard," Freida smiled, "I really do appreciate everything you've done, but Dr. Guild is a lost cause. Even if we got him to overturn his decision, which is doubtful, he will make me pay. He could also stand in the way of your funding requests, or make life difficult for Patrick. That's not a risk I'm willing to take."

Patrick protested, "I can fight my own battles, Frieda."

"Son, this is not about you." Richard turned his attention back to Frieda. "So what are your plans?"

"First, I need to find out if I can qualify without spending time in the Obstetrics ward. If I can't, then I need experience in another hospital. I could do that on a volunteer basis, perhaps."

Looking pensive, Richard said, "Good idea. Lilian and I have, between us, plenty of friends in the field. We should be able to help you."

"Frieda, you are following a well tread path." Kathleen added, "Just the other day I was reading about Elizabeth Garrett Anderson, an English doctor. She was so determined to become a doctor, she studied French and qualified in Paris. She then returned to England where she has set up a women's hospital in London. I believe she still works there. She appointed our own Elizabeth Blackwell, God rest her soul, as Professor of Gynecology. Those two women and others in their field are inspirational. Things may not have changed enough, but they have improved since they first wanted to become doctors. At least you don't have to leave your home or set up your own hospital."

"Although moving to London to work with Dr. Blackwell could be fun," Patrick suggested, making his parents laugh. Frieda wondered what he meant. Was it a hint for her to consider a future abroad?

Richard changed the subject, "Frieda, are you hungry? I'm starving and I would like to treat my family to a meal."

She felt Patrick looking at her. Family, that's what he thought she was too. Despite being ravenous, she shook her head. "Thank you, Richard but I ate earlier. I'm exhausted and am on shift later."

"Please, Frieda, come with us. It's been ages since we went out as a family."

Patrick's words increased the pain in her heart. "No, but thank you."

Kathleen stepped forward, kissing her on the cheek. "Sleep well, darling; tomorrow will be better. Just wait until Lily hears about this. She's bound to have an opinion or two."

Everyone laughed before Frieda gratefully made her escape.

# CHAPTER 4

Freida walked into the hospital canteen the following Monday morning to grab a coffee. She yawned as the busy night on the wards caught up with her. When she pushed the door open, she could have groaned out loud. It was too late to close it as she'd been seen by a number of her fellow medical students.

She forced a smile when Martin Caldwell was the first to acknowledge her. He normally pretended she didn't exist.

"Morning, Frieda, we were partying at my place yesterday. Drank too much of the old man's champagne. We need some fine doctoring this morning, don't we?" He looked at his friends, some of them laughed but some, she noticed, had the grace to look uncomfortable. "We all have serious headaches."

"Plenty of water and some aspirin will cure you." Frieda responded, trying to keep the smile fixed in place.

"Aren't you going to ask what we're celebrating?"

Frieda waited for him to elaborate. She knew he was baiting her, but she refused to give him the satisfaction of playing his stupid games.

"Got confirmation of our positions, assuming we pass our finals. Isn't that something?"

"Yes, it certainly is. Congratulations." She moved away from the group, toward the kettle, but he couldn't let her go.

"Did you get the position you wanted? Baby ward, wasn't it?"

She heard the door shut behind her but didn't turn. What should she say to Caldwell?

"Frieda has another project lined up but I won't bore you with the details, Caldwell. Dr. Guild has been looking for you since seven."

She turned at the sound of Patrick's voice. Caldwell paled, knocked back the coffee and ran. His friends soon dispersed, leaving Frieda alone with Patrick. He moved closer to her, his lovely eyes lit up with pleasure as he looked at her.

"Don't mind that idiot. He'll do well to pass his exams with the grades he's been achieving lately." He smiled at her, causing her stomach to do a funny flip. The back of her neck grew hot. She didn't look him in the eyes, not wanting him to see how his presence affected her.

"Why did you do that?" she demanded, angry with him but not knowing why.

"What?" he sounded genuinely confused.

"Interfere like that. Don't you think it's bad enough that they all believe I'm only here because of your father, and now you are acting like my protector?" She slammed the cup on the counter, the contents flowing over. Irritated at herself for losing her temper, she looked around for a towel to mop up the mess.

Patrick touched her arm.

"Frieda, what's gotten into you? I stood up for you just like I'm sure you would for me."

"You mean the next time you find out you don't qualify for a job because of your sex?" she retorted. She knew she wasn't being fair, but she was too frustrated to care. She was a better doctor than Caldwell could ever be. That guy wouldn't even touch a patient unless they came from a certain class.

"Frieda, that's uncalled for. I'm not Guild. I don't make the rules."

"No, you don't. But I can fight my own battles, thank you."

He moved closer to her. She could feel his stare, and when she looked up at him, he looked furious.

"I don't understand you. I thought friends stuck by one another."

"I can look after myself, Patrick. I've been doing it a long time."

He gazed at her for a few seconds, before asking, "Have I missed something? 'Cause you seem to be really fed up with me. I thought you were tired on Friday night, but after this morning, I'm wondering if there's something I did?"

"I've no idea what you are talking about," she replied stiffly. "Don't you have somewhere else to be?"

He didn't take the hint.

"Frieda, on Friday you refused to come to dinner, this morning you jump down my throat, and now you can't wait to get rid of me. That's not how friends behave."

"Friends! We're more like brother and sister according to you. I have somewhere to be. See you later." She marched off, heart thumping with fury. She had to pass the final exams and then she would shove her results down Caldwell's throat. Or maybe up his nose.

She couldn't think about Patrick. He'd made his position clear. She had to forget about her dreams in which they got married and worked together in New York. Maybe it was time to leave. Lilian had offered to give her a reference for the women's hospital in New York or the one in Pennsylvania. She had also suggested she consider London to get more varied experience. London seemed a bit far to travel, but she might consider getting out of New York. Then she wouldn't have to see Patrick anymore. If she stayed in the city, even working at another hospital, she could still run into him at the Sanctuary or when she went to visit Elsa. She wasn't sure she could cope when he started courting someone. It was bad enough to watch the nurses flirting with him. He was rich, talented, and handsome, yet genuine and kind; he could have his pick of women. Why had she ever thought he would consider her?

## CHAPTER 5

$\mathcal{T}$he following Saturday afternoon, Frieda waited for Maria to come out of the Triangle. Maria didn't see her as she walked outside, chatting to a couple of the other seamstresses. How happy she looked, her face a big smile.

"Frieda, you're early! What's wrong?"

Frieda smiled at the good-natured teasing about her awful timekeeping, but Maria wasn't fooled. She tilted her head as she looked at her. "You're more tired than usual, you have a sad look in your eyes, and that smile couldn't be more forced than the one I gave Mr. Blanck earlier."

That did make Frieda laugh. She knew how much Maria and the other women despised the Triangle Shirtwaist Kings as the papers called Blanck and Harris.

Maria put her arm through Frieda's. "Come on, let's

29

go to Charlie's . One of his cakes will help put a smile on your face. Then you can tell me why you look so miserable."

"I don't want to ruin your day."

"Frieda, it can't be that bad."

They walked the few blocks to Charlie's in silence, navigating their way through the packed streets. It was payday and the shoppers were out in full force.

Frieda followed Maria into the small Italian diner. The staff greeted Maria like a long-lost relative, kissing her on both cheeks. Frieda glanced around, the tables were busy with mostly male clientele. Not surprising given the delicious aromas coming from the kitchen. Charlie's wife, mother, and his daughters all worked in the family business providing Italian home cooked meals to the local community. Like many other nationalities, Italian men came to New York ahead of their families. They worked hard and saved whatever they could to bring their loved ones to America. Charlie's provided a little touch of home comforts. Somewhere not only to get a decent low priced meal, but to talk of home in the native language.

Frieda slid into the two person booth opposite Maria who ordered for both of them.

"Now tell me what's wrong?" Maria ordered.

Frieda looked everywhere but at her friend, "Nothing."

Maria whistled, "That bad?"

Frieda glanced at Maria, swallowing hard, knowing there was no point in trying to convince Maria there was nothing wrong. "Everything."

"Start at the beginning. Is it Patrick? Or the hospital?"

"Both. Neither. Maria, who am I fooling? Patrick sees me as his sister and the hospital doesn't want female doctors. Nobody does. Do you know it was easier to train as a doctor back in the 1890's than it is now. More of the female colleges are closing but getting a place in medical school is only a start of the challenge. You have to have a job when you graduate and few hospitals want to employ women. Those that do expect you to have experience. But how can I get that when I can't get a placement on the wards?"

Maria took her hand. "Frieda, slow down. You aren't making a lot of sense. You're already in medical school. You haven't been kicked out have you?"

Frieda shook her head.

"Good. So the fact it's harder to get in, while not fair, doesn't apply to you. You haven't graduated, yet, so why are you worried about finding a job? You know there are loads of places to work as a doctor. This isn't like you, you're normally so positive. What happened?"

Frieda told her about the interview with Dr. Guild and the comments of the other medical students.

"It's so unfair. I scored higher than that idiot Caldwell on every test. He won't touch a patient who comes in from the tenements. You should see how he treats the children. Yet he's guaranteed a job. Just because…"

"He's a man. We know it's a man's world, Frieda. That's why we need women like you to fight back. You knew from the start this wasn't going to be easy. You're just overworked and exhausted. When was the last time you took two days off in a row?"

Frieda shrugged her shoulders.

"You can't work all the time," Maria lectured.

The coffee and cakes arrived, interrupting them. Maria chatted in Italian to the young server making her laugh. Frieda wished she had some of her younger friend's optimism. There was a time when she thought she could conquer the world. She knew being a female doctor wasn't going to be easy, but she thought they would treat her fairly. That was the worst of it.

Maria stirred her coffee. "So tell me about Patrick. Why do you think he sees you as a sister? That's not the impression he gave me."

"Maria, you think everyone is in love with everyone else. You are the original romantic."

Maria blushed prettily. "I just want everyone to be as happy as I am. I can't believe I have only known Conrad a few months. I feel like I've known him forever." Maria's expression clouded for a moment. "I just wish Papa had met him."

A tear escaped as Maria took a gulp of her coffee.

"Your father would have liked him. From what

you've said, Conrad is everything your Papa was. Kind, considerate, and a good worker. He invited Gustav and young Alice to live with him and even got Gustav his old job back."

"He's lovely, but he's not Italian and that would have been an issue for Papa. Mama too."

"Has she still not come around to the idea of having a German-Irish son in law?"

"Frieda, he hasn't proposed yet!" Maria protested, her cheeks turning scarlet.

"'Yet' being the operative word. We both know he will and you will say yes."

A shadow of doubt appeared in Maria's eyes.

"We aren't talking about Conrad, we're talking about Patrick. Tell me what happened."

Frieda relayed the story of how Patrick had told her over Christmas how glad he was that she was part of the family; how he had tried to insist the family dinner Richard wanted wasn't complete without her. Then she told Maria about what had happened after he stood up for her with Caldwell.

"Did his head need stitching back together?" Maria asked. Frieda wasn't following.

"Frieda, you bit his head off after he did something kind. No wonder the man is confused. You're giving off the wrong signals. You don't get a man to marry you by shouting at him or treating him like the enemy."

"Marry? I didn't say anything about getting married."

"Not in so many words, but I know you've thought about it. I've seen that dreamy expression on your face when Patrick's around. I haven't seen what you're like when you're alone with him, and I'm not sure I want to after what you just said."

Frieda poked her tongue out but Maria ignored her.

"When we were at dinner in the Sanctuary, when Lily was talking about her factory, you couldn't keep your eyes off one another. Frieda, I would bet my wages he feels the same as you do."

Frieda's hopes flared, "You would?"

"Yes I would. Maybe he does consider you part of his family, after all you have grown up in his shadow. Kathleen and Lily are like aunts to you, mothers even. So he may act more familiar with you than he would another woman, but a man doesn't look at his sister the way Patrick looks at you."

Frieda couldn't stop her hopes rising. "So what should I do? I can't ask him out, and he has never asked me anywhere."

Maria rolled her eyes, "He asked you to dinner."

"With his parents," Frieda retorted.

Maria wasn't accepting any excuses. "He still asked. You acting like a bear with a sore paw isn't going to help him take the first step, is it? You have to treat a man delicately."

"How do you know so much about men?"

"I'm Italian aren't I? Italy is the home of romantics. Or is that France? Anyway, I've seen my sister, my cousins, Benito's wife," Maria screwed up her face at the mention of her sister in law, "They all got the man they wanted, and it wasn't by shouting at him."

Frieda didn't care that Maria was younger than she was. She had more experience with men, having a married brother and a courting sister as well as a boyfriend. Frieda knew she needed help, "So what do you suggest I do?"

"Apologize for hurting his feelings. Ask him questions, make him feel important. Mama says when you want something from a man, you have to make him think it was his idea. When they came to America first, Papa wouldn't let Mama work. No matter how hard things were, he refused, saying an Italian man always supported his family. Mama knew they couldn't afford to live on Papa's earnings. But he was a stubborn man with too much pride. She said she dropped a few comments about how wives of his friends were able to buy eggs and butter during the week. How embarrassed she was at not being able to bake a cake to celebrate an engagement, a birth, or something else. Papa loved mama, and knew keeping a clean home and being a good cook was important to an Italian woman. Weeks later, Mama dropped a couple of hints about how Mrs. Milano or Mrs. Cornelli were making a few cents from home making artificial flowers. Mrs. Maltese, on the other hand, was out working in a factory with her daughters. Soon Papa started talking about how wonderful it was in America that you could earn money from home without going out to work. Mama was working on her artificial flowers in no time, and Papa thought it was all his idea."

Frieda smiled as Maria recounted the story, but when her friend stopped and stared at her, she couldn't relate it to her and Patrick.

"I don't see how to apply that to Patrick."

"For an intelligent girl, you can be very dumb, my friend." Maria smiled to reduce the insult. "You want Patrick to court you, to show you how he really feels. So get him to take you to tea or to see a play or whatever it is doctors do in their time off."

"I can't ask him out." Frieda felt like a parrot repeating the same objections, but she had to make Maria listen.

"Frieda, you aren't going to do the asking. You just plant the seed and let him take the hint."

They finished their cakes, left a tip for the server, and walked out into the noisy streets. Maria was meeting Conrad; Frieda planned to go back to the Sanctuary and enjoy an early night.

As they walked, Maria spoke about her sister Rosa's upcoming wedding.

"Mama is putting on a brave face, but at least Rosa

gets to marry in a church and in white. The neighbors won't have any reason to talk about the Mezza's." Maria imitated her mother's accent, making Frieda laugh. "I wanted to tell her all the neighbors would be too scared to say a word given he's a Greco, but I had to let it pass. I have to be careful with Mama, especially when it comes to her Rosa."

Frieda picked up on Maria's hurt. "Maria, your mother loves you too. This wedding is her way of dealing with the grief of losing your father. She doesn't mean to be harsh with you. Be patient."

Maria stopped suddenly causing the person behind her to walk into her. Maria apologized and pulled Frieda to the edge of the sidewalk.

"You need to take your own advice, my lovely friend. Is Patrick working tonight?"

Surprised at the change in topic, Frieda replied. "Yes, at least I think so."

Maria darted over to a stall holder selling fresh donuts. She bought two and returned.

"Maria, I can't eat another cake."

"They aren't for us, silly. Take them to the hospital as a peace offering. Say you're sorry for biting his head off."

"I'll look silly."

"And? Do you want him or not?" Maria kissed Frieda's cheek. "Go on, off you go before you spend too much time thinking about it. Good luck, and don't forget to let me know how it goes."

Maria gave her a friendly push in the direction of the hospital and had disappeared before Frieda could pull her thoughts together.

"Why not?" she said, not realizing she'd spoken aloud until people stared at her. Grinning, she picked up her skirt and walked faster in the direction of the hospital.

# CHAPTER 6

*T*he hospital waiting room wasn't too busy, and Freida found Patrick having a coffee while reading some notes. He yawned as he read. She saw the dark shadows under his eyes. How long had he been on duty? He glanced up and caught her staring at him. A wary expression darkened the blue of his eyes.

"Frieda?"

She thrust the bag of donuts at him. "Here, these will help your energy levels."

He sniffed appreciably, "Fresh donuts. What's the occasion?"

He looked at her, and she tried to speak but couldn't. What had Maria told her to say? Her mind went blank. She panicked realizing she looked like a right fool standing in front of him, opening and closing her mouth like a fish.

"Frieda?"

"Sorry. I wanted to apologize for snapping at you, the other day. I don't know what came over me. The donuts are a peace offering."

"That's real sweet of you, Frieda, but you didn't have to come all the way to the hospital just to see me."

"I wanted to." Oh great, now she sounded desperate. "What I mean is, it would be awkward with us working together, you know if there was an atmosphere between us."

He looked more confused than she sounded. She wished Maria was here. This wasn't going the way she wanted it to.

"Don't you like them?" she asked, pointing at the donuts. He took a bite.

"They're delicious. Remind me to annoy you more often. I could get used to having donuts bought for me." He turned to get a plate. "Would you like to share?"

"No thank you. I had cake at Charlie's with Maria."

"How is she?"

"Good. She was asking for you." Darn it, now he'd know they were talking about him. "I mean you and the rest of the family."

"I see." He ate the rest of the donut in silence.

Frieda couldn't think of anything else to say, and the lingering silence grew uncomfortable. "I should go home. I hope you don't have too busy a night."

"Looks like a quiet one. Thanks for the donuts. I'm glad we are friends again. I missed you."

"Did you?" Her voice sounded so squeaky.

"Yes, I did. I love talking to you and seeing you every day."

She smiled as her stomach twisted, her heart raced.

"Elsa and Richie have been asking for you as well. They miss you too."

Her stomach hardened as if he had punched her. He only saw her as a friend of the family. She tried to stay smiling as he added, "You should come over to the house one day when you finish work early. They'd love to see you."

"I will. Bye Patrick."

He replied, but she couldn't tell what he said due to the noise drumming in her ears. A voice in her head calling her a fool. What did you think he'd do? Take you in his arms and profess his love? Her cheeks flamed as she walked through the halls, out of the hospital. She declined a cab, preferring the fresh air to cool her face. She was a complete idiot. That was the last time she was ever taking romantic advice from Maria.

## CHAPTER 7

FEBRUARY 1911, NEW YORK

*M*aria Mezza trudged through the melting snow, greeting various stall holders she knew as she took the familiar route to her job at the Triangle Shirtwaist Factory. Her sister chattered on about her upcoming wedding to Paulo Greco. Maria tried to appear interested, but nothing could make her warm to her sister's fiancé. He was a thug and always would be. He treated Rosa well, if giving someone extravagant presents was a sign of love. Maria questioned where the money came from to buy these gifts, he didn't appear to have a real job. He worked a few hours a day in a barber shop one day, but the next he'd be behind the counter of a small store.

"Maria?" Rosa hissed.

"Sorry, what?"

"You weren't listening to a word I said. What's wrong with you?"

Maria didn't need her sister snapping at her. "Rosa, I'm tired. You snore in your sleep, you kept me awake."

"I don't snore. Take that back." Rosa stopped walking, hands on her hips.

Maria kept moving. They'd be late, and she didn't want her wages docked. She hated her job at the Triangle with a passion. It wasn't the work so much; it was the place. Working so many floors up, being locked in for ten hours a day made her feel like a trapped rat. She particularly resented being searched every day as she was leaving. As if she was a common thief.

Conrad suggested they both stay working there until Lily's factory was up and running. Then they would leave to work for Lily. When they'd saved enough to marry, he would work and she could go back to school and train to be a teacher. He was adamant she wouldn't remain a seamstress after they married.

Sighing, she linked arms with her sulky sister. "Sorry Rosa. I'm bad tempered today."

"You are! Wait until you get married, if you ever get engaged." Rosa glanced at her, but Maria kept her face expressionless.

Conrad spoke about the future, after they married but he hadn't proposed yet, and she worried about the evil eye. Mama had told them the old stories of how when you planned things to be wonderful, the evil eye could ruin them out of spite. Maria claimed not to be superstitious, but she didn't want to tempt fate.

"I know you're excited Rosa, but can we please talk about something other than weddings or houses or babies? Just for today, please."

Rosa opened her mouth to protest but closed it again, shrugging her shoulders. "What do you want to talk about then?"

Maria didn't care so long as the word Paulo didn't come into it. "Want to come to Frieda's with me on Wednesday?" she suggested.

Rose screwed her nose up. "To that place."

Maria snapped, "It's a woman's sanctuary, not a brothel, Rosa."

Horrified, Rosa glanced around her quickly as she made a sign of the cross. "Keep your voice down, Maria. What if someone overheard you? Our reputations would be in the gutter. If you want to go visit that place, it's your choice. I have better things to be doing."

Thankfully, they'd just reached the Asch building, or she'd have been tempted to throw her sister into the slush piled up on the sidewalk. Frieda was her closest friend, and Rosa couldn't even say her name. She was meeting Frieda outside the Asch building, but she didn't clarify that to Rosa. Her sister could go jump.

# CHAPTER 8

"Good morning my beautiful Italian girls. How are we this morning?" Joseph, the elevator operator, greeted them, his eyes dancing, his face lit up with a smile.

Every day he smiled and flirted with all the ladies, from the oldest to the youngest.

"How can you be so cheerful every day?" Maria once asked him after a difficult day at the factory.

"Why not? I have a full belly, a happy home, and I can look after my family as I have steady work. I am a fortunate man. My life is better than some."

Maria couldn't disagree with him. There was always someone worse off than you.

This morning she forced a smile, trying to swallow her rage at Rosa as she greeted him, "Morning, Joseph."

They flew up to their floor and were sitting at their

respective machines less than ten minutes later. She glanced around to see who was in to chat to, she had a few minutes before the machines would start.

She knew most of her fellow workers now. Angela and her sister, Bernadette, had worked with her at the old factory but left after Reinhart's harassment of the young girls became too much. Leonie Chiver waved to her. Maria walked over to where the younger girl sat, she looked thinner than ever, and much older.

"Leonie, want to come for a walk at lunchtime? The snow's melting. We can grab a hot cup of coffee?"

"I'd love to, Maria, but just for the walk."

Maria agreed, but as she made it back to her own work area, she calculated she had enough change to buy coffee for the both of them. She might even have enough to buy Leonie a donut. The girl looked even worse close up, worry lines making her look like she was frowning. Frieda had told her about Leonie's spell in Jail during the strike, the depth of poverty she lived in at home with her invalid mother and younger siblings. Leonie's father was alive and well, but had skipped out on his family some years previously. Maria took her seat and checked to see her needle was threaded and ready to use. They should arrest men for desertion, make them break rocks like other prisoners and pay their wages paid directly to the family.

"Maria, you'll turn the needle crooked with that face. What's wrong with you?" Anna Gullo asked. Her half teasing, half serious expression made Maria feel guilty. Anna had been very good to her, she shouldn't cause her supervisor a moment's worry. Anna was the reason she had a job, having ignored Maria's role in the strike.

"I was thinking about men who desert their families."

Anna glanced in Leonie's direction before rolling her eyes. "If he was my man, I would hit him with something hard. Make him think twice. Poor Leonie, at her age she should have fun. Instead, she is old before her time."

There was no time for more conversation as the machines started with a roar.

# CHAPTER 9

*L*unch time came, and she spotted Conrad making his way to her workspace. Most of the workforce ate their lunch at the window sills, but she preferred to escape the building, if only for a few minutes.

"Walk with me?" he asked.

"I've plans. You should have spoken earlier," Maria teased.

"You are a popular lady. Who is my competition?" He pretended to push his chest out as if jealous, making her giggle.

"Leonie Chiver. I asked her to come for a walk. She looked miserable this morning."

"Why can't I come too? Instead of one pretty lady, I get to have two on my arm."

She poked him in the chest. "I won't share you with anyone."

His eyes warmed as he gazed back at her, his glance moving to her lips. Her heart beat faster. He wouldn't kiss her now. Would he? They were at work. He broke the moment by calling over her shoulder.

"Leonie, would you mind if I tagged along with you and Maria?"

Maria exhaled, trying to control her racing pulse. Being this near to him was disconcerting as she wanted him to pull her into his arms. She turned to greet Leonie.

"You two go ahead. I don't want to intrude," Leonie replied. Maria caught the look of disappointment on the younger girl's face.

Maria put her hand out to stop Leonie from heading back to her workspace.

"It's Conrad who's intruding. Come on Leonie, that coffee is calling me."

The three of them rode the elevator downstairs. Conrad bought them all a coffee and a hot donut from the street trader at the edge of Washington Square gardens.

"We don't have a lot of time, but I can never resist a donut," he said as he handed the cakes to the girls. Leonie looked ready to refuse but Conrad added, "I can't eat alone, so you two can get indigestion too."

Maria loved him even more. She watched the young Leonie devour the donut. The girl was what, fifteen if even that, yet she looked to be much younger. Her clothes, while clean, had been mended so often, it was hard to tell how much of the original dress remained.

"How is your mother, Leonie?"

Leonie's face fell. "She's in a lot of pain, but she refuses to take the medicine the local drugstore recommends. She says it makes her feel funny, like she is dizzy."

Conrad finished eating before saying, "Your mother should see a real doctor. Some drugstores lace those bottles with alcohol or worse."

Leonie didn't answer. Maria guessed she was wondering how to pay for a doctor.

"Frieda's friend Patrick visited your mother during the strike didn't he?" Maria hinted.

Leonie's face blossomed, she looked almost pretty. "Yes, he was so lovely. Mama liked him, said he was gentle. He didn't hurt her."

"So why doesn't she see him now?"

Leonie looked at something in the distance.

"Leonie, talk to us. Maybe we can help?" Maria offered.

"Our landlord, he's increased the rent. He said if Mama had money to pay for doctors, she could pay more for the house. He suggested Mama can pay in other ways, but Mama got annoyed. I've never seen her so upset. She won't see Patrick or even Frieda anymore. She's too afraid to upset Mr. Murdoch."

Conrad flushed, his eyes lit with anger. Maria put a hand on his arm, afraid he would scare Leonie who was timid enough already.

"I'm seeing Frieda on Wednesday. We'll call to see your mother. Then maybe we can help work something out." Maria waited for Leonie to say something. The girl didn't look convinced.

"It's worth a try, Leonie. Your family have friends; you don't need to face any of this alone."

For a second she thought Leonie would refuse, but instead the girl gave her a shy smile.

"You are very kind, Maria. Mama would enjoy chatting to you and Frieda."

"Good. We best get back before they send a search party out for us." Maria took Leonie's arm and squeezed her hand. "Have faith, Leonie."

They walked back in silence, Maria thinking of what Joseph had said. There was always someone worse off than yourself. She caught Conrad's gaze over Leonie's head; he was angry at what the landlord had done, but still he smiled at her, a smile that warmed her from her toes up.

# CHAPTER 10

## THE SANCTUARY

*L*ily and Kathleen sat in the office going through paperwork. Neither relished the task, but they had to keep their records accurate. Not just for the city inspections, but also to keep their accountant and attorney happy. Charlie had suggested the Sanctuary keep an attorney when families sued over organizations stealing their children. Not that the Sanctuary ever took away a child without the parent's permission.

"Where's Frieda, today? Is she at the hospital, or is it the day for home visiting?" Lily asked. "I haven't seen much of her since you told me about her meeting with Dr. Guild."

Kathleen's lips thinned at the mention of the doctor. "At the hospital, but knowing Frieda, she will do some home visits later. She's working even harder now, maybe she hopes she can change that man's mind.

Patrick says he never gets to chat with her anymore, and she doesn't come to see Elsa as often."

"Do you think something happened between Patrick and Frieda?"

Kathleen glanced at Lily, an unreadable expression in her eyes. Lily waited for an answer, but when one wasn't forthcoming, she asked again.

"Have you noticed how they look at each other when they think nobody is watching? I used to think they would announce they were courting, but lately it's as if Frieda is avoiding Patrick, don't you agree?"

"Lily, you are always trying to play matchmaker."

"No, I'm not!" At a look from Kathleen, Lily laughed. "Well, maybe I am. But that aside, she used to light up like a Christmas tree when Patrick came into the room. Now, she looks miserable. I don't think it's just because of Dr. Guild, but maybe I'm wrong. I can't help feeling something else has happened. Surely you've noticed?"

"I have, but I try to ignore it. I think I should stay out of it."

Confused, Lily came out from behind her desk to sit beside Kathleen. "Why? Don't you like Frieda?"

"I do, I love her. Who wouldn't? She is a credit to her family, turning her whole life around after what happened." Kathleen fell silent.

"But?" Lily prompted.

"I don't want her throwing away everything to get

married." Kathleen put her hands up to her mouth as if wondering how those words had escaped.

Lily didn't hide her surprise. "It's early to be talking about marriage anyway, they haven't even gone out alone for one evening. Now it looks like they never will."

Kathleen didn't answer. Lily took Kathleen's hand, genuinely worried now she was missing something. "I thought you would like them to get married. They are well suited. He brings her out of her shell, and she adds a calming influence."

"Yes, I know all that. And I know they would wait for her to qualify and everything. But Lily... we both know if she gets married, her life as a doctor will be over. It's been so hard for her to get accepted into the study program, even with Richard's backing. She's worked and struggled so hard. Dr. Guild made his feelings clear about her future at the hospital. It will be difficult for her to find another job, and if she was to get married now, then that was all for nothing. And as for Patrick, Richard thinks he could make a wonderful surgeon. If he settles down, he won't want to spend years studying."

Stunned, Lily stayed silent. She didn't want to offend Kathleen and knew some of what she said was valid, but what was more important, a future career or happiness?

"Do you think I'm horrible? I mean, what mother

wouldn't want her child to be happy. I know Patrick loves Frieda, even if he hasn't completely realized it yet. I love Frieda already. She is like a part of our family."

Lily hugged Kathleen before drawing back, keeping her arm on her friend's shoulder.

"Kathleen Green, you are a wonderful mother, and nobody could ever question your love for all your children. But I wonder whether Patrick sees Frieda more as a sister or a young woman. She wears her heart on her sleeve, but he is more difficult to read."

"I don't think he sees her as a sister." Kathleen paused as if considering her next thought. "She's Frieda. She's always been around. Maybe he takes her for granted a little."

Lily would not confirm or deny that remark. Kathleen was her best friend, but as Patrick's mother, Kathleen wouldn't want to hear anything that sounded like criticism.

"Kathleen, I think you are underestimating both Frieda and Patrick."

"How? They can't change the world. You, of all people, know the attitudes of our society."

"They don't have to change society. They just have to make it work for them. Patrick is supportive of Frieda's career. I think together they can find a way if they decide they want to be a couple. They might even open up their own practice. In fact, we could employ both of them right here at the Sanctuary."

"Lily, you can't fix everything by throwing money at it."

Stung, Lily bit back. "I'm not. You and I both know how much the people in our community need qualified doctors. Lillian Wald is doing wonderful work in reducing the infant mortality rate. Frieda has told me so much about her, I've asked her to come to dinner tomorrow evening. You and Richard should come, too. Maybe we could also ask Patrick and Frieda. We can see how they react to each other."

"I suppose there is no harm in that. But don't try matchmaking. You will embarrass both of them."

"Me?" Lily adopted an innocent expression, but when Kathleen laughed, she did too. Her attempts at matchmaking were legendary, though not always for the right reasons. More than one couple whom she thought were well suited had hated each other. So much so, Charlie had told her to give up and concentrate on the stuff she was good at. Things like setting up Sanctuaries and building factories. Although she would need more help if she was to get the factory off the ground.

"Why do you look like you sucked a lemon, Lily?"

"I know I said I wouldn't let it upset me, but the progress on the factory is so slow. Anne and her friends have been wonderful, but I thought we'd have it built by now." She still hadn't got over her disappointment in not being able to locate the factory in Little Germany. She'd settled for a site nearer the Sanctuary. Anne Morgan had raised a lot of money, so they purchased the land in cash.

"Lily Doherty, you have no patience. Look at what you have achieved already. You've bought the site and the foundations have been dug. The weather didn't help, but with Spring coming, things will improve."

Lily paced the floor.

"Tell me Lily, what's the real reason you are so bent out of shape."

Lily wanted to share, but would Kathleen think she'd lost her mind? She wondered if she had.

"Lily, please. I know you aren't happy. You seem more troubled with every passing week. I won't say a word to anyone, not even Richard. I promise." Kathleen coughed, reddening slightly. "Is it our age?"

"Age?" Confused, Lily glanced at her friend who seemed embarrassed. It took a moment to dawn on her. "You think I'm going through the change?" Maybe she was, although she was a little young for it, wasn't she? What age did the change happen?

"Richard says it can lead to mood swings and depression. Not to mention taking up a project although most women re-decorate their house not build a factory."

Lily stopped pacing. "You've discussed me with Richard?"

"No, of course not. He was talking about some patient of his, and I just recognized some symptoms.

Don't you look at me like that, Lily Doherty. You have been a giant pain in the…" Too much of a lady to finish the sentence, Kathleen let it hang.

"Tell me how you really feel," Lily retorted.

"See! That's what I'm talking about. I'm concerned for you and you just laugh in my face. I may be your oldest friend Lily, but that doesn't mean you can't be insufferable. I'm going home." Kathleen stood and marched to the door. She slammed it shut behind her.

# CHAPTER 11

*L*ily stared at the shut door, shocked to her core. Despite being Irish, Kathleen rarely lost her temper and never with her. Lily sat on the edge of the couch, playing with her hands. She should go after her. Maybe it would be better for Kathleen to calm down. The door opened, admitting Kathleen. She still looked mad, but also a little shamefaced. "Left my coat." She picked up the coat, but took a long time to move to the door.

"Please don't go. Sit down. I'm sorry. I didn't mean to hurt your feelings."

Kathleen stayed silent. Lily glared up at her friend. "You could apologize, too. You called me some horrible names."

"I said you were insufferable and you are. I don't

take it back." Kathleen looked like she was struggling to keep a straight face.

"At least I don't flounce out in a temper."

Kathleen glared at her, "Flounce! Who's flouncing? I left."

"And took the door with you." Lily took out her hanky and held it in the air. "Peace?"

"A peace flag is white."

Lily glanced at the pink hanky and giggled. Kathleen joined in before she took a seat beside her.

"Sorry," they both muttered at the same time.

Cook arrived with some tea and cake just at that moment.

Lily took the tray from Cook. "Thank you, Cook, but we didn't order anything."

"I heard that door slam shut, wonder they didn't hear it in Florida, the noise it made. Tea will calm both of you down. At least, it better, or I will have something to say." Cook tottered off. Lily and Kathleen exchanged another glance before dissolving into giggles again.

"I think we just got told off, Kathleen. She's rather scary when she's mad."

"It's chocolate cake. She can get mad anytime she likes. You pour while I cut the cake."

They ate and drank in silence. Lily caught Kathleen glancing at her a few times.

"Lily, if you don't want to tell me what's wrong,

that's fine. But please don't pretend everything is alright. Remember, I will always stick by you, no matter what."

"Kathleen, I think I'm losing my marbles."

Kathleen didn't comment and kept her face steady.

Lily hesitated, but then once she started talking, she couldn't stop. "It started after that horrible fire in Newark last November, where the twenty-five factory workers died. I keep dreaming the Sanctuary is on fire and people are trapped inside. I can't get to them to help them. The smoke is too thick. In the next dream, it's a building on fire but not one I recognize. It's the same theme though, I can't get inside to help. I... it's getting to the stage, I'm too scared to go asleep."

Kathleen put her cup down and took Lily's cup and plate and set them on the table. Then she sat beside Lily and pulled her into her arms, stroking her hair as if she was a child like Elsa.

"Lily, you're torturing yourself. The Newark fire and finding Alice brought back memories of the Slocum tragedy and all that entailed. Your dreams are about nearly losing Teddy, those hours when you thought he was dead. It was a horrible time, and it's no wonder you still get nightmares."

Lily shook her head. It wasn't about Teddy or Alice or any of the children. The people she saw in her dreams were adults.

"I have to get the factory built. I can't explain it,

65

Kathleen. It makes little sense to me, but something seems to push me to get the factory finished and operational," Lily sobbed, "I know I'm a mess. I keep snapping at Charlie and the children. Teddy told me to go on vacation, a long one."

"That's not a bad idea, love. You're exhausted. When was the last time you went away for a few weeks? That time you went to Clover Springs to see Charlie's family? That was when the children were little."

Lily pulled away, stood up, and started pacing once more. "I can't leave New York. I have to get the factory working, employ people in a safer environment, get people out of the sweatshops. That's when the dreams will stop. I know it."

"Lily, you can't save everyone. You've done more than most."

Lily didn't want to see the concern on Kathleen's face. She knew she sounded like a demented old woman.

"Lily, we will get our heads together. All of us. Mr. Prentice, Sadie, Father Nelson, everyone you can think of. There must be a way to speed things up."

Relieved Kathleen didn't seem ready to take her to the insane asylum, Lily asked, "You think I'm right? The dreams are a sign."

"Yes, but not in the same way as you do. You can snap and snarl as much as you want, but those dreams mean you need a vacation. And you won't take one until that blasted factory opens. So, come what may, I will beg, borrow or harass people until we open the factory doors. Then, my dear, occasionally insufferable friend, you are going on vacation for at least a month."

"A month!" Lily protested.

"Those are my terms. If you want my help, you agree to them. Otherwise I am out of here." Kathleen stood up and held out her hand, "Deal?"

Lily knew when to give in. She shook Kathleen's outstretched hand. "Anyone ever tell you, you drive a hard bargain Mrs. Green."

"I learned from the best," Kathleen smiled before glancing around her. "Where's my pen? We need to make a list of invitees for Mr. Prentice's party."

"I didn't hear about a party."

"Neither has Mr. Prentice. But he will soon enough. After I get Sadie Prentice involved and on board," Kathleen winked before taking her seat at the desk. She moved the papers out of the way before making a list of who's who in New York.

Lily stared at Kathleen, feeling a little sorry for Mr. Prentice. He wasn't a fan of large social occasions, but with Sadie and Kathleen's combined input, the party would be something to give New Yorkers to talk about for a long time. It should raise a lot of funds.

## CHAPTER 12

### WEDNESDAY 15 FEB 1911

"*Y*ou look happy tonight, Maria. Got plans with a certain charming Irishman?" Joseph closed the elevator door.

Maria smiled at Joseph's greeting. "Not tonight. I'm meeting a friend." She giggled as Joseph put his hand over his mouth, pretending to be shocked.

She played along, "Don't worry, Conrad knows. He's fine with it."

Joseph rolled his eyes. "Conrad is too nice. Now if you were my lady, I wouldn't let you out of my sight for five minutes."

Maria laughed off his flirting. He didn't mean it. He treated all the women the same, regardless of their age. She watched in amusement as he made a forty odd year old grandma blush with his remarks. Joseph was a tonic. She hoped to convince him to come and work for Lily when the new factory got built. Not that she'd mentioned it. It was too early, and she didn't want to jinx Lily's plans.

She waited for Frieda outside, her friend late as usual. No doubt she had got caught up in something at the hospital. Rosa walked down the opposite sidewalk, clinging to Paulo's arms like a drowning swimmer with her rescuer. Maria waved but her sister ignored her. Or maybe she didn't see her.

Frieda waved as she crossed the street, avoiding an automobile and a horse and cart. She was slightly out of breath. "Maria, sorry. You should have waited inside. I got caught and --"

"It's fine. I know you will never be on time. The day you get married, they better tell you the ceremony starts an hour before the scheduled time."

Frieda blushed, her scarlet cheeks only making her eyes look greener and her hair more burgundy. Frieda was beautiful inside and out. Maria put her arm through Frieda's and together they walked toward Charlie's for dinner.

"Frieda, I have to talk to you about Leonie."

"What's wrong with her? Well, apart from having to support a whole family when she is but a child herself?"

"Exactly Frieda. She is skin and bones. Conrad bought her a donut the other day, and she devoured it. I'm really worried about her. Her mother isn't any better, she's been taking some tonic, which makes her dizzy. Conrad said it was probably alcoholic."

"He could be right. Many of the cheaper tonics are nothing but alcohol. They don't cure any illness, but the patients feel better for a time at least."

Shocked, Maria didn't know what to say. Frieda glanced at her.

"Why didn't Leonie come to the hospital? Patrick would be happy to visit her mother."

"I know, but she seems scared. Something about her landlord. I didn't understand exactly what she was talking about. I sensed she didn't speak freely as Conrad was there. She was embarrassed, poor little thing. So I wondered if you felt like visiting tonight. We could go together?"

Frieda's smile dropped. Maria rushed to reassure her.

"We don't have to go. I know you find going into Little Germany difficult."

"No, we must go. I can't be selfish. We should bring some food with us. Otherwise we might embarrass Leonie." Frieda searched in her purse. "Only I didn't bring much cash with me."

"Why don't we take dinner from the cafe? I can get something later at home."

Frieda beamed. "You are full of good ideas. Lead on Miss Mezza. As we walk, you can tell me all about the delightful Conrad. Is he the reason your eyes are sparkling?"

Maria blushed, although she knew Frieda was teasing.

"Conrad came to see Mama at the weekend. She wasn't very welcoming, but she didn't throw him out."

"It still bothers her that he's not Italian?"

"Yes. Isn't it stupid. He's got a great job, he's a kind, wonderful man, and I…" Maria put a hand to her mouth.

"Everyone who has seen you together knows you are a match made in heaven. Apart from your mother. Did he stay for long?"

"Yes, ages. I thought Mama would get upset, but she seemed to thaw toward him. I think she would have asked him to come back for another visit." Maria frowned.

"But?"

"My brother, Benito turned up. Mama treats him like the prodigal son, although he does nothing to help her. He made it very clear Conrad wasn't welcome. Mama turned ice cold, too. I could kill my brother." Maria gasped, "Sorry, Frieda."

"Don't be silly. Hans and I used to fight when he was alive. I'm sure I threatened to kill him sometimes, too." They were standing outside Charlie's. "Should we buy the food from here or somewhere nearer Leonie's house?"

Maria looked at Charlie's regretfully, "I think nearer so it stays hot. We don't know if they have a fire lit."

Both girls shivered. The wind was chilly, especially as darkness fell. They jumped on a streetcar heading toward Leonie's house. If it was earlier, they could walk, but at night the streetcar was safer. It didn't go as far as Leonie's house, but it got them most of the way there.

Frieda looked around as they crossed the street. "I will speak to Lily and Kathleen. They can arrange for some food baskets and maybe some coal, too. Let's see what they need when we get there."

They walked faster as it got colder.

"So how are things with you and Patrick? Did he like the donuts?"

Frieda sighed, her eyes clouded in pain.

"He did, and he said he was glad I apologized as he missed me."

"That's wonderful Frieda, but why the long face?"

"He said he was glad we were friends again, and invited me to go visit Elsa and Richie."

"Friends!" Maria rolled her eyes. "For an intelligent man, he's stupid."

Frieda sighed louder. "I don't know what to do now. I'm really tempted to go out with the next man I see."

With that, she bumped into an old grandfather with no teeth. She apologized, trying not to look at Maria. When the man had walked on, they burst out laughing.

"Come on, Frieda, there's a pie shop up that street. We must work on your romance later."

They bought some beef pies and some bread and milk. Frieda added some broken biscuits as a treat for Leonie's younger siblings. Then, carrying their shopping, they made their way to Leonie's apartment just in time to hear loud shouting.

# CHAPTER 13

*W*ithout hesitating, they ran to help. The shouting grew louder. An overweight white man with protruding teeth sent spittle over everyone as he roared at Leonie's mother. Leonie was standing like a statue, her arms around Carrie, her younger sister. The man had the older twin boys in a vice-like grip. They were fighting like madmen, kicking and hitting, but they were no match for the older man.

"What's going on?" Frieda asked, using her hospital voice. "Who are you and why are you shouting at my patient?"

The man turned on Frieda but didn't lower his voice. Disbelief and suspicion clouded his face.

"*Your* patient?"

"I am Dr. Frieda Klunsberg. Mrs. Chiver and her children are my patients. Who are *you*?"

Maria watched in admiration as the man shrunk back, his grip on the twins slipping. One boy gave him a kick, and he released both of them with a grunt. He reached out, hand raised, but Frieda stood between him and the children. Frieda pushed the boys behind her.

Maria spoke up. "Shall I get the police? I saw an officer on the lane back there." She hadn't, but how would he know?

"Don't need no coppers. I called to collect the rent. She's late again." The man snarled, but he didn't look as confident as before.

"Do you usually behave in such an aggressive manner, sir" Frieda looked like an avenging angel. Her eyes blazed with rage and indignation flowed out of her very bones.

"I ain't done nothing. They have to pay, or they leave. Simple as that."

"We paid." Leonie spoke up, "We've paid twice. He said the landlord put up the rent. Mama paid him when he visited while I was at work."

Frieda gave the man a dismissive look. "So this… man isn't your landlord?"

"No." Leonie sounded slightly more confident.

Frieda moved closer to the stranger. Maria watched as her friend almost hit him with her finger as she pointed at him.

"Get out and don't come back. You have no

authority to be here. I won't have anyone upset my patients, do you hear?"

"Two women won't tell me what to do."

"Won't we?" Frieda raked her eyes from the top of his head to his feet and back again. "Maria, could you please fetch the policeman? Ask him to telephone Inspector Griffin."

The man's gaze shifted right and left, telling Maria he recognized the name. "Now wait a minute, don't be hasty. I'm leaving."

Maria glanced at Frieda, her friend was shaking, not with fear, but anger.

Frieda put her hands on her hips. "Not yet, you aren't. I want you to hand back the extra rent you took."

"I ain't got it." He wouldn't look at them. Maria knew he was lying.

"Maria," Frieda's voice held firm. Maria took a step toward the door.

"Hold your horses. Here." He threw pennies and dimes at them before stamping out. He slammed the door. The building shook and pieces of plaster fell off.

# CHAPTER 14

*F*rieda coughed as dust-covered everything. Glancing around, she saw things were even worse than they had feared. One look at Leonie's mother told Frieda that her condition had deteriorated rapidly since she'd last visited during the strike. That was eighteen months ago. Why hadn't she come back sooner?

"Maria, why don't you and Leonie sort out dinner while I examine Mrs. Chiver." She didn't wait for a response. She tried to be gentle, but the woman was very ill and fragile. "You are very good to come to see us, Frieda." Mrs. Chiver whispered. Frieda had to strain to hear her.

"You should have asked Leonie to come get me. I should have come sooner. I'm sorry. I let you down."

Mrs. Chiver gripped Frieda's hand, "It was my pride

79

that let me down, Frieda. I refused to admit I couldn't keep my family together."

"Yes, you can. You just need some help. Why don't you try to eat a little beef pie, it will help build you up."

Johanna ate less than a small child before announcing she was full. Frieda's concern grew.

"Maria, I will find a telephone and call the hospital. We need an ambulance. Leonie, do you have a spare nightgown for your mother? She isn't well, but she will feel better once I get her the right medicine. She just needs some tests to find out how we can help her." Despite putting a positive spin on her announcement, Leonie's sister, Carrie, burst into tears again.

"My little ones, I can't leave them here." Leonie's mother fretted.

"We will take them to the Sanctuary. Lily can send some men over to pack up the rest of your things." Frieda wished Tommy and Mini-Mike were here to help. Lily had spoken about these men with such fondness, but they were dead now. Caught up in some stupid gang war.

Frieda phoned to order the ambulance. She wasn't at all sure Leonie's mother would leave the hospital. Then she flagged down a cab to take Maria, Leonie, and the children to the Sanctuary. It was quicker and safer, although more expensive, than trying to find their way by streetcar. Relieved when the cab driver recognized her, she told him someone at the Sanctuary would pay him.

"Don't you worry none, Dr. Frieda. Pieter is my name. You helped my missus birth my son. Do anything for you so I would."

"Pieter, would you know a trustworthy man willing to look after this house and the family's belongings until I can get back tomorrow? The landlord's agent was here earlier."

Pieter spat on the ground. "That man is scum. I have a friend who will do it for a hot meal. He's been out of work for a while, but I'd trust him with my family."

"I will pay him tomorrow. Thank you, Pieter."

She went back inside to tell Maria the cab was waiting, and ask her to accompany the girls to the Sanctuary.

"I don't have money for a cab, Frieda," Maria's cheeks burned.

"They keep a jar at the Sanctuary for just such an emergency. Don't worry. Pieter, the driver, is a patient of mine, or at least his wife is. He'll look after you. Leonie, can you tell your siblings they will be safe, and your mama too?"

Leonie nodded, her large eyes too big for the small pinched face. Frieda kicked herself again. If she had visited earlier, maybe this poor child wouldn't look so brow beaten.

# CHAPTER 15

*P*ieter dropped Maria, Leonie, Carrie and their brothers at the Sanctuary. Lily opened the door, insisting on paying the cab driver and giving him a tip on top. She ushered the children inside to the main sitting room. The room was lovely and warm. Maria felt herself thawing out.

"Maria, so nice to see you again. Who are these lovely children?"

Lily behaved as if people arrived at the Sanctuary every day carrying a bag of belongings. Maria admired the other woman's calm.

"This is Leonie Chiver and her siblings. Leonie works with me at the Triangle."

"Welcome, Leonie. Are you the girl who joined the strike with Frieda?"

"Yes, Ma'am. We were in jail at the same time." Leonie whispered the word.

"Yes, she told me. What are you children called?" Lily asked the younger twins, but they took a step back to hide behind Leonie.

"They are Carrie and Morris, ma'am," one of the boys said, "I'm Sam and he's Alfred." The boy looked at his brother, "we're eight years old."

The younger twins played dumb, holding onto Leonie as if they would never let go. Lily smiled at them.

"Are you hungry? Cook made a cake earlier. Would you like some?"

They remained silent. Maria intervened.

"Lily, if you don't mind, I can take the younger ones for cake while you speak to Leonie. Frieda has taken her mother to the hospital."

"No, we want to stay with Leonie." Carrie and Morris shrieked in unison.

"Why don't we all eat in here." Lily bent down to Carrie's level. "Carrie, Morris, I promise nothing bad will happen here. You and your brothers are safe, and Leonie will stay with you."

Leonie protested, "I have to work in the morning."

"Yes, you do but the twins can stay here and you can come back in the evening." Lily spoke confidently and smiled, but it did little to help the frightened children.

Carrie and Morris moved closer to Leonie, but didn't speak.

Starving and anxious about the walk home alone in the dark, Maria moved to the door.

"Where are you going, Maria?" Lily demanded.

"I should get home."

"Not until you have something to eat and warm up a little. Please stay, Maria. I haven't seen you for at least two weeks."

Maria couldn't hide her stomach grumbling. The noise made everyone laugh, even Sam. Lily grinned.

"I think that's enough evidence to tell Cook you're staying for tea."

Maria's cheeks reddened, but she didn't really mind. She had helped put the children at ease, and she loved Cook's baking.

# CHAPTER 16

*A*fter they had eaten sandwiches and cake, a yawning Carrie allowed Leonie to take her up to a bedroom. Lily arranged for the whole family to stay in one room. There were two beds and a mattress on the floor. Leonie and Carrie shared while Morris took the mattress. Sam and Alfred took the other bed.

"Please try to rest, Leonie. Frieda will come and tell you how your mother is when she gets home."

"Thank you, Miss Lily." Leonie's eyes hadn't lost their fearful look.

Maria could imagine how she was feeling. She'd been worried sick about her Papa, but at least her sisters had Mama to lean on. Poor Leonie had nobody to help her. Maria spoke up, "Leonie, we are all your friends, and we will do as much as we can to help you.

Lily, Kathleen, Cook, and the other ladies who live in the sanctuary all understand what you are going through. Please try to get some sleep."

"Thank you, Maria, for bringing us here, and to you, Miss Lily, for letting us stay."

"Call me Lily, Leonie. We will see you in the morning." Lily closed the bedroom door, and led the way downstairs.

She ushered Maria back into the sitting room. "Take a seat for a few minutes, and tell me everything."

With the Chiver family settled, Maria told Lily about the state of their apartment, the horrible rent collector, and the lack of food or anything else in the house.

"Frieda looked very concerned for Leonie's mother. The poor family. Nobody should live like they do. Even during the strike, when things got bad for us, we managed."

Lily's face turned crimson, her foot tapping as anger over the family's situation flooded through her. "Poor Mrs. Chiver trying to cope with illness and the children, never mind that man. Frieda was right to pay someone to protect their stuff overnight, but I don't think they should go back to that apartment. They can live here for now until we know what is happening with their mother. Would Leonie leave the Triangle and work here, do you think? I don't have space at the moment, but I'd give her a job as soon as a position arises."

"I'm sure she would." Maria wanted to say she'd take the job, but she couldn't. The Sanctuary's mission was to help people like Leonie's family. She was rich in comparison.

"Maria, get a cab home. Your mother will worry and you look tired. Conrad won't be happy with me for keeping you up late."

Maria blushed as Lily kept talking.

"Conrad's a wonderful young man. He and Gustav have been very useful. Their ideas for the factory will help a lot. If the builders ever work. All they seem to do is drink tea." Lily stood up. "Don't mind me, Kathleen says I like to grumble. Would you like to take the rest of the cake home with you? Give your mother a treat?"

"Thank you, Lily. Mama has a sweet tooth. At the moment, I need to give her more reasons to love me." Maria put her hand over her mouth, startled she had spoken her thoughts aloud.

Lily took Maria's hand and squeezed it. "Your mama loves you, sweetheart. She's grieving for her husband and we often lash out at those we love. Give her time."

Maria hesitated, not wanting to be disloyal to her family, but she needed reassurance.

"It's been over a year. When will she forgive me?"

"She has nothing to forgive, Maria. It wasn't your fault you were there with him during his final moments while she was at home. In time, she will be thankful he didn't die alone. She has to work through her feelings. But she loves you Maria, she shows you in little ways every day. She always has your lunch ready for work, she keeps your clothes clean and your home tidy."

Maria pushed her hair out of her eyes. She wanted to believe Lily.

"Trust me. When you have children of your own, you will understand your mother better." Lily put her finger under Maria's chin and forced her to meet her gaze. "How about we add some cookies to that cake?"

"Thank you, Lily. Not just for the cake, but for listening."

"I am always here. You come and see me anytime you want. Bring Conrad, too. In fact, why don't you both come on Sunday? Gustav and Alice are coming to tea and bringing a Miss Baker. She works at the orphanage where Alice used to live. Alice speaks of her like a guardian angel. I'm curious to meet her."

"We'd love to come, thank you, Lily."

Maria took the cake, cookies and other things Lily had wrapped up. Lily whistled for a cab, surprising Maria. She'd never have believed a lady like Lily could make that sound, but it worked as a cab arrived promptly.

Maria hesitated, she didn't have the money for the fare, but Lily had thought of that already. As she made her way home, Maria counted her blessings. She didn't know what she would do if she lost Mama or anyone else in her family. They might not be perfect, but they supported each other in their own way. She'd make an extra effort with Rosa from now on.

# CHAPTER 17

Frieda held Leonie's mother's hand while Dr. Richard Green examined her. Frieda suspected Johanna's liver was failing. Despite Johanna's color, her shriveled up body, and her yellow pupils, Frieda hoped Dr. Green would find a different cause. Her hopes died as he delivered his diagnosis.

"Mrs. Chiver... Johanna... there is no easy way to say this. I..."

"I'm dying," Johanna whispered.

"Yes, ma'am. I'm so sorry. If there was anything we could do, we would, but in cases like these, the best we can do is keep you comfortable. The pain must be unbearable."

Despite the agonized expression in her eyes, Johanna put on a brave face, "I get by."

Frieda turned her head so Johanna wouldn't see her tears.

"Is there anyone we can get for you? A family member?" Dr. Green asked.

Frieda took over. "I'll speak to Leonie, Johanna's eldest daughter. There is nobody else." Frieda didn't want anyone asking for Johanna's husband.

"I'll go get you some morphine for the pain, Johanna. Try to rest a little."

Frieda thanked Richard before taking a seat beside Johanna's bed. When he left, Johanna reached for Frieda's hand.

"What will happen to my young ones? Leonie, she tries, but she's too young to look after the little ones. She's at work all day." Johanna's voice was fainter than before.

"Do you have any family? A sister or a close friend?"

Johanna closed her eyes, Frieda assumed she had drifted off to sleep. She waited, holding the woman's hand, praying her suffering would be over soon. Richard returned to administer the morphine injection.

"Why didn't she come to see us before now?" he asked.

"It's my fault. I should have visited."

Johanna moved her head slightly and then opened her eyes. She spoke in short sentences, trying to get the words out but struggling.

"Not your fault. You were kind to us. Dr. Patrick, too. Mine. I had too much pride. Didn't want people to know I couldn't cope." Johanna struggled to sit up. Richard and Frieda supported her as a nurse gave her more pillows.

"There's nobody, Frieda. Any family I had, gave me up for dead a long time ago. They didn't agree with me marrying Jacob Chiver. Said he was a no good, lily livered son of a rattlesnake. They was right too. But I was in love, thought I knew best."

"Do you know where he's at?" Richard asked.

Johanna shook her head, violently. "No, and I don't want to. He's never to get his hands on my children, especially the children. He wouldn't treat them right. Beat them when they were little. He tried treating Leonie like... like a wife."

Frieda exchanged a look of horror with Richard. Was it the morphine talking? Sometimes people hallucinated.

Johanna spoke faster than before, as if desperate to get the words out.

"That's why I got rid of him. I knows people feel sorry for me, said he left me. I ran him out of town. Told him I'd get him one night when he was asleep if he ever set foot in my house again. I sharpened a kitchen knife. I wasn't going to kill him. I told him what I'd do. He'd never be able to hurt another girl again. You should have seen his face. Worked, too. I never saw him after that. I don't know whether he's alive or dead. I don't care neither." Johanna fell back on the pillow.

"Rest now. Let the morphine work its magic. I'll look after your children, Johanna, I promise. You know Lily and Kathleen from Carmel's Mission? They'll help me." Frieda brushed the hair back from Johanna's forehead, massaging the woman's temples. "That's it. Relax and sleep. We will talk more tomorrow."

Frieda sat by the bed as Johanna slept, still holding her hand. She cried silently for this poor woman and her children back at the Sanctuary. Why hadn't she done more? She knew Leonie was struggling during the strike. She should have kept visiting; she should've helped more.

She sensed someone watching and looked up to find Patrick standing a little away from the bed, as if he was afraid to intrude.

"Frieda, Dad said you were here. You should be at home, resting."

"I can't go home. I failed her," Frieda looked at Johanna.

"You didn't fail anybody, Frieda. you can't cure everyone. We're doctors, not God."

"Don't you think I know that! But I should have checked up on the family. So should you! Why didn't you go back to visit them? You knew she was sick. You could have helped --" Frieda stopped, horrified by what she had said. Attacking Patrick would help no one.

"Frieda, I went back. Mrs. Chiver didn't want me to visit anymore. She said she was feeling better, and my time was best used looking after those that needed me. I had my final exams, and it was hard to find time to study and... Don't you know how bad I feel?"

She did, and she could see her own emotions reflected in his eyes. Guilt, anger, and regret.

"I didn't mean what I said. I know you did your best. I just.... I feel so angry. Why do good people die and horrible people live long healthy lives?"

"That's not a question I can answer." Patrick examined Johanna, noting her breathing and pulse rate on her chart.

"How long?" Frieda whispered.

"A day or so. You should bring the children in to say goodbye. But wait until the morning. Dad gave her a large dose of morphine so she will sleep for hours. She needs the rest."

Frieda stood and kissed Johanna on the forehead.

"I will be back soon. Don't let go, Johanna, until I come back with your children, you hear?" Frieda's voice shook.

Patrick stood back to let her pass. "She'll be in a deep sleep for a while after the morphine. Let her daughters sleep tonight."

"Patrick…"

"You go, I'll stay with her." He didn't look at her. She wanted to reach out and touch him, to apologize for her words, her anger. But he was so distant and cold.

With a last look at Johanna, she left.

## CHAPTER 18

When Frieda got back to the Sanctuary, it was after three in the morning. Everyone was asleep, Patrick was right. It was pointless waking Leonie and her siblings now. She would see them first thing in the morning.

She lay on her bed, but sleep wouldn't come. Every time she closed her eyes she saw Patrick's wounded expression, the hurt in his eyes. She couldn't believe she'd attacked him like that. He didn't deserve her censure or her judgement. He was a wonderful, committed doctor.

* * *

She must have fallen asleep as gentle knocking on

her bedroom door woke her. Lily poked her head around the open door.

"Frieda, I'm sorry to wake you, but Leonie and the twins are wondering how their mother is. Leonie will have to leave for work shortly."

"Lily, what are you doing here so early?"

"I slept in one of the empty beds." She came into the bedroom, softly closing the door behind her. "So how is she?"

"Bad. She will die soon. Richard gave her morphine. Patrick is with her, but he said to let the children sleep."

"The poor woman and those children. What will they do? Will you be able to track down the father?"

"No, definitely not." Frieda told Lily the story Johanna had told them last night.

Lily wasn't shocked, she'd heard similar tales far too often.

"They will have to stay here for the moment. Based on what Maria said, their apartment is barely habitable. I wish I had space for Leonie to work here. If the factory was built..." Lily fell silent.

"I know, Lily."

"Do you want me to be with you when you break the news?" Lily spoke gently, her eyes full of concern.

Tears sprang into Frieda's eyes at Lily's thoughtfulness. "Please. I know I should face them alone, but I feel so guilty. I should have checked up on Mrs. Chiver before now."

"Frieda, would checking on her have stopped her getting whatever is killing her?"

Frieda shook her head. "I don't think so."

"Then you can stop talking like that. We can only do so much. Wash your face, and I will bring the children downstairs. We will get them breakfast before we go to the hospital. I guess someone should tell Leonie's work."

"Maria will do that. She is bound to guess when Leonie doesn't turn up. I can't see the boss giving Leonie time off though." Frieda got out of bed. "The Triangle bosses are not known for their charity."

Lily sighed. "Let's pretend they are and deal with the consequences later. Better to ask for forgiveness than to ask for permission, right?"

Frieda flashed Lily a smile, trying to ease the concern written all over the other woman. Then she turned to wash her face. Lily took the hint and left.

With a glance in the mirror, Frieda left soon after. She was about to break the children's hearts.

Carrie and Morris reacted as expected, crying for their mother, but the older twins worried Frieda more. They just stared at her. Leonie didn't shed a tear, just looked more downcast than she usually did.

"I knew she was worse than she let on. What will happen now?" Leonie asked.

"Don't worry about that for now." Lily said. "You will stay here for now. Have breakfast, and then we will

101

all go to the hospital. Your mother wants to see you. After, we will go back to your apartment, pack up your things, and bring them here."

"We lose our home and Mother, Leonie?"

"It wasn't ours, Sam. You don't want to be there when that man comes back, do you?" Leonie spoke harshly, her despair getting the better of her.

Sam shook his head, his eyes on Leonie. She didn't say another word. Frieda wanted to shield the youngsters, but couldn't blame Leonie. Overnight she had become a parent and sole earner of this little family.

Frieda took Morris by the hand. "Why don't we see what we can rustle up for breakfast. Do you like porridge?"

Morris screwed up his face. "I don't know. What is it?"

"It's a bowl of warm oats. I love it. Try it and see for yourself. It will keep you warm inside."

"Can we bring ma some?" Morris said, his eyes lit up with hope.

"Yes, Morris. She might like that." Frieda didn't know how she kept her voice steady. She wanted to scream and rant about how unfair life was, but that wouldn't help anyone.

Breakfast passed quickly with Cook spoiling the children. She packed a small basket for Morris to take to the hospital.

Frieda whispered, "Cook, I don't think Johanna will eat anything."

"I know that, Frieda, but it will do that child good to think he's helping. Poor little thing. He looks no older than a toddler."

"He and Carrie are almost four. Their older twin brothers are eight, and Leonie is fifteen, or thereabouts," Frieda whispered for fear the children would hear her.

Cook made the sign of the cross before giving her eyes a quick wipe with the corner of her apron. Then she started washing some pots. She'd scrape the metal off the bottom at the rate she was scrubbing.

Lily came in to tell them the cab was waiting outside. Morris and Carrie moved to Leonie's side, but she seemed unaware of her younger siblings' need for reassurance. Lily helped Morris into the cab before handing him the basket of food, "Can you carry that, Morris, or is it too heavy?"

"No, I can hold it."

"Carrie, you climb into that seat beside Morris and then I'll sit beside you. Sam and Alfred can sit in the back. Frieda can sit beside Leonie. All set, off we go."

Frieda could tell Lily was forcing her voice to sound cheerful. No doubt she was dreading the hospital visit too.

As they neared the hospital, Frieda's stomach turned over. Would Patrick be there? Would he still be angry or would he accept her apology? Morris put his hand into Frieda's and asked, "Does Mother look scary?"

Cursing herself for thinking about Patrick and not these poor children, she put her arm around Morris. "No sweetheart, she looks the same as yesterday. Maybe a little more tired. She is on very strong medicine to help keep her comfortable."

Morris paused as if to consider what Frieda had said before asking, "Will she know us?"

Frieda wasn't sure of the answer, so she avoided the question. She hoped Johanna hadn't lost consciousness for the sake of the children, although for their mother, it would bring relief.

# CHAPTER 19

*P*atrick was at Johanna's bedside. He greeted Lily with a kiss on the cheek, and then shook hands with Leonie. He barely looked at Frieda.

"Johanna, your children are here," he said softly, brushing Johanna's hand to wake her. He addressed the youngsters, "Your mom is tired, but she's been asking for you."

"Mama, wake up. Please. I want to go home," Carrie cried, pushing her way past Frieda and climbing up on the bed. She sat on the edge, stroking her mother's hair. "We have a picnic for you. Cook is very nice and she gave me cookies."

Carrie pulled at her mother before glaring at Patrick.

"What have you done to Mama? Why isn't she listening to me?"

"Carrie, be quiet. Mother will be cross if you make a spectacle of yourself," Leonie admonished her sister.

Johanna's eyes opened and lit up when she saw her daughters. "My children, give me a kiss." Carrie kissed her, not moving out of the way for the others until Frieda intervened.

"Sit here, Carrie, on the seat. You can hold your mother's hand."

Carrie sat down and held onto her mother in a vice-like grip. Johanna grimaced but when Frieda tried to loosen the child's hold, Johanna whispered, "No. Let her hold me."

Frieda bit her lip, trying to remain brave. She listened as Johanna told each of her children how much she loved them, and how they would have to stick together in the future. Johanna picked something individual to say to each child. "Carrie, your drawings will hang in art galleries. My darling Leonie, grown up before your time. Your designs will dress smart ladies all over New York. I'm so proud of you." Johanna's voice slurred slightly as she battled tiredness and pain to speak. She held Morris's hand as she told him how she loved the way he made her laugh. Then to the older twins she said, "Sam, you must keep practicing your writing. They will make your stories into books one day. Alfred, dear, solemn boy, you will be a scientist or a doctor. Someone special to help people like me. You all make me so proud."

Johanna closed her eyes again, but just as Frieda was about to usher the children outside, Johanna spoke again.

"Now be good and go wait in the hall with Dr. Frieda. I need to speak to Miss Lily for a moment."

The younger twins protested, but at a look from their mother, they left. Frieda shepherded them outside, leaving Patrick and Lily behind. Patrick came out to call them back inside a few minutes later.

"Children your mother wants to see you."

Frieda wrapped her arms around her stomach as she watched the children hug and kiss their mother goodbye. Lily came to stand at her side, her arm around Frieda's shoulders, her eyes just as glassy. Then Johanna called for Frieda and Patrick.

"Thank you both for all you did for me."

Frieda couldn't reply. Patrick said huskily, "I wish all my patients were like you, Johanna."

Johanna smiled. Her eyes went back to her children, huddled around her. Carrie on one side, Morris on the other, with Leonie supporting Morris from behind. The older twins stood behind Carrie.

"Leonie, look after my babies. I love you."

For a few seconds, they stared at their mother.

"Is she dead?" Leonie whispered, still looking at her mother.

Patrick responded, "No, she's sleeping for now. You can stay with her. I'll make sure nobody disturbs

RACHEL WESSON

you." His gaze met hers for a second before he left the room.

Lily indicated for Frieda to take a seat beside her, but Frieda needed to go to Patrick. He looked like he wanted to cry.

"I'll be back in a few minutes."

She left the room wondering if it had been Patrick who arranged for a private room. She found him on the roof of the hospital; it was where they went when they had a harrowing crisis.

"Patrick."

"Not now, Frieda. I haven't slept in hours. I don't want to say something I shouldn't."

Taken aback by his tone, she kicked herself for hurting him.

"Patrick, I want you to listen to me. What I said yesterday, I didn't mean it. I was hurt, angry, confused, tired, and all the above. You did what you could, more than that for Johanna. I'm sorry."

Silence.

"Patrick, I…"

"She's dying. I didn't save her. You were right in what you said. Other things distracted me. I can see that now. I will do better. From now on, I will focus solely on my work. Next time, maybe the patient won't die because of my neglect."

He turned his back and stared out over the city.

Horrified, Frieda took a move closer. He stiffened and she hesitated. Without turning to look at her, he said in a tone that brooked no argument.

"Go back to Johanna's children. They need someone now."

## CHAPTER 20

The city buried Johanna on Saturday morning. The family didn't have the money for a funeral. Johanna had made Lily promise not to waste money on her funeral, but to help her family instead. When Lily protested she could do both, Johanna said she didn't need a fancy coffin to meet her maker.

Lily asked Father Nelson to say a few words in church at his usual Saturday morning mass, despite Johanna not being a member of his congregation. Leonie refused to go to church, insisting on returning to work.

Lily took the younger children to Father Nelson's church, feeling they needed to mark their mother's passing. They listened as he said some nice things about their mother. Father Nelson hadn't known Mrs. Chiver, but he chose a sermon on the merits of having a wonderful mother and a happy home. Lily exchanged a sad smile with him when he greeted them as they filed from the church.

"Will the children stay with you, Lily? I could try to find them a place if you wish," he asked.

Carrie and Morris gripped Lily's hands tighter.

"No thank you, Father. They will stay at the Sanctuary for now. Leonie, their elder sister, works at the Triangle. She will be home before the children have to go to bed."

Once back at the Sanctuary, the four siblings returned to their room. Lily came up with some food but they were fast asleep, curled up in a ball together on one bed. How young and innocent they looked. She stared at them for a few seconds. How was she going to help this family? The children couldn't live here forever. The mission hadn't been set up as an orphanage. Maybe Bridget could help?

*Dear Bridget,*

*I know Kathleen wrote you the other day and updated you on everything happening here. This is just a short note to say we buried Johanna Chiver this morning. I am at a loss how to help her, and wondered if you would have space in Riverside Springs. I know it's a lot to ask, but we really don't want to separate the children. Leonie is only fifteen years old but feels responsible for her siblings. She appears quite serious at first but underneath, I think there is a wonderful young woman just waiting for a chance to thrive rather than survive.*

*The eldest twins, boys of eight, are as different as chalk and cheese. Sam is outgoing and confident, while Alfred is very serious and a real worrier. The younger twins are almost four, although you'd never guess from their height. Carrie is such a sweet little thing with her blonde hair and sea-blue eyes, I'd keep her if I could. Her twin, Morris, has a mop of blonde hair and although his eyes shine with innocence, he is always up to mischief.*

*Johanna made me promise the children's father would never gain custody. I don't know where he is or if he is even alive. I believe it's in the best interest of the children to get them out of New York. The story Johanna shared with me about this man makes him the last person innocent children should live with. I will deal with the legalities if questions should arise.*

*Johanna begged me not to let the children end up on the orphan train. Bridget, it was the first time I saw the woman cry. She was adamant the family needed to stay together, especially the younger two, Morris and Carrie. Leonie has a job at the Triangle Shirtwaist, she is a seamstress. Perhaps Bella would have enough work to give her a job? Despite Morris's mischievous smile, all are well behaved. Johanna did a wonderful job with them.*

*You are my last hope. I know you will do your best. Kathleen said things were going well in Riverside Springs, so I am keeping fingers and toes crossed you can take these children.*

*Looking forward to hearing from you soon,*
*Love always,*
*Lily.*

Lily posted the letter before she could think twice about asking for help. She knew Bridget would try her best, but Kathleen's older sister had a heart complaint, and they preferred not to worry her. Still, this was an exceptional situation.

When Leonie got back that evening, she refused to discuss anything, instead pleading a headache, and asking to go to bed. Lily didn't push her. She had space for now, and the family needed time together. She would wait for Bridget's reply before saying anything to Leonie.

For now, she had to re-arrange the lunch for Miss Baker and the others. It was too soon for the Chiver children to witness a party atmosphere in the Sanctuary.

\* \* \*

Frieda suspected Patrick was avoiding her. He

usually worked a similar shift pattern, but she found herself partnered with Dr. Hamilton instead.

When she saw Patrick at a distance, he looked haggard. He barely acknowledged her, and the one time she had walked over to his table during lunch, he'd claimed an emergency and left almost as soon as she sat down.

She stopped him one day, trying to apologize.

"Patrick, please talk to me. I know you're angry. I wish I could take back what I said."

"Why? You were right. I wasn't focused and Mrs. Chiver died. I won't let it happen again." He looked at the clock. "Excuse me, Frieda. I'm due in theater."

She watched him walk away, not knowing what to do.

"Frieda? Dr. Klunsberg? Are you with us?"

Frieda jumped as a nurse pulled her arm.

"Frieda, do you need a cup of coffee? Dr. Hamilton called you several times. I think his patience is running out."

Frieda ran a hand through her hair. "Please tell Dr. Hamilton I will be right there. I just need to wash my hands."

As she walked into the bathroom, she forced herself to breathe slower. She had to work here, to be professional. She couldn't allow herself to fall apart because Patrick couldn't bear to see her. It would blow over.

He'd come around in time. Wouldn't he? What would happen if he didn't?

Days passed and still he avoided her. She tried to apologize again, but he brushed her off. Eventually she gave up.

# CHAPTER 21

Saturday afternoon, Frieda crept into the Sanctuary, hoping to get to bed without meeting anyone. She was beyond tired.

"Frieda, there you are. We haven't seen you all week. You look shattered."

Frieda tried to smile at Lily's remarks. She was mentally and physically exhausted. Influenza had broken out in some tenement buildings and the hospital had been busier than ever. But that wasn't the sole reason for her exhaustion. Patrick continued to avoid her, only speaking to her when necessary. If she looked tired, he looked like death warmed up.

"Are you coming down with something? You can't afford to neglect yourself, Frieda."

"I'm just tired, Lily. It's been a long week."

Lily put her head to one side, but for once didn't

argue. Frieda turned for the door.

"Are you free tomorrow for afternoon tea?"

Frieda suppressed a groan. She'd forgotten Alice, Gustav and their friend Miss Baker were coming to tea. Lily had invited Maria, Conrad and Patrick too. Was he coming?

As if Lily read her mind, she confirmed, "I've had a note from Patrick to say he's too busy and sends his regrets. Maria and Conrad also canceled. Maria has a cold."

Frieda's stomach lurched. Did Maria have influenza? Lily must have seen the fear in her face as she rushed to reassure her.

"Maria has a cold, that's all. Conrad came around earlier to say he was taking her chicken soup his mother used to swear by. Cook gave him some cookies for Maria's mother. I swear, Frieda, I have a good mind to go around to Mrs. Mezza's and give her a piece of my mind. Why would you not want your daughter to go out with such a wonderful young man?"

Frieda didn't want to discuss romances. Not now, her heart was breaking. She pretended to yawn.

"Lily, please excuse me, but my bed is calling."

Lily wasn't easily put off. "You will come tomorrow, won't you? Alice will be upset if nobody is there to meet Miss Baker. She thinks the world of the lady. It will be good for the Chivers too. I can't get a word out of the younger children. They don't speak unless it is to

Leonie. Cook has tried tempting them with many wonderful creations, but even chocolate cakes cannot raise a smile. I'm worried about them. I haven't heard from Bridget yet."

Lily had told Frieda about writing to ask if the four children and Leonie could move to Riverside Springs. Frieda wondered if it was wise to leave Leonie in the dark about the plan, but figured Lily knew best. If Bridget didn't have room, they would have only raised Leonie's hopes for nothing.

Guilt flooded through Frieda. She hadn't spent a minute helping with the Chiver family, and Lily looked tired too. Lily rarely admitted to being worried, preferring to put a positive face on at all times.

"I'll be there." Frieda couldn't bear to upset Alice either. Plus, if she spent time with the twins, maybe her mind would stop replaying images of Patrick's face.

"Are you going to eat something before you sleep?"

"No thank you, Lily. I will eat later."

Frieda climbed the stairs, each step feeling like a mountain. She hoped she'd sleep, but as usual when her head hit the pillow, her guilt over what she'd said and done overwhelmed her. It was her fault Patrick looked so awful and Kathleen was worried about her son. Lily hadn't asked the Chiver family to come to the sanctuary, that had been her decision, and now she was letting Lily carry the burden alone. She owed her friends a lot better.

# CHAPTER 22

*S*unday morning, after a restless night tossing and turning, Frieda woke to a gorgeous smell wafting up from the kitchen. She followed the delicious aroma downstairs to find Cook up to her ears in baking.

"Morning, Frieda. I got apple pies in the oven and some cookies already baked. Bread's fresh this morning. Would you like some ham and eggs?"

Frieda reached for an apron. "I'm not hungry, Cook. Let me help you. What can I do?"

"Sit down and have something to eat for a start. You didn't eat a pick last night. You can't fight off influenza and goodness knows what else is in that hospital if you don't eat properly." Cook flapped a cloth at Frieda, directing her to sit at the table.

Frieda didn't bother trying to defend herself. Cook was as ornery as a mule when she got her mind set on something. Frieda sat sipping a cup of coffee as Cook dished up a plate piled high with eggs, bacon and biscuits.

Frieda protested, "I can't eat all that."

Cook gave her a stern look, making Frieda feel like a five-year-old. She picked up her fork and ate. Her mouth watered as the food tickled her taste buds. She had the plate finished in no time.

Cook took the dirty plate. "See. You listen to me from now on, young Frieda. All that studying is all and well and good, but nothing is better for ya than a decent breakfast." Cook re-filled her coffee cup. "Plain simple food can cure a lot of ailments including a broken heart."

Startled, Frieda glanced at the older woman, wondering if she was talking about her, but the woman was staring out the window.

"I thought those children would go to church, their mother being the religious sort and all but they said no." Cook's voice wobbled. "Still, I guess a bit of wintery sunshine might do them good."

Frieda glanced out the window in the garden at the back. The elder boys were sitting together on the wooden bench under the tree. They didn't appear to be chatting, but maybe they were whispering. Carrie and Morris were playing with something on a blanket on the grass.

"Might take them a bit of time to appreciate

anything good, Cook."

"Aye Frieda, I guess you're right. Something wrong with this world when young kiddies like that are left all alone."

Cook ran her cloth over her eyelid. Frieda wanted to hug her, but knew that would really upset the older woman. Cook liked to pretend she could cope with anything.

"You really outdid yourself Cook, everything looks fabulous." Frieda did her best to distract the older woman. "And the smell has my mouth watering, despite that great mountain of food you just fed me."

Cook beamed before looking at her clock.

"Is that the time? They'll be here any minute. Frieda, go pretty yourself up and take off the apron. Lily must be running late, as usual. We need to show Miss Baker we run a good house here."

Was Cook nervous? She was used to entertaining Lily and Kathleen's friends and various visitors who called to discuss charitable functions.

"Cook, Miss Baker is our guest not an inspector."

"She runs that home for delinquent girls, doesn't she?" Cook shuddered. "I know those places. We should burn them all to the ground. As if any child is born delinquent. It's the badness in life that ruins innocent children."

Frieda sighed. Cook had decided Miss Baker was the enemy. Cook intensely disliked anyone who didn't

123

treat children with kindness. Frieda rushed to rectify the older woman's misunderstanding.

"Alice speaks of Miss Baker like she was her guardian angel. I think you might like her. At least give her a chance. Everyone deserves that."

Cook grumbled as she headed back to her stove. Cook had a heart the size of the ocean, and took each child who came to the Sanctuary to her heart. She would have been a wonderful mother if her life had taken a different path.

Frieda ran upstairs, changed, and was down again in fifteen minutes. She grabbed a cloth and some polish and gave the sitting room a quick dusting. Cook was right, they had to put their best foot forward. As she cleaned, her thoughts flew to Patrick. Was he working today or just avoiding her?

"Frieda, darling, you look sad."

Startled, she jumped. She hadn't heard Kathleen come into the room. "I was miles away." She gave her friend a kiss on the cheek, looking behind her. "Where is Richard?" she asked.

"Patrick stayed at the hospital last night, again. Richard went to pick him up. I'm worried about Patrick, Frieda. Mrs. Chiver's death has taken a huge toll on him. No doctor likes to lose a patient, but this is worse than that. It's almost as if he blames himself."

Frieda tried to make her voice sound normal. "She was a lovely woman. I guess that makes it harder."

Coward! Why can't you just admit you made him feel responsible? Your harsh words are the reason he works so hard.

Kathleen looked unconvinced but thankfully Lily and her husband, Charlie, arrived with their guests.

"Frieda, Kathleen, Alice would like you to meet someone." Lily said, taking off her hat and gloves.

Alice led a woman by the hand into the sitting room. Frieda couldn't get over how young Miss Baker was, she couldn't be much older than Patrick.

She didn't look at all like Frieda had imagined. She'd expected someone formal with a pinched face after all she had heard about the horrible home where Alice had lived. Miss Baker's round, plain face lit up with a hesitant smile. An anxious, eager to please expression in her eyes. The poor woman was nervous.

"Frieda, Miss Kathleen, this is Miss Baker. She's lovely, but shy. I said you'd be nice to her." Alice looked at them so earnestly, Frieda couldn't hide her amusement.

"Alice, you make us sound like ogres. Miss Baker, it's lovely to meet you. I'm Frieda, I've heard a lot about you."

"Please call me, Emily. I've heard a lot about you too. Especially about your work in the hospital. Alice is rather a fan."

Alice nodded, clinging to Emily's arm. "I will be a doctor when I grow up."

"Are you Alice? I thought you enjoyed sewing?" Gustav ruffled her hair. Alice leaned into her father's side.

"Pa, I told you ages ago. I changed my mind." Alice glanced out the window. "Who are they? Those children. They look very sad."

Frieda glanced outside before saying, "They are, Alice. Their mother died a week ago."

"Can I cheer them up?" Alice asked.

Frieda put out her hand to take Alice outside. "Let me introduce you."

"No, Frieda. You stay here with Miss Baker. I'm a big girl."

Alice ran outside, leaving the adults staring after her.

"Gustav, your Alice is just blossoming." Kathleen said.

Miss Baker spoke up. "Alice was always so caring for others. She always tried to help others, even when she was little."

"Please come in and sit down, Gustav and you too, Emily. You don't mind if we call you Emily, do you? Would you like tea, coffee, or water?" Lily asked. Frieda went to the kitchen to give the drinks order to Cook before heading to the garden. Alice had got the children talking. Frieda stood listening, hoping her presence wouldn't stop them chatting. She listened as Alice explained her background.

"Mutti died when I was younger. On a boat. You were lucky to have your mother with you for so long."

"But she's gone now," Alfred retorted.

"Not really. She's up in Heaven and looking over you. Someday you will see her again." Alice bent to pick up some stones. "Do you want to play a game? Miss Baker taught me."

Alice showed Sam and Alfred how to play a game with some stones. When they had the hang of it, she showed Carrie and Morris an easier version. Soon the children were laughing as each tried to be the best. Frieda caught Leonie staring at her and beckoned her to come to the kitchen door.

"Why don't you join us adults and leave the children to it, Leonie?"

"No, thank you Frieda. I can't speak. My heart, it hurts so much and I feel so… so guilty. I can't give my family a home. I won't be able to keep my promise to mother."

Frieda hugged the girl. She couldn't tell her everything would be okay. She pushed the hair back from Leonie's eyes.

"Leonie, you have friends now. You aren't alone. We will all help you as much as possible. Lily and Kathleen are working on solutions." Her words fell on deaf ears.

"But we can't live here, Frieda. Not forever. How will we stay together?"

"I don't know the answer. But whatever happens, even if the children go to live somewhere else, we will make sure you don't lose contact."

Leonie paled. Frieda insisted she sit on a chair and put her head down between her legs. Only when the color came back to Leonie's cheeks did Frieda relax. She insisted Leonie drink some water.

"You can't send them on the orphan train. That was Mama's greatest fear. Some people in our community suggested it. But Mama knew they could separate twins, send them to different homes, different States. She begged me not to let that happen." Leonie sobbed. "I won't ever find them."

"Leonie, please don't think the worst. Your mother spoke to Lily and explained how she felt. Lily and Kathleen will do their best, I promise."

Leonie chewed her fingernail, her eyes on her siblings.

"You look exhausted, why don't you go for a nap? The children are having fun with Alice. Let them forget, if only for an hour. They need it, and you need sleep. When the visitors leave, we can sit down with Lily and Kathleen and ask them for an update."

"Yes Frieda." Leonie's flat reply worried Frieda. It was almost as if she had given up hope.

Leonie didn't move immediately. Frieda wished there was something she could do to make Leonie's situation more bearable. But what?

CHAPTER 23

*W*hen she returned inside the sitting room, conversation was also on the orphan trains. Frieda helped Cook with the tray of drinks and then took a seat, listening to Miss Baker.

"I've tracked down Isabella, Alice called her Issy. I've also found Chloe, but there's no sign of Dawn."

"Alice was anxious about Issy." Kathleen glanced at Frieda before addressing Miss Baker again. "From what she described, I imagine it would have been difficult to place a troubled girl."

Emily smiled, lighting up her plain face. Frieda caught Gustav staring at the woman, his eyes wide with admiration.

"That's what I thought too, if I'm honest. But April Lawlor, I mean Mrs. Baxter as she is now, she visited with Issy. Her new family loves her. They told Miss

Lawlor if their own child was half as spirited as Issy, she might have lived past the age of three. Issy has brought a light back into their lives."

Kathleen smiled, "It just goes to show there is a place for every child. We just need to find it."

"Have you told Alice?" Frieda asked. Alice had told Frieda about Issy pinching her and saying nasty things. Frieda had tried explaining Issy was probably just as frightened as Alice was, but trying to hide her fear.

"Yes, she didn't believe me until I showed her the letter from Miss Lawlor. She's happy. She and Issy didn't always get along, but they seemed to have bonded on the train."

"Is April Lawlor working with you?" Lily asked.

Kathleen interrupted, "Good grief, Emily must feel she has gone back in time to the inquisition with all our questions."

Emily shook her head. "It's fine. I know you ask out of concern, not nosiness. April isn't working for us, not officially. She's had trouble finding work as a teacher, the references from her last job not being too good."

Kathleen flushed bright red, "Deadman's Creek townspeople should be ashamed. She was a wonderful person and teacher."

"I agree, Kathleen, but I'm also a little grateful as now April has time to check on our girls. Mrs. Twiddle," Emily scowled as she said the name, "has a lot to answer for." Emily looked tearful.

Gustav interrupted, "Alice still asks for Dawn. She was the girl who helped her most at the orphanage, but Emily, I mean Miss Baker, hasn't been able to track her down. Not for want of trying," Gustav added with a glance at Emily. Frieda saw the girl blush. Gustav was in his late thirties, over ten years older than Emily Baker, yet it was obvious there was a mutual attraction between them.

"I'm scared to push too hard. I suspect they may give me bad news on Dawn. She had, what some call, a history. None of it was her fault, but people don't see that. Her brother, Jem, was a handsome, charming devil who thought nothing of family loyalties. His job was to protect Dawn, yet he betrayed her in the cruelest manner. I never thought she'd last long at waitressing." Emily turned red. "The Harvey girls, they have a certain reputation to uphold. And they work hard, too. Dawn was a hard worker, but she had dreams of a fairy tale life. I worry she fell in with another man."

Poor Emily was crimson, probably wondering how she would get herself away from the topic.

Frieda tried to help. "Emily, we can guess what may have happened to Dawn. Perhaps you could tell Alice, she found a new family and is happy too."

Emily looked upset, "But that's probably a lie."

Frieda didn't care about small lies if they were for a good reason. "Sometimes it is kinder to tell a lie than for a child to know an ugly truth. I think Alice has had enough ugliness to last her a lifetime. When she is older, if she remembers Dawn, she may work out the story for herself. She mentioned Jem to me and how sad Dawn was about him running off. That's all she needs to know."

Lily stood behind Frieda's chair. "I agree. I know Father Nelson probably wouldn't, but this is real life. Now, what else has been happening at the orphanage, Emily? I heard you've changed the name."

The relief on Emily's face at the change in the topic was obvious as the woman became more animated.

"I always hated the name. I don't think any girl or boy is delinquent, at least not at first. Most of the girls in our orphanage are there because of poverty. Their parents are dead because of illnesses spreading like a fire though the tenements, or accidents at work. Being poor isn't a fault, so why give them such a horrible start in life?"

"Well said, Miss, I mean Emily." Charlie clapped.

Emily's crimson cheeks showed she wasn't used to getting praise. She glanced at the man beside her. "It wasn't me who changed it. Gustav suggested it. He suggested a new name for a fresh start."

"So what did you decide on?" Charlie asked.

"It's not my decision, but the city's. I wanted to call it 'Hope Orphanage' but they would only agree to changing it to 'Home for Girls'. The official who came to see me said my job was to get rid of orphans, not keep them in the city."

Lily snorted. "Sounds like the typical response from Tammany Hall."

"I love the girls in the home like they were my own children. I want them to be happy and have the best start in life. The Orphan Train program isn't always the answer." Emily blushed as she glanced around the room, possibly remembering Kathleen and Lily's work with the orphan trains. "I don't mean to be offensive. I know some children find wonderful homes. April wrote to tell me of her personal experience. She found a lovely home. But then you have Alice's story."

"Nobody here could be offended by anything you say, Miss Baker, I mean Emily." Lily interrupted. "We all have our misgivings about the orphan trains, some more than others."

Frieda studied Lily, wondering if her reservations were the reason she was pushing the factory building so hard. Lily was always motivated to help the poor, but lately she was more driven, less patient, as if something was pushing her on.

Emily distracted Frieda as she thanked Lily.

"Some children need to stay in New York. They might be like Alice and have a living parent. Others have siblings and extended family they want to stay close to. Or at least, know where they live." Emily wiped a tear away. "I apologize. Matron always said I was too emotional and cared too much."

"Matron was wrong. You can never care too much about children," Lily hastened to reassure the younger woman.

Frieda noticed Gustav give Emily a hanky and rubbed her hand quickly before pulling away just as fast.

"Let's have lunch as I can hear my beloved husband's stomach growling." Lily glanced at Charlie who shrugged.

"It's been a long time since breakfast."

Everyone smiled.

Lily spoke. "Emily, if you don't mind perhaps myself and Kathleen can call on you on Tuesday or Wednesday? I think there may be ways we could work together for all the children."

"Yes, I would like that. Thank you."

"Don't thank her, knowing our Lily she has a few schemes in mind." Kathleen teased, leading the way into lunch.

Gustav pulled out Emily's chair, allowing her to sit. Frieda wished, with all her heart, Patrick was here and would do that for her. She wondered how Maria was feeling and whether her afternoon was going any better.

# CHAPTER 24

*M*aria sneezed over and over again. She wished Conrad would leave, it wasn't nice for him to see her in such a state. She must look so ugly with her red nose, streaming eyes, and she smelled twice as bad. Mama had insisted on her swallowing a vile garlic based tonic. Maria could smell it coming off her skin.

Conrad appeared oblivious as he sat at the table opposite, talking away to her mother about different subjects. They'd spoken about the weather, then politics for a while, and now they were discussing different recipes for chicken soup.

Maria shuffled in her seat, earning herself a rebuke from her mother. Conrad spoke up.

"Perhaps you should go to bed, Maria, and sleep it off. The chicken soup will work its magic too."

RACHEL WESSON

"See, listen to the man." Turning to Conrad, Mrs. Mezza said, "She is too stubborn. All morning I tell her to go back to bed, but she insists on helping me with these flowers. Now she sneezes over everything."

Conrad winked at Maria, but she saw he was careful for her mother not to see him. "Maria is strong willed, Mrs. Mezza, but I think that is because she takes after her mother."

Maria bit back a groan at the look on her mother's face. Conrad hastened to add, "I mean you are an obviously strong woman, raising a family by yourself, and doing such a wonderful job. Your children, your home, and this baking is a credit to you. Your husband was a lucky man."

Maria relaxed slightly as Conrad's charm worked it's magic on her mother.

"Si, I guess I am a little stubborn and strong willed. My Benito used to say I was. He was a wonderful husband and father, a good provider." Mama's voice wobbled, but she didn't weep.

Conrad spoke up. "I wish I had met him, Maria speaks so highly of him and you. I'm so grateful you allowed me to sit with you today."

Maria disguised a laugh with a cough as her mother became tongue tied. Mama's prejudice towards non Italians was no match for Conrad's charm offensive. Mama gave her one of her looks. Maria stared at her feet. Now would not be a good time to catch Conrad's eye.

"Do you go to church, young man? I assume they brought you up in the real faith, that of your mother?"

Maria crossed her fingers and held her breath. This was serious. If Conrad told her mother the actions of his mother's family had done little to endear her religion to him, he might as well leave now.

"I go to see Father Nelson regularly. You've heard of him? A catholic priest in charge of the orphan trains."

Maria knew he spoke to Father Nelson about the new factory, so technically he wasn't lying, but it wasn't what Mama meant. She hoped her mother didn't quiz Conrad any further.

"Yes, a good man. He does a lot for the poor in New York. I've never heard a bad word said against him."

"He's a character for sure," Conrad answered. Maria noticed he didn't catch her eye. She stayed silent too, not wanting to get involved in pulling the wool over her mother's eyes. She sneezed again and brushed her watering eyes with a hanky. The silence grew uncomfortable with the three of them shifting in their seats.

"Mrs. Mezza, I know this is not how things are usually done. Normally I would ask Maria's father for permission, but in his absence, could I ask you?"

Mama looked ill for a moment, glancing around her as if she wanted to escape, but Conrad kept talking.

"I would like to court Maria properly. I want the world to know I intend for her to become my wife. When I have more to offer. A better home and job, but also at a time you deem to be respectable given your loss."

Maria couldn't have loved Conrad more. She silently begged her mother to agree. When Mama remained silent, Conrad stood up.

"Perhaps I have been too hasty, but I love your daughter. I would like her hand in marriage. What do you say?"

Mama stood up, looking tiny next to Conrad.

"You are an honorable young man and a hard worker. I appreciate the respect you've shown me."

Maria allowed her hopes to soar. Conrad had won Mama over.

"But these are trying times. My other daughter, she wishes to marry an Italian."

Maria wanted to shout, "An Italian gangster!" but a look from Conrad kept her quiet.

"As Rosa is the elder daughter, it is only right that her wedding take place first. I will allow you to court my Maria, but I can't give you permission to wed. Not yet. I must pray and seek guidance."

Maria sighed, but still it was better than she'd imagined. Mama hadn't said no. Not yet anyway.

Conrad coughed. Maria sent him a look, begging him to stay silent, but maybe he misinterpreted it. He spoke up, "Is it the fact I am not Italian that causes you the most concern, Mrs. Mezza?"

Maria almost bent under the table thinking her mother would explode, but the older woman sighed and took her seat.

"Young man it is, but not for the reasons you believe. I do not think Italian men are all wonderful. But marriage is difficult." Mama's voice cracked. She took a couple of seconds to compose herself before speaking again. "You think it is easy when you are young and in love but then the hard times come. When you share similar backgrounds, faith, religion, traditions, it makes for an easier life."

"Sometimes." Conrad added.

Maria didn't want to look at Mama. She sensed Conrad had pushed too hard.

"Si, sometimes." Mama spoke softly before she stood up. "You asked for my permission. Please respect my wishes. One more thing, I do not wish this to be discussed with anyone, particularly not Rosa."

"I won't say a word, Mrs. Mezza. Thank you for your time and your hospitality." He held out his hand and she shook it.

Glancing at Maria, he said, "Maria, listen to your mother and go to bed now."

Mama laughed as she escorted Conrad to the door. "Maybe you will handle my Maria."

As the door shut behind him, Maria waited at the

table. Would Mama say something? Mama returned to her seat and picked up some of her artificial flowers.

"What are you sitting here for? You heard the man. Get yourself to bed."

"Mama, do you --"

"Not now, Maria. Leave me with my thoughts, please, child. And remember, not a word to your sister. Rosa needs her moment to shine."

Maria heard the emotion in her mother's voice. She guessed she was missing Papa even more than usual. Maria wished he was here, she'd always been able to get him on side quicker than her mother.

She kissed the top of Mama's head and went to bed. Conrad had declared his feelings. That was all she needed for now. As she fell asleep, she wondered if Frieda had taken her advice and spoken to Patrick. She hoped things worked out well for the couple as they were meant to be together. Just like her and Conrad.

rieda lost count of the number of times she had tried to speak to Patrick, but he always rushed off with some excuse or another. It was all very well, Maria telling her to be nice to him but if he wouldn't stay in the same room as her, never mind speak to her, how was she going to achieve anything? She shut the door of her bedroom, having decided she was doing too much thinking by staying on her own. She'd go help Cook or keep company with the Chiver children for a while. Anything to stop thoughts of Patrick tormenting her. She was so deep in thought, she nearly walked into Kathleen as she came up the stairs.

"Frieda, there you are. You look peaky, are you sure you are getting enough rest?"

She didn't have time to answer as Kathleen kept talking.

"I wanted to ask you for your help in organizing Patrick's birthday. You know how we always celebrate it on St Patrick's day. This year I think we should arrange a get together in a restaurant just for the adults. What do you think?"

"I guess."

Kathleen ignored her obvious lack of interest. "I think the place you go to with Maria sounds good. What did you call it? Charlie's? I love Italian food and so does Richard. Patrick will eat anything. Maria and Conrad should come, too. Who else do you think we should invite?"

"I'm not sure I can make it, Kathleen. I may have to work."

"Nonsense. Richard will sort that out. I've already asked him. Now why don't we pick a day to go shopping. We could get our hair done and enjoy some time together. What do you say?"

Frieda studied Kathleen, her expression seemed innocent, but why was she going to all this trouble?

"I don't know, I have a lot on at the moment."

"Don't be boring, Frieda. Lily hates shopping. I'd love a day away from everything. Please say you will come. You could try out one of those new hair styles you were talking about."

Frieda's hand went up unconsciously to her hair. Would he notice her if she got her hair cut short? Maybe he'd hate it.

"I don't think you should go too short though, I mean men like women to be feminine don't they?" Kathleen kept chatting as if Frieda had agreed. Frieda decided she might as well give in. It would be easier in the long run.

* * *

THE TWO OF them had a wonderful time at the stores. Frieda didn't think about the hospital once as Kathleen kept her occupied, telling her stories or getting her to try on various outfits. Kathleen insisted on buying Frieda a new skirt and two shirtwaists. One blouse was the most delicate thing she had ever seen, embroidered with fancy stitches. Kathleen took her to a hairstylist who cut and styled her hair so beautifully, Frieda had to pinch herself.

"Wait until the others see you! You don't look like Frieda, you know. You look like a well to do, upper-class young lady about to head to finishing school. Perhaps in France?"

Frieda laughed at Kathleen's comments, but her hands brushed the soft material of her new skirt. Kathleen had insisted she change as soon as they purchased it.

"Seriously, you look so ladylike. I guess it's because I'm used to seeing you coming back from another tiring day at the hospital or up to your tonsils in study materials. You look sophisticated and almost carefree."

Frieda took her friend's arm and guided her to a small cafe. "Please sit down for a few minutes. I don't know where you get your energy. I'm exhausted."

Kathleen looked a little guilty. "I suppose I have been making you try on lots of outfits. I just get so excited watching you grow from the young girl we know and love into a wonderful young woman."

Kathleen was speaking in rather a loud voice. Frieda blushed as people turned to look at her. "Everyone's staring at us."

Kathleen looked around. "Who cares? Why shouldn't they stare, you look stunning. I can't wait to see the men's faces when they get to the party on Friday. They won't believe their eyes."

Frieda tried to keep her face expressionless. She didn't want Kathleen to know she was dreading Friday night. What if Patrick ignored her in front of her friends? She'd be mortified.

The dinner was cancelled. Kathleen looked furious when she told Frieda Patrick was stuck at the hospital. Frieda couldn't help wondering if it was an excuse, not that she could say that to Kathleen.

## CHAPTER 26

"What's in the post?" Kathleen asked as she walked into the office where Lily was already working.

"A letter from Bridget. Want to read it to me?"

Kathleen opened the envelope. There were two letters, one for Kathleen and one addressed to Lily.

"You forgot your glasses again, didn't you Lily?" Kathleen couldn't resist teasing Lily who hated admitting she couldn't see without the new glasses.

"Are you going to laugh at me or read the letter?" Lily retorted.

Kathleen cleared her throat and read aloud.

*Dear Lily,*

*What a sad world we live in. Johanna Chivers sounds like a lovely woman taken in the prime of her life. We would love to help. We can offer the twins a*

145

*place in the orphanage here with us. To be honest, it will be a struggle to feed four more children, but we couldn't dream of separating them.*

*Bella can help with Leonie, but not as much as we would have liked. Her business is going well but she can't afford to take on another seamstress full time. What she can offer is a commission based position where Leonie could earn a percentage of all the sewing jobs she completes. It's not ideal, but it's the best we can do. The town is increasing in size and hopefully soon things will pick up. But there is some competition from these mail order catalogues. Their prices are very cheap and difficult to compete with. I try not to worry about our little town, but my neighbors feel like family. Speaking of which, tell Kathleen our younger siblings are barely recognizable these days. Carolyn says to remind Kathleen to write.*

Kathleen glanced up at Lily. "I should write more. I just run out of things to say."

"You? I never knew you to be short of words, Kathleen Green."

Kathleen smiled at the teasing, but she knew Lily understood. It wasn't a lack of things to say, but a lack of time. She seemed to have more work than hours available. Still, she must make more of an effort.

She continued to read,

*Leonie would be welcome to live at the orphanage too if she'd like to be near her siblings, but would the*

*Sanctuary be able to pay a little to support her? I hate asking, but things are a little stretched at the moment. We just invested in a massive tractor. Geoff Rees says it will help us increase our production of wheat. I don't like it but Carl says we have to embrace new technology or we will lose the orphanage.. I love my husband, but sometimes his need to use the latest inventions is rather irritating.*

Kathleen stopped reading, raising her eyes to meet Lily's. "I didn't realize things were so bad in Riverside Springs. Why didn't Bridget write and ask for help? She is so independent, it's beyond annoying."

"Bridget never wants to worry anyone, least of all you. She knows you would fret. We can help her."

Lily sounded so confident, but Kathleen had seen the accounts at the Sanctuary. The regular contributions they all made to the running of Carmel's Mission only went so far.

"How? We just asked her to take on five more people? The children and Leonie may be too many to manage."

Determination transformed Lily's facial expression. "We will find a way. Do more fundraising or increase our own contribution. I won't let that family suffer any more misfortune, and I'm not sending them to different homes. I made a promise and I intend to keep it."

Relieved Lily was back to fighting form having been

in the doldrums for the last few weeks, Kathleen returned to reading the letter.

*I am sorry you are both dealing with so much pain and suffering. On a happier note, the McDonagh twins Megan and Eileen wanted me to tell you they are having their babies christened on New Year Eve. I miss my sister and would love if you could persuade her, Richard, and the children to come visit. They could drag you with them, Lily. Can you believe it is almost twenty years since the Collins family landed on your doorstep? How time flies past.*

*With love always,*

*Bridget.*

Kathleen looked up from the letter, her eyes glistening. "Lily, can you believe Megan and Eileen are all grown up? I keep seeing them sitting on Mrs. Fleming's floor."

"What age are they now? Twenty-two or three? Remember, Megan was dead set on coming back to New York. Now she is a farmer's wife with a new baby and couldn't be happier."

"Geoff Ree's nephew made her head spin, or at least that's what Bella wrote. I'm glad they both found such good husbands after everything they went through."

Kathleen sniffed, trying not to remember the horrible things that had happened to Megan and Eileen after they had found them a home via the orphan train. Thank God Bella was so insistent on checking up on the twins, or goodness knows what would have happened to them.

"Lily, what will we do? Would Leonie take on a position like that?"

"We must discuss it with her. She won't need to earn much if we take care of her room and board. She earns a pittance at the Triangle and is used to giving up her wages to her mother. At least in Riverside Springs, she is safer than staying in New York. Her father could find them easily as it's no secret they are living here." Lily stopped talking, causing Kathleen to look at her.

"What is it? You're worried about something, Lily." Kathleen tried to ignore the shiver down her back. Lily didn't look well, she was too thin and smiled less often than before.

"Does Bridget ever ask you about Maura?" Lily asked.

What had prompted Lily to ask that? Had she seen her?

Kathleen couldn't speak for a second as painful memories. Her older sister had run off after robbing the Sanctuary and injuring Bella. Nobody had heard of her since.

"Have you seen her?"

"No, I haven't. You know I would tell you if I heard anything. I was just thinking about your family and wondered."

Kathleen stared at Lily's face, wondering if she was telling the truth, but her friend held her gaze. She knew Lily wouldn't lie to her, not an outright lie, but being best friends, they were protective of one another.

"No, Lily, Bridget never brings Maura up in her letters. Nobody does. Do you think she will ever come back, Lily? I know what she did was horrible, but I wish I knew she was safe. Happy too."

"I don't know, Kathleen. Stranger things have happened, as we both know. I shouldn't have asked about Maura, I'm sorry. For now, let's concentrate on sorting out Leonie and her siblings."

Kathleen played with her wedding ring as she considered the options.

"Leonie may find a nice young farmer and settle down to have her own family."

"Kathleen are you going all romantic on me again?" Lily teased.

"No! I just think living in New York means Leonie will always feel responsible for her siblings. If they are happy living with Bridget in the Riverside orphanage, she could find a life of her own. That's worth considering, isn't it?"

"Yes, Kathleen, it is. I was only teasing. Come on, get your coat on and let's see how the factory is progressing. Maybe you could frighten the builders into working harder."

Kathleen threw the envelope at Lily but did so with

a smile. Good old Lily could always cheer her up. The news from Bridget was good. It would be better if Leonie could have a well-paid position, but overall it was a good offer.

\* \* \*

LILY DIDN'T CATCH up with Leonie until the following Friday. They were all having dinner together, Frieda too.

"Are you coming to Susie's engagement party, Leonie? I'm going so we could go together."

Lily glanced at Leonie, who looked torn. She caught the younger girl looking at her siblings.

"Leonie you should go. Cook will be here to mind the children. She'll tuck them into bed with a story while you have some fun. You deserve it after working so hard."

"You think it would be okay?" Leonie asked.

"I think it's a wonderful idea. I hate the thought of Frieda coming home alone so the two of you will be company for each other."

Leonie glanced down at her dress. Lily could guess her thoughts.

"I have some clothes in the spare room. You should look through them to see if there is something suitable in your size. There should be. We get so many donations from different people. Carrie, will you help Leonie find a dress for the party?"

The little girl jumped up immediately. "Come on Leonie, it will be fun!" Leonie took Carrie's hand and together they went up to find new dresses. "Leonie, you will find one for me, too, won't you?"

Frieda didn't hear Leonie's reply.

"Well done Lily, I thought it would upset Carrie if Leonie went out."

"I think she was, but she's at that age where she is young enough to distract. Will you talk to Leonie about the offer Bridget made? I spoke to her earlier, but she is worried about being a burden. She thinks Bridget has only offered because of Kathleen."

"I'll talk to her. I wish I could visit Riverside Springs. It sounds like a lovely place to live."

"Maybe we could go to the christening and catch up with the Chivers after Christmas." Lily glanced closer at Frieda's face. "Do you want to leave New York?"

"Maybe. It sometimes seems a little small."

"When you are trying to avoid someone you mean?" Lily prompted.

Frieda turned scarlet.

"Frieda, don't get embarrassed. I know how you feel about Patrick, and I know you think he doesn't feel the same. In time, things may change. But if you ever need to talk, you know I am here. I won't tell anyone what you say, not even Kathleen. So if you need an ear, I am here."

"Thank you, Lily." Frieda glanced upstairs as they

heard the girls laughing. "That's a nice sound, isn't it. I better get ready or we will be late."

"Where is the engagement party?" Lily asked.

"On the streets outside the building, Susie lives in. She is marrying a man from work. Conrad and Maria invited me. Maria says I need to live a little. It should be a huge street party. The Italians like to celebrate. Susie has invited everyone, she is such a kind girl. She even invited the Jewish girls, but a lot of them have to go to Temple tonight."

"It's good to have the different communities mixing. Only by getting to know one another, can people see we are all the same." Lily pushed Frieda toward the door. "Go before I get up on one of my soapboxes. Enjoy yourself."

" $\mathcal{L}$ eonie, you look so pretty. Your hair really suits you. You look like a Gibson girl."

Leonie blushed at Lily's praise. The young girl's smile brightened up her whole face, her eyes gleaming with excitement and possibly a little nervousness too.

"We have to go or it will be over before we get there." Frieda said bustling Leonie out the front door.

Cook fussed around the younger girl.

"Not likely, those Italians party until the early hours. You be good and don't let any fancy young men turn your head, Leonie. You hear me?" Cook handed them each a parcel. "I baked a few cookies for you to bring with you. I made some chocolate ones Maria likes so much."

Frieda kissed the older woman on the cheek. "You

have a heart bigger than America. Thank you." Frieda took Leonie's hand. "Come on. Let's go."

They were lucky, catching a street car almost immediately.

"Have you been to a party like this before, Frieda?"

"A few times. Maria always invited me. I can't always go because of the hospital."

"Do you enjoy working there?" Leonie shuddered. "I couldn't do it. All that blood and guts."

"I have more good days than bad, so yes, I like it. Do you like your job?"

To her surprise, Leonie said yes. "I love to make things, and I'm lucky to be working at the Triangle."

"Lucky?" Frieda couldn't hide her surprise. Maria hated that factory.

"Yes, I know Maria doesn't like it but it's much better than it was at the old place. We have more room to breathe with the high ceilings and light from the window. We have electric sewing machines. At the last place we had slow ones. You should see some places my friends work. In badly lit basements and they work longer hours than we do. I think I am lucky."

Chastened by the younger girl's gratitude, Frieda wondered just how many people in the tenements now surrounding them worked in worse conditions than those at the Triangle.

"There you are. Not too late tonight. It must be your

doing, Leonie. Frieda is never on time." Maria's voice broke into Frieda's thoughts.

"Hilarious, Maria," Frieda pouted, pretending to be insulted. "If you're mean, I won't give you the present Cook sent."

"Cookies, please tell me they are chocolate. I love them."

Leonie and Frieda exchanged glances and giggled as Maria almost inhaled her first cookie. "I think she meant you to share them!" Leonie mumbled, her words causing Maria to blush.

"Let's find you some plates. You must taste Mama's frittata."

"What's that?" Leonie whispered to Frieda.

"A dish made from potatoes and other ingredients. Mrs. Mezza is a very good cook. Try some."

Some Italian musicians played various instruments as couples danced in each other's arms, some under the watchful eyes of their parents. Frieda saw Leonie dancing with the same young man a few times. He kept making Leonie laugh.

"You having a good time?" Maria asked her.

"Yes, look at Leonie. It's so good to see her laugh and forget her troubles for once."

"Yes, she's having fun but why aren't you dancing my friend? Aren't my Italian friends good enough for you?" Maria teased. "Conrad give Frieda a drink."

Frieda took the drink from Conrad as Maria

said, "I'm going over to check on Mama. Last time I saw her, our neighbor, Mr. Maltese, had taken her out dancing. She was breathless, but I think she had fun."

She took a drink and coughed.

"Too strong for you?" he teased. "You're probably used to a more refined wine."

"I rarely drink," Frieda said, putting her glass down on the table behind her. "I heard you are helping Lily with her new project."

Conrad rolled his eyes. "I'm not cut out to be a boss. Those builders work so slowly, I want to roll up my sleeves and lend a hand."

"Don't let Lily or Kathleen hear you saying that, or you just might end up becoming a brickie."

Conrad laughed before someone called him to come over.

"Go. I want to find Leonie." Frieda spotted the girl on the other side of the street.

"Are you having fun?" Even as she asked, Frieda knew the answer. Leonie looked so young and carefree.

"Frieda, taste this. I've no idea what it is, but it's delicious. The spices burst into flavor."

Frieda took a bite of the vegetable dish. It was good. A young man appeared carrying two drinks. Leonie's face flushed bright red.

"Frieda, this is Deleo. He works at the Triangle. He's training to be a cutter."

"Nice to meet you Deleo."

Deleo bent his head in greeting and muttered something, but Frieda couldn't hear him. Judging by his color and his shifting from one foot to the other, he was very shy.

"Leonie, we should head home soon. We both have to get up early tomorrow."

"One last dance, please Frieda. I love dancing. Please."

For a second Leonie's facial expression mirrored that of her sister, Carrie, begging Cook for an extra cookie. Just like Cook, Frieda couldn't resist the plea in those big brown eyes.

"Okay, but then we have to go. It was nice meeting you, Deleo."

Frieda walked back to Conrad and Maria. Why was Maria scowling? She followed her friend's gaze to see Maria's sister Rosa wrapped around a young man. Maria's mama stood to the side, her face a mask of disapproval.

"I take it that's Paulo?" Frieda whispered to Maria.

"Yes! Look at him making a show of my sister. Poor Mama looks like she will have a heart attack. But she daren't do anything."

"Why?" Frieda asked.

"Paulo is a Greco. Around here, he may as well be the President. Nobody will touch that family in case they end up swimming with the fish. In cement boots."

Frieda stared at the young couple. Paulo looked just as infatuated with Rosa as she was with him. Still, Mrs. Mezza was looking more upset by the minute, holding her hands in front of her as if she was praying. Frieda saw other people staring at the couple when they thought nobody else was looking. Maybe she should intervene.

She walked toward the couple, holding out her hand.

"Excuse me for interrupting your dance, but I wanted to offer my congratulations. Rosa, you will be the most beautiful bride," Frieda ignored the girl's widened eyes. She turned to Paulo and extended her hand to him. "You must be Paulo. I'm Frieda, a friend of the Mezza family. I've heard a lot about you. I hope you will both be very happy together."

Frieda held Paulo's gaze for a moment, sensing the aggression behind the over-cultivated appearance. He didn't look like a killer with his well-cut suit of clothes and manicured hands. You could be forgiven for thinking he lived in a better class of neighborhood, his appearance a contrast to those of the working men around him. She kept staring, waiting for him to say something, showing she wasn't afraid of him. At first, she wondered if he was angry, but he smiled.

"Nice to meet you, Dr. Klunsberg."

She didn't blink or make any movement to show she was surprised he knew of her. She guessed this was a trick he used to intimidate other people. To show how well connected he was.

"Frieda, please. I'm not at the hospital now. I must go and greet your mother, Rosa. I'm sure she wants to tell me all about the wedding."

Rosa glanced toward Paulo before she took the hint. "Mama can talk about nothing else. Come and we will find her. Paulo has friends to talk to."

Rosa led Frieda over to Mrs. Mezza, and the two of them described the wedding plans in great detail. Frieda caught Maria's gaze out of the side of her eye and saw her friend beam her approval.

Mrs. Mezza asked Rosa to get them all a drink. When her daughter had moved out of earshot, Mrs. Mezza leaned in and whispered her thanks to Frieda.

"My Rosa forgets about her reputation. She is a good Italian girl, but that monster she's taken up with, he will treat her as he wants. Thank you for intervening like you did. The whole neighborhood was staring at them. Benito, my poor husband, sometimes I am glad he didn't live to see this."

"Mrs. Mezza don't worry too much. Paulo seems to care for Rosa, and I'm sure your daughter will want for nothing. Lily says sometimes we have to accept things we don't agree with as we have no power to change them."

"Your friend Lily is a wise woman. She is the lady

who runs that home for..." Mrs. Mezza looked around before she whispered, "fallen women."

"Lily runs Carmel's Mission to help all those who need help. Some are women who may have made difficult choices. Lily believes nobody should be judged for their actions." Frieda wasn't shy about telling people about the work Lily did. She couldn't understand people who went to church every week, judging those who often took the only route they could to avoid total destitution.

Mrs. Mezza blinked a few times before saying, "I may have misjudged Maria's friends. You have been good for my family, Frieda. I will never forget your kindness to my Benito. He was much impressed by you back in the hospital."

"Mr. Mezza was a true gentleman. Now, I best go find my young friend and head home."

Rosa came back with their drinks. "Thank you Rosa, I was just saying goodbye to your mother. It's getting late."

"It is. I think I shall go home too. Rosa, find Maria please, it's time to go home."

"But Mama...."

"Rosa Angelica Mezza, don't make me tell you again."

"Yes, Mama." Rosa fled, leaving Mrs. Mezza to wink at Frieda.

"I can keep my girls in line. Sometimes."

Frieda found Leonie and took the streetcar back to the Sanctuary.

"I had such a wonderful time. The Italians are very nice, aren't they? I don't get to speak to anyone at work, they do not allow us to chat. I always thought there was a barrier between us and them but we are all just people in the end aren't we?"

"Yes, Leonie."

As she lay on her bed, Frieda wondered if Mrs. Mezza would ever come around to Conrad and Maria getting married. They belonged together, anyone could see that. What would it take for them to get their happily ever after?

# CHAPTER 28

SATURDAY, MARCH 25TH, 1911.

*M*aria crawled out of bed, her head aching from lack of sleep and a little too much wine. Rosa was still snoring, so Maria shook her sister awake.

"Come on, sleepyhead. We'll be late."

"Can't we stay in bed and pretend we're sick?" Rosa groaned.

"I'd rather face the bosses than mama if we tried that excuse. Get up or will I have to throw cold water at you?"

Rosa jumped out of bed. "You wouldn't dare."

Maria grinned. "I don't have to, now do I?"

Rosa's response was to throw the pillow at her before rushing to get washed and dressed. They had to run part of the way to the Asch building but got there just before the clock struck eight. Joseph was waiting as usual with a smile on his face.

"You two had a good time at the party last night. I've lost count of the sleepyheads I've taken up to the ninth floor today."

"Joseph, I saw you still dancing as we were leaving. How can you be so cheerful?" Rosa grumbled. Joseph's smile got bigger.

"I had a fabulous time with my friends, got to dance the shoes off my feet and had plenty to eat. Your mama is a wonderful cook, those cookies you had were the best I've ever tasted."

Maria didn't correct him by telling them the cookies had been a gift.

"Maria, I'm meeting Paulo this evening. He's taking me uptown, come with us?"

"No, thank you, Rosa. I have dinner plans with Conrad, and then I will go home to Mama."

It was a poor excuse. She could have suggested Paulo and Rosa come to dinner too. Mama could look after herself, she'd surprised everyone with how well she was coping after losing her husband. Maria avoided Paulo as much as possible. She knew it annoyed Rosa, but she couldn't be in his company for long. He had an air of suppressed violence about him. She wasn't as much frightened by him as disgusted her sister was marrying such an individual. Mama and Benito didn't like him either, but Benito had warned them not to

166

show it. The Greco family had a reputation for a reason.

"Have it your way." Rosa stormed off. Maria didn't enjoy falling out with her sister. Sitting down at her machine, she resolved to make it up with her later. Rosa had been nice to her when she was ill last week. Since Papa's death, they had made more of an effort to get along for Mama's sake as much as anything else.

At lunchtime, Maria went looking for Rosa. "Come have lunch with me."

Rosa didn't even look up.

"Rosa, don't ignore me. I will go out with you and Paulo another night. You'd prefer to be with him alone, anyway, wouldn't you?" Maria teased, but still no response. "I heard he was taking you to see Madame Sherry."

Rosa glared up at her. "Who told you that? Mama would kill me if she heard I was in a dance hall, let alone seeing…" Rosa's rant slowed as Maria clapped.

"Got you talking to me. Now come have lunch. I won't tell Mama about the dance hall. I know how much you love dancing. See the show with your head held high. Everyone says it's hilarious. If you are old enough to be engaged, why can't you choose your own entertainment?"

Rosa pushed her unfinished work aside and picked up her small purse. "I guess you get those ideas hanging around with Frieda, Sarah, and their friends."

Maria hated how Rosa put her friends down all the time. She wondered how Sarah was. Despite her friend's fiery temper, she missed her and the friendship they had built up during the strike. She could still see Sarah's face as she called Maria a scab for breaking the strike. Sarah had vowed never to speak to her again. She hadn't either. Anytime Maria saw Sarah in the street or at a store, the girl ignored her.

Maria opened her mouth to retaliate but closed it again. They would only argue. Gritting her teeth, determined to keep her temper under control, she asked Rosa, "So, the park or the store?"

"The park. I need some fresh air after all this." Rosa glanced around the room. Linking arms, they made their way to Washington Park. They'd only have about twenty minutes to enjoy people watching, but it was worth it. The sun was warm on their backs as they walked to the little square with its curving walls.

Maria loved watching all the different people who walked in the gardens. Children from the tenements chattering in various languages, running in between wealthy ladies scurrying through the park to visit some genteel townhouses on the far side of the park. These ladies looked anxious, as if they would catch something by sharing the same air as the poorer community. She wondered what it would be like to visit one of the big houses. Frieda had told her about the ones she saw during her fund-raising efforts on behalf of the Sanctuary. The dazzling chandeliers, carpets your feet sunk into, silver ornaments, mirrors everywhere. Someday, she hoped to accompany Frieda on one of her trips. She'd enjoy dressing up as a lady. Her mind savored an image of Conrad dressed up as a gentleman; he'd look so handsome all the rich women would envy her.

"Ow!" she exclaimed as Rosa poked her in the ribs, "what did you do that for?"

"What were you thinking about? You have a stupid big grin on your face, that Italian stall owner thought you were smiling at him."

Maria blushed as she caught the admiring gaze of the overweight, fifty odd year old trader. Giggling like a schoolgirl, she took Rosa's arm and scuttled across the main path away from him. She waved to a few of the Italian Nonna's she recognized. They were enjoying the sun too, their shopping at their feet as they gossiped with a neighbor.

With all the benches occupied, Rosa threw her coat on the ground as a blanket.

"Real hint of summer coming now isn't there?" Rosa smiled as she stretched out her feet in front of her. "Maria, I know…" Rosa hesitated.

"What?" Maria prodded.

Rosa glanced at her under her eyelashes. "I know you don't like Paulo, but could you try to be pleasant? I love him. So very much. He is kind to me."

Maria bit into her bread so she wouldn't have to agree with that remark.

"Maria please. When we marry and have children, I want them to know their Auntie Maria. I will tell them not to listen to her mad ideas, though." Rosa rolled her eyes and giggled.

It was so unusual for her sister to tease her, Maria wanted to say yes. "I'll try. With Paulo, I mean. As for your children, I will have the girls wearing pants and the boys in dresses."

Rosa laughed, making Maria laugh too. They chatted about the future, coming up with more ridiculous stories of what it would be like. Maria wiped tears from her eyes. Her sides hurt from laughing.

Rosa glanced at the watch Paulo had given her. "Maria, we'll be late. Come on." Standing up, she held her hand out for her sister. "We might fight a lot, but I love you, Maria."

Shocked into silence, Maria took her outstretched hand and walked back to the Triangle. The women in the elevator were so chatty returning to the ninth floor, Joseph Zito wanted to know if they were planning another party. He protested that too many people were still tired and some hungover from Susie's party the night before.

# CHAPTER 29

*T*he afternoon passed quickly. The sun being out helped people to smile. Everyone was in high spirits looking forward to the weekend. Anna Gullo walked around the floor distributing their weekly pay packets. Maria stood as Anna came closer to her station. She didn't want her supervisor to see she had packed away most of her things in anticipation of leaving work.

Anna smiled as she handed out the pay, teasing some girls including Doris who was getting married the next day. Maria glanced across the floor toward the windows and saw Rosa taking her pay packet from blonde Mary Levantal. She smiled, but Rosa didn't see her. Probably already planning her time with Paulo. The seconds ticked by. Their work day was almost over.

Maria was out of her chair and over at the dressing room almost as soon as the machines stopped. A woman was there before her, already singing. Maria joined in, humming "Every little movement has a meaning all of its own." She didn't have a good singing voice, but she loved the song. She checked her reflection in the mirror, at the last minute tying a scarf around her neck. The older girl next to her laughed.

"Not like that. Like this." The girl said as she corrected Maria's scarf. "Now your Irishman will be happy."

Blushing, Maria looked away.

"Don't be shy, young love is a good thing. Enjoy it before you have a load of children and can't remember the last time you spoke to your man."

"Don't talk like that, Sylvia," her friend said. "Give the young ones some hope. Doris is getting married tomorrow."

Maria joined in the good natured teasing before leaving the dressing room to head to the freight elevator. Sylvia followed behind her. "Maria, I was just teas-" Sylvia paled, grabbing her arm, her fingernails digging into Maria's skin. "Maria, what's that? It's smoke."

Maria stared in horror as smoke rose near the windows. Someone screamed behind them.

"It's in the staircase, too. Mary, Mother of God, what shall we do?"

Maria didn't answer Sylvia. Rosa. She had to find her sister. She saw what looked like flames coming from the windows. Some areas around the sewing tables were already on fire.

"Maria, the fire escape." Sylvia pulled her, but Maria shook her free. She had to find Rosa. Sylvia ran toward the iron doors of the fire escape. Maria lost sight of the woman in the ensuing chaos. Women running and hollering surrounded her, but fear glued her to the floor. The thick black smoke caught the back of Maria's throat. Panicking, Maria couldn't see through the smoke. Where was her sister?

The girls still sitting at the machines climbed up on the machine tables. Chairs and baskets blocked the narrow aisles, so moving from table to table seemed safer. Maria tried to scramble up onto the table nearest her, but her skirts hampered her progress. Esther, a young girl who sat near her, held out a hand to Maria and pulled her up onto the machine tables.

"Try to get to the front elevator. This way," Esther said.

Esther climbed from one machine table to the other. Maria saw some girls fall backwards into the fire as she moved carefully from one table to the next, frantically searching the room for a sign of Rosa.

Mounds of boxes hindered their progress. It was getting harder to see, to breathe. Some girls fled toward a door and she followed them. But when they tried to open it, nothing happened. Thinking the girl was too weak to open it, Maria pushed her out of the way to try for herself.

"It's locked. I can't open it. Stop pushing, it won't help." She screamed again and again. No amount of kicking, screaming or pushing could open it. As the crowd behind them thickened, Maria was sure she'd be trampled or pinned against the door. She tried to find another way out.

A girl shouted above the noise. "The elevator. We have to get to the elevator."

Maria didn't know who was screaming at her, but she and Esther followed them, anyway. They pushed past their screaming workmates, but there was no way out there either. What would they do?

"Maria, where are you? Maria Mezza" She heard someone, a man, calling for her. Conrad. What was he doing on this floor? Trying to breathe slowly, she pushed toward the voice.

"There you are," his voice shook with relief. He took her hand. "Come on, we have to get out quickly."

"Conrad, my sister? Rosa is back there somewhere."

"She's probably already outside. She's worked here longer, knows the exits. Come on, we don't have much time." He looked around. "Don't let go of my hand. Promise? No matter what? We will try for the other elevator. Over that way." He pointed before looking at her.

She nodded, gripping his hand tightly as possible.

With her other one, she grabbed Esther's hand and insisted she follow them. Together, the three of them headed toward the elevator, but the crowds pushed them back.

Coughing and retching they battled through the smoke. The heat was unbearable. A flash of fire lit up Conrad's face. She saw her fear mirrored in his expression. He looked around them, trying to find their route of escape. A shadowy figure called out. "Conrad! This way," The man's voice came closer. Maria recognized it but couldn't place it.

"We got the door open to the Green Street exit."

Maria's brain froze. She couldn't remember which side of the building was Green Street. The combination of fear and smoke was making it hard to focus.

The man spoke again, calling her by name. "Maria, trust me. I know the factory like the back of my hand. Years ago, I helped the boss set up the factory."

Gustav, Alice's father. That's who was helping them. "Put your scarf around your head, Esther. You too, Maria. Wrap it as tightly as you can. Conrad, you follow behind and I'll lead the way. We'll get you girls out, just don't look up. It's hot."

Understatement of the century, but Maria didn't care. She pushed Esther in front of her. Gustav pushed through the door. "Green Street exit this is. We have to make our way down."

When they got to the next floor, Esther stopped and

wouldn't go on. She pushed down her scarf, screaming, "We can't go through there. Are you trying to kill us? The fire's everywhere!"

"Shut up, Esther, and do what I tell ya." Gustav's firm tone calmed Esther. "Good girl. Put that scarf back. You listen to me and we'll get out. Otherwise we all die."

Esther did as she was instructed. Conrad patted down Maria's scarf. She could feel his hands through the heat. "You're smoldering and not in a good way," he whispered in a raspy voice. Then they were off again. The heat was unbearable, and more than once Maria was tempted to take the scarf off to breathe.

They kept moving downward, floor by floor. Little by little it seemed easier to breathe, but she still didn't take the scarf off, not until they heard the fireman.

"Steady on there now. You are almost down. Ladies, you can remove the scarves now. Gents, take care of those ladies."

Esther darted for the door, but the same fireman blocked her. "Not outside yet, Miss. We'll tell you when. Just wait here. You are safe."

Maria couldn't breathe or see. She clawed at her throat as if she could open it more. She felt her legs give way and grabbed for Conrad as she passed out.

# CHAPTER 30

$\mathcal{M}$aria opened her eyes to find herself on the ground floor, seeing Conrad's face hovering over her.

"Thank God, you gave me a fright passing out like that. How do you feel?" he asked as he helped her to sit up properly.

How did she feel? Rather numb. Spotting Esther standing to her side, alone, she asked, "Where did Gustav go?"

"He muttered something and took off. The firemen tried to stop him, but he shrugged them off. He knows many people working here, maybe he's gone to check on them." Conrad's voice sounded different, rougher than usual.

A group of firemen protecting the small group of factory workers distracted her. She searched the faces of the female workers, but Rosa wasn't there. She didn't recognize any of the women, some of whom were crying, others calling out asking if she had seen Sur-ka or Mary Leventhal or Anna Gullo.

Maria stood up with Conrad's help. Gripping his hand, she asked some women if they had seen Rosa. Nobody had. Everyone fell silent at the cries for help, and screams from the upper floors floated over them.

Maria counted backwards, trying to distract herself from the horrible sounds around her. Screams, thuds, an explosion. She gripped Conrad's hand tighter. He pulled her closer. Esther stood near them, her eyes scanning everyone who moved.

"Esther, who are you looking for?"

The girl didn't seem to hear her. Maria reached out to touch her arm. Esther jumped.

"Did I hurt you? Are you burned?"

"I have to find my sister and my brother. I should have stayed to look for them. I have to get back up there." Esther tried to push her way through the firemen but couldn't.

Maria rushed to her friend's side. "Esther, you can't go back up there. Let the firemen do their work. Come over here."

A fireman stepped forward. "Listen to your friend, lady. There's nothing you can do for those up there."

Maria caught the expression in the fireman's eyes,

but she didn't want to recognize it. She wanted to see hope, not resignation. She put her arm around Esther's shoulder but took it away as the girl flinched. She lifted Esther's hair, grimacing at the horrible burns. "Esther, we have to get you to the doctors. You must be in agony."

Esther brushed off her concern. "I want to stay here. Wait for Joseph and Fannie, my brother and sister. They will look for me."

Conrad and some other men spoke with a fireman. Maria watched Conrad's expression, seeing his eyes turn glassy, his face losing all color.

She moved to his side. "It is Rosa?" Even as she asked, she knew it was stupid to think the fireman would know her sister.

"What?" Conrad took a moment to understand. "No, he wants us to go outside."

If that was all the fireman wanted, why did he take the men aside. Why not just tell them all to move? Suspicious, she looked closer at the other male workers. They wouldn't meet her eyes either. She glanced at the women. Some of them were crying, others staring into space.

Conrad took her hand. "Stay close to me. I don't want to lose you."

"We're only going out on the sidewalk." Why was she arguing with him? He knew something. What?

"It's chaos out there. Lots of people looking for their

179

loved ones, friends, neighbors. Just keep beside me." Conrad turned to Esther. "Come on my other side, Esther, and hold my hand. The three of us stick together until we all get out alive."

Alive? What was he talking about? They were safe now, weren't they?

Maria sagged against him, not releasing her grip. The firemen directed them across the street into the doorway of a store where others had gathered. Maria turned to look at the factory, but Conrad pulled her head against his coat. "Don't look, Maria. Don't look."

She pulled against him, knowing he was protecting her. But from what? She saw the fire engines, firemen and police. The nets, the ladders. They were too short, the ladders. They didn't reach to the top, not even to the windows where the blazing flames were pouring out.

"Maria, stop it. Torturing yourself won't help anyone."

Esther screamed beside her before fainting. Conrad released Maria and helped to lay Esther on some coats.

"Stay here, look after her. I'll get someone," he said.

"Don't leave me."

"I'll be back. She saved your life. Look after her, Maria."

His firm tone spoke through her panic. She owed Esther everything. Kneeling by Esther's side, she cradled the girl's head on her knees, trying to position her friend in such a way as to prevent hurting her more.

"Esther, everything will be okay. Conrad will find someone to help. Open your eyes. Please."

Esther's eyes fluttered. "Maria, did you see? The pavement?"

Maria shook her head. "Don't speak. Just rest." Where was Conrad with a doctor? She didn't want to think about what Esther had seen. After everything, what had been so horrid it caused her to pass out?

# CHAPTER 31

*C*onrad came back alone.

"There aren't any spare doctors. They're busy. We'll take her to the hospital." The whole time he spoke, he avoided her eyes. She wanted to scream at him to talk to her, tell her what he had seen, what scared him, but she was too frightened. She knew it was bad, but she didn't want to know for certain.

Maria spotted Gustav walking down the sidewalk, his red eyes staring out of his blackened face. He looked... lost.

Conrad moved forward to shake his hand and then hug him. Instead of shaking Gustav's hand, Maria hugged him too. She held him as his body shook and then he pushed her away.

"I saw you and Conrad, and I couldn't leave you behind. Not after what you did for my family," Gustav's raspy voice testified to how much smoke he'd inhaled. "I'm sorry about your sister. Any sign of her yet?"

Maria shook her head. "No, Conrad offered to search for her, but then Esther fainted, so he went for a doctor. I spotted Rosa's boyfriend, Paulo. I didn't speak to him, but he'll search here. She may have gone looking for me. We need to get Esther to the hospital."

Conrad squeezed Maria's hand. "Firemen said we should get Maria and Esther checked out. Both got a little singed by the fire."

"I'm fine." Maria protested, "I can cut the burned ends of my hair out, but Esther has a nasty burn on her neck. We've been waiting for news of her brother, Joseph, and older sister, Fannie."

Gustav offered young Esther his arm. "Come on Esther, let's get you down to the hospital. Your family will look for you there. Can't leave a burn like that to fester, could get infected."

The girl took his arm without a word, leaving Maria and Conrad to follow them.

They walked in silence. Every so often, Conrad shuddered, but he didn't cry. Maria brushed away enough tears for both of them. The streets were full of people, some crying, others covered in soot walking in a daze. She saw people on the ground, doctors trying to mend broken legs, nurses cleaning wounds. Ambulances passed them. Nearer the hospital, the crowds seemed to intensify. She moved closer to him.

"Thank you for saving me. You risked your life coming back for me."

"I don't have a life without you." Conrad didn't look at her, but tightened his grip on her arm and maneuvered their way through the assembled crowds.

Some were obviously looking for their families. The looks of horror and desperation were enough to tell that. She looked round for Rosa or Paulo. She didn't see anyone else she recognized either. Not until they reached the hospital did she see some familiar doctors.

"Maria, are you hurt?" Patrick Green moved quickly to her side.

"No, thank you, Patrick."

Conrad gave her a look. "Ignore her, Doctor. Her hair got burned, and she swallowed a lot of smoke."

"Only as much as you did, Conrad," Maria responded. She pointed at Esther. "Patrick, I mean Dr. Green, could you look at Esther? She took off her scarf, she was frightened, and she got burned."

"I'll help your friend, but try to find somewhere to sit and drink milk. They think it helps with smoke inhalation. Frieda will be happy to know you are okay. We all are."

# CHAPTER 32

She let Conrad lead her to an empty chair before he went in search of milk. The surrounding chairs filled up quickly, as did the room. More and more survivors came into the hospital with their families. Like her, many were missing sisters, brothers, and sometimes mothers and fathers.

One boy was missing his mother, two sisters, and a brother. Maria wanted to help him, but when she tried to stand, her legs wouldn't work. She sat back down just as Conrad returned, a cup of milk in hand.

"Drink that." He pushed it into her hand. She met his eyes, but he wouldn't hold her gaze. Her heart hammered in her chest. Was it Rosa?

"You know something. What? Tell me."

"I can't," he whispered, his face ashen.

"It is Rosa? Did you find her?" She stood up,

spilling some milk. She handed the cup to one of the other workers. "I can't drink it, but the doctor said it would be good for us."

She turned back to Conrad. "Tell me."

"It's not Rosa."

"What then?"

"Not here, Maria. Come outside."

She followed him outside stunned to see the crowds gathering, all muttering and mumbling, but nobody was shouting.

"Maria, oh my God. I can't get the images out of my head. There are loads of them in there with all sorts of injuries. I don't know how the nurses and doctors do it." He angrily brushed a tear away. "What do I look like? Whining like a boy."

She wrapped her arms around him, not caring who saw her or what they thought.

"Conrad, you saved me and Esther today. You should be proud."

"Gustav saved all of us."

"Yes, but you came back for me first. Otherwise, Gustav wouldn't have found me. They'd have crushed me against that door. Why was it locked? Why did nobody know where to go? What about Harris and Blanck? Did they get out? I haven't seen them."

"They survived. And their kids, too. Not that I would want anything to happen to those lovely little girls, but their fathers? How they can walk around with their heads up, I will never know. They should be here supporting everyone, but my guess is that they're in hiding."

"Or filing their insurance claim forms knowing those two," Gustav said, coming up behind them.

Esther wore a bandage around her neck. Gustav spoke as Esther just stared into space, "We should tell Esther's mother she is safe. Maybe they know something about her brother and sister. What will you do?"

Mama! How could she have forgotten her mother? She'd be fretting at home. "I've got to go home. I checked with the nurses. No patient with the name Rosa Mezza has been admitted. She just seems to have disappeared."

Maria caught Conrad and Gustav exchanging glances, but someone distracted her. Looking into the crowd, she recognized Mr. Maltese.

"Maria, have you seen my wife, my daughters? Rosaria? Lucia? Please, you must have seen them. They walked to work this morning." His facial expression begged her to tell him they were alive.

She had seen the family on her way to work. Lucia was joking around, making her mother and sister laugh. She'd shared the elevator with them but couldn't remember seeing them later in the day.

"I'm sorry, Mr. Maltese. I didn't see them. I've lost Rosa. Have you seen her?"

Mr. Maltese shook his head, his eyes wide with terror.

"Mr. Maltese, don't wait here." Conrad said. "I know your wife, a lovely lady. I've searched this hospital for Rosa and didn't see your wife or girls. They took some injured to Bellevue hospital. The police have taken the bodies to a temporary morgue. That's all we know for now. Would they have gone home?"

The man muttered in Italian. "I was at home, nobody came. I waited, and then I heard there was a fire. The building, the smoke, those bodies. My girls, where are they?"

Conrad offered his advice. "Mr. Maltese, speak to a police officer or a fireman. They may know more. I would go with you, but I must get Maria home."

"Yes, her mama will worry." Mr. Maltese wrung his hands, his eyes darting one way and another before he wandered away.

# CHAPTER 33

*C*onrad led Maria away. Maria hoped the man would find his family. Could they have all died? Knowing Lucia and Rosaria, they wouldn't have left their mother behind, and Mrs. Maltese might not have been able to jump up on the tables. Getting up above the fire was one common theme to the stories of how some had survived. Maria shuddered.

"Are you cold?"

"No, I was thinking of the Maltese girls, they wouldn't have left their Mama. Nobody would run away and leave a parent in that inferno." Yet she'd done exactly that only in her case, it was her sister.

He read her thoughts. "You can stop thinking like that right this second, Maria Mezza. You didn't desert Rosa, you couldn't know if she had got out or not. She worked at the Triangle longer than you did. You had to save yourself, that's what she would have wanted."

Maria couldn't answer. It was uncanny how he could read her mind. She huddled closer. Glad of his support even though he'd suffered too. He hadn't lost family, but many close friends and co-workers, plus they'd never forget the sights they'd seen.

Conrad put his arm around her waist to support her physically and mentally.

"Paulo may have found her and taken her home. Come on, we will try to find a cab."

But there wasn't any, and they had to walk back. Their journey slowed by meeting other survivors or those still looking for missing family.

"Maria, Maria Mezza!" Maria turned in response to her name being called. Sarah, her friend from the 1909 strikes, flung her arms around her.

"Thank God you are safe, Maria. I worried about you and prayed for you."

It was just like she and Sarah had spoken last week. As if they were still close friends.

"Sarah, it was horrible. Just like you said. They locked the doors."

Sarah didn't look shocked, she knew what working in the Triangle was like. "Don't worry about that for now. How are you? Rosa? Your friends? Did you see Katie and Rosie Weiner? They're sisters and good friends of our family."

Thrilled to give someone good news, she nodded. "Katie is fine. I saw her after on the sidewalk. Someone said they took her to Bellevue hospital for her hands or maybe her feet. I heard she jumped onto the elevator. The top of it or something, but she's alive. I didn't see Rosie."

Sarah hugged Maria. "Thank you, Maria, her mother will be so happy to hear about Katie. Maybe Rosie went to the hospital with her. So many dead and injured. How will they recover? I best get back. I'm so glad I saw you. I pray you will find your sister. Good luck."

With that, Sarah left. "A good friend of yours?" Conrad asked as they continued down the street.

"She was. We were friends during the strike, but she was very cross when I went back to work. I broke the strike, and she hated me for it. We haven't spoken since."

"Looks like she got over it. Those things mean little in times like this."

He was right, nothing mattered now but finding Rosa alive. As they drew closer to the apartment, her walk slowed.

"Want me to wait here?" Conrad asked. "Your mama might not welcome my presence. Times like this are for close family."

"No, don't go." Maria gripped his arm so hard she made him wince. "I'm terrified. What if she isn't there? What if she didn't make it out?"

"Shush, darling. We will know soon enough. Don't expect the worst. Come on, dry your eyes. Your mama needs you more than ever now." He kissed her on the tip of her nose, and taking her hand once more, strode around the block to her apartment. Nodding at people staring at them, he pulled her alongside into the apartment. Only when they got to the door did he stop.

"You can do this, Maria Mezza. Go on."

The door opened just as he finished, and her mother's screams rang in her ears. A string of Italian followed with her mother kissing her and behaving like she was the prodigal son. Out of the corner of her eye she saw Benito standing up, his arms folded as he eyed Conrad. Sophie and Louisa hung in the background, arms around each other, tear stained white faces.

Mama held her away, looking over her shoulder, "Where's Rosa? Why isn't she with you?"

Maria glanced at Conrad before she looked her mama in the eyes. "Mama, she's not here?"

"No Maria, she was with you. You left here together this morning. You come home together." Mama spoke forcefully, as if she could will Rosa to appear. "Rosa, where is my Rosa? My girl, where is she?" Mama paled and crumpled.

Before Benito could move, Conrad caught Mama before she fell to the ground. Maria pulled a chair out and together they pushed her mother onto it.

"Take your hands off my mother!" Benito roared.

Maria turned on her brother. "Benito stop. Conrad saved my life. That's not the way to treat our guest. Louisa, some water for Mama." Maria forced her mother to drink some water. "Have you seen Paulo? He went back to look for Rosa." She threw the last remark over her shoulder at their brother, who was still glaring at Conrad.

"No, he hasn't graced the door either. Who would have thought my sisters would bring such shame to our family? Paulo is bad enough but at least he's Sicilian this one–Irish ain't you?"

"American actually. Maria, I'll go back to the factory and look for Rosa." When she moved to go with him, he shook his head. "Stay here. Your mama needs you. I will be back soon." He kissed her on the cheek regardless of her brother, and left before she could stop him.

Furious, Maria roasted her brother, "You jack-ass!" She had never used the term before, but it suited her brother. "What gives you the right to throw your weight around? That man saved my life. He came back into the fire and rescued me. You should be out there looking for our sister, our neigh-bors. There are hundreds, yes, hundreds of girls miss-ing. Go. Get out now before I say something I regret."

Benito gave her a dirty look before grabbing his hat. He banged the door shut behind him. Maria glared at the door for a few seconds as she tried not to cry with frustration and grief.

Maria turned to her younger sisters, who shrank back from her. They were used to Rosa's tantrums, but Maria was usually the quiet one. "Louisa, Sophia, come here and give me a hug."

"Phew - you need a bath, you smell rotten," Sophia grumbled but Louisa just clung to her. She hugged both before giving them chores to do. "Louisa, you go check on our neighbors. See who has some food prepared and borrow some. Mama will pay them back tomorrow, won't you, Mama?"

Her mother uttered something unintelligible from the table where she remained sobbing. If only Papa was here. But it was best he wasn't. Poor gentle Papa would have blamed himself for bringing his girls to a city that let them burn.

All night they waited, joined by some of their neighbors who were also missing family members. The men toured the hospitals and the morgues; the women stayed home saying rosaries. The priest came to sit with them, but Maria couldn't face him. She went to sit on the doorstep for a while, but the need to do something grew stronger. She returned to the apartment. "Mama, I have to go to the hospital. Maybe there is some way I can help. I am going out of my mind sitting here doing nothing."

Her mama's look chilled her blood. "We are praying, Maria."

Praying. That hadn't kept Rosa safe, had it? "Yes, but I need to do something practical. I need to be active. I can't sit anymore."

Her mother looked like she would argue, but decided against it.

"Be careful, Maria. I can't lose you." The "too" hung in the air. Maria grabbed her coat, kissed her sleepy sisters on the hair telling them to go to bed and then left the house. One neighbor said she would walk with her. She couldn't talk and was glad the woman felt the same way. As they walked, more joined them en route to the hospitals and morgues. Maybe she should check the morgues, but she couldn't face that. It was almost like admitting Rosa was dead. She pictured her sister as she had been at lunch, her eyes lit up chatting about Paulo and their plans for the future. So full of life. She had to be okay.

# CHAPTER 34

*A*t the hospital, Maria found Frieda, her friend, almost asleep on her feet. Her apron had blood and soot stains on it, her hair tumbled from its bun, and her eyes spoke volumes about the sights she'd seen.

"Maria! Patrick told me you were safe, thank goodness. I was so worried. And Rosa?"

Maria gave a slight shake of her head. "What can I do to help? I have to do something. The time is passing so slowly. Benito, Conrad, and others are out looking for her. I can't sit waiting. I need to help. I need to stop thinking, stop seeing..." She spoke fast, trying to hold back the tears, but they came anyway.

Frieda put her arms around her, escorting her to an area dispensing tea and coffee. She gave Maria a hot tea with lots of sugar. Maria grimaced at the taste, but Frieda insisted it was good for shock.

"You could translate for us. We have so many Italians waiting for answers on their loved ones. Some nurses are trying to help, but they would be better with patients. Can you do that?"

Yes, Maria could do that. She went to the waiting area and soon was caught up helping families of other victims. Some knew their loved ones were in the hospital and waited for news. Others were hoping to find their wives and daughters. A few were waiting for a priest. All were grieving. Time passed a little faster.

Maria hurried back and forth. She loved being able to impart good news. The sign of a smile breaking through the worried faces lifted her spirits, but they were few. Other families had to deal with the fact their loved ones had lived until reaching hospital, only to lose their fight. She avoided the priests. They weren't all like Father António, but they could have done more to help the strike. Maybe if the strikers had won, this wouldn't have happened. The doors wouldn't have been locked for starters. The fire buckets might have been full of water. The hoses may have worked. She didn't want to think about that.

It was early morning before Conrad found her. She quailed at the look on his face, all hope gone. "Where?"

Conrad moved closer, taking her hands in his. Her whole body shook, a mixture of anger and grief. Some had survived, why hadn't Rosa?

"Paulo identified her, he recognized her watch. He

said he gave it to her as a gift." He put a finger under her chin making her look up at him. "I'm so sorry, Maria. I'll take you home."

Recognized her watch? Her stomach churned. Rosa, her beautiful sister, had burned. She had to see for herself. Otherwise she wouldn't believe Rosa was dead.

"Bring me to her."

"No, Maria." Conor spoke firmly. "You need to go home. Paulo won't tell your mother. He has other people to find. His cousins or something."

She didn't want to face Mama. She didn't want to be the one who broke her heart, not again. Mama had only just forgiven her for Papa dying. She'd never forgive her for leaving Rosa behind.

"Why didn't I go back for her? Why didn't you make me go back for her?" She beat his chest with her hands. "You should have looked for her, rescued her! She can't be dead."

Conrad held her as she railed against the news, throwing hurtful accusations at him.

"You never liked my sister. That's why you left her behind, isn't it?"

"I'm sorry, so sorry." Conrad murmured repeatedly, holding her in a vice like grip. She glanced up and saw people staring at her. Their grim, shocked faces highlighting their grief. She wasn't the only person to lose someone. Taking a deep, shaky breath, she composed herself. She had to be the strong one.

"Maria, please let me take you home. I know you're angry with me and you have every right. I should have gone back in to find Rosa."

She ignored his words. Actions spoke louder. He'd insisted she get to safety, even if that meant leaving Rosa behind. Rosa sat near the windows. All the girls working near her desk had died. Maria pushed those thoughts out of her head.

"Benito, does he know?" Not that her brother would volunteer to tell Mama.

"I haven't seen him, but it is possible he is still down there. So many people, not just families but others. Rich people, all dressed up in their fancy clothes."

Maria barely registered what he was saying, but she glanced up at his last remark.

"What do they want? They didn't help us when we needed them to support us with the strike. If they had, maybe we wouldn't be dealing with this now."

Conrad shrugged. "I don't know. Come on, you look as if you could sleep on your feet. Let someone else help. Rest and grieve."

She wanted Rosa home, healthy and happy. She didn't want to grieve. She'd done enough of that for Papa. Her sister with her dreams of getting married and having a family. All gone.

CHAPTER 35

*F*rieda searched the wards looking for Patrick, but he was nowhere to be seen. Where was he?

"Frieda, have you seen Patrick?" his father asked.

"No, Dr. Green. I assumed he was in surgery with you."

A nurse passed by at that moment. "Dr. Green went down to the factory site some time ago."

Frieda and Richard exchanged a look. Heart thumping, Frieda tried to breathe slowly. "Why would they need a doctor down there? I thought they had taken all the survivors to hospital."

"They did, but it's something to do with an elevator shaft. The firemen used water to put the fires out, but they didn't know some people had tried to escape by jumping into the elevator shaft. Someone came to the hospital, a police officer asking for volunteers and Dr. Green, I mean Dr. Patrick Green rushed off."

Frieda saw her concern mirrored on Richard's face. He took her hand, "I can't leave, I have too many patients. Theater is backed up right now."

She glanced at the full waiting room. She shouldn't leave either, but Patrick had run into danger. What if anything happened to him?

A nurse's voice broke into her thoughts, "Dr. Klunsberg, another ambulance has just pulled up."

Frieda rushed to help, followed by Richard. The ambulance doors were open.

"Could do with some help in here."

Patrick's voice. Frieda rushed to assist. She climbed in, her heart failing at the sight in front of her. Patrick looked awful, his face streaked with soot, his eyes bloodshot.

"Frieda, it's Leonie. Blood pressure is too low, can barely take it. Come on Leonie, don't give up now. We got you out of there. Fight. You're so brave, jumping into the elevator shaft. Carrie and your brothers will be so proud."

Patrick kept talking to Leonie as Frieda and Richard helped to steady her trolley as they walked into the hospital. Patrick gave Richard a lowdown of injuries he found.

"Probably missed some, Dad. The light was rather dim. She's soaked, but as far as I can see there's no external bleeding. Not anything more serious than a couple of cuts and bruises and a gash on her forehead. There may be internal bleeding; her pulse is erratic and blood pressure dropping."

"Patrick, stand down, lad. We'll take it from here. You go wash up, get some clothes and some food."

"But Dad --"

Frieda pulled Patrick's hand. "Let your dad do his thing. She couldn't be in better hands." She stared after the trolley wheeling Leonie away, stamping down her urge to scream in frustration. It was all so unfair. None of the workers deserved to die or be injured. Leonie couldn't die too. She just couldn't. She blew through her mouth trying to stop the tears.

Patrick clasped Frieda's hand and pulled her to him, to the cheers of those surrounding them. She felt him shuddering in her arms; he was crying. She held him until his body stopped shaking, not wanting to expose him to ridicule. There were still some who would look down on men who cried in public.

"You're in shock, Patrick. Drink this." She handed him a hot drink prepared by a nurse. "You need to have a bath and go to bed. Go on now. You're exhausted."

Frieda wanted to follow Patrick, but she couldn't be seen going into the staff quarters. It was one thing for them to embrace in a public hall, but she had her reputation to protect. She stared after him as he shuffled off, like a sleepwalker.

Leonie. She had to find out how she was, but a voice from behind stopped her.

"He's a hero, that man of yours, ma'am."

Frieda turned toward the voice. A fireman, almost covered in black apart from white streaks down his face and his red eyes, stared back at her.

"Are you hurt? Has a doctor seen you?" Frieda asked, moving closer as her eyes assessed him from head to toe. There was no obvious sign of injury, but with the amount of dirt, she couldn't be sure.

The fireman held a hand up.

"I had to come and see if the girl made it. We didn't even know she was down there. Could have drowned the poor little darling. We didn't know how to move her, she was so weak. Your man, that doctor fella, he climbed down into the shaft and told us what to do. He's a real hero."

Frieda blushed at the fireman calling Patrick her man. She quickly recovered her composure.

"You are all heroes. I heard how your men went up toward the fire and broke down a door on the sixth floor, allowing some workers to escape. If it wasn't for you and the men like you, more would have died."

The fireman didn't look like he agreed. "We all feel so helpless, ma'am. Angry, too. If that place had the sprinkler system we recommended, we'd have saved more. They didn't even do regular fire drills and some survivors have told us how there was fabric lying about everywhere."

Confused, Frieda was about to ask what he expected given it was a shirtwaist factory.

"I don't mean the material those poor girls were working on. There was a mountain of waste material which hadn't been collected. Some say the fire started on the eight floor yet most of those who died worked on the ninth. There are lots questions that need answering." The man seemed to realize he was talking out of turn. The fire inspectors should investigate the cause before a fireman commented on it.

Frieda put her hand on his arm. "You are a hero. So are your men. You put your lives at risk to help those who needed you. When did you last eat? We have a small kitchen. I could put together a sandwich."

"Thanks lady, but I best get back to the lads. You look after that doctor of yours. He's one of the good men." The man hesitated, "Could you tell me if she will live?"

Her smile fell. "Leonie is very badly injured, so it's too early to tell, but I can say she is in the best hands. Dr. Richard Green is one of the best doctors in New York as well as being a burns specialist. He is also the father of the doctor you met."

The fireman raised a hand to his head and left before she remembered to ask his name or his fire-house. Frieda checked a couple of patients before she was free to check on Leonie's prognosis.

# CHAPTER 36

*F*rieda pushed the hair back from her eyes, blinking rapidly as she did so. She was beyond tired, but they had to keep going. There were so many casualties, not just those injured in the fire, but family members who'd collapsed or gone into shock on hearing of the loss of their loved ones. Leonie was still in theater, not a good sign, but Frieda couldn't think about that. She had another patient to worry about, the young woman lying in the bed.

"Nurse, she's woken up. Nurse."

Frieda looked up as the nun called to her. She didn't correct her. Most people didn't like being treated by a trainee doctor, never mind a female one. She smiled at the girl in the bed, relieved to see her focusing normally.

"Good evening, Celia, how are you feeling?"

"I was just telling her it was a good job she protected her hands. What presence of mind for such a young lady." The nun bustled off to see someone else, leaving Celia with a big grin on her face.

"It's lovely to see you smiling, if rather surprising under the circumstances. Is the pain not bad?"

"I was just thinking about the nun. She is praising me for having presence of mind. Not that at all. I just paid off my fur muff, and I wasn't leaving that behind, fire or no fire!"

Despite herself, Frieda giggled. Celia joined in. Patrick found them laughing.

"Ladies? Frieda?" He asked, the concerned look on his face making Frieda stop.

"Sorry Doctor, it was my fault. I made the nurse laugh. Don't get cross with her." Celia sat up straighter in the bed.

"I'll try not to," Patrick said, giving Frieda a sly wink. She had to turn away for fear of giggling again. What was wrong with her? It was neither the time nor the place.

Frieda sought refuge in her profession. "Celia has a broken arm and finger and a nasty gash on her head. Dr. Hamilton stitched that up. She was lucky. She jumped and slid down the center cable to floor five."

Admiration lit up Patrick's face. "You're a brave young lady. So many of you were."

Celia's eyes clouded over. "Doc, can you give me

anything for my dreams? I can't get the sounds out of my head. Just something to tide me over."

Patrick nodded. "A sleeping tonic will help you rest and give your head injury a chance to heal. Do you have family we should notify?"

"The nun said she will send someone round to tell them. Thanks Doc, you get on and see to someone else. Better yet, go home and rest. You look as tired as the nurse does. She should nurse you better."

Patrick sent Frieda a look, sending the butterflies in her stomach dancing. "That sounds like a great idea. What do you think, *nurse* Frieda?"

Frieda walked away before he saw her scarlet face. She almost fell over a young man practically crawling along the corridor.

"Here, let me help you. Patrick, Dr. Green, help me, please." Frieda shouted as she grasped the man under one shoulder.

The man said something in Yiddish. Frieda answered in German, and between the two of them she understood he was looking for his father. "I left him behind. I didn't think it was serious. I can't believe I came out without him. What type of son am I?" The man muttered repeatedly as Frieda and Patrick led him to a spare bed. There they pushed him onto it, Patrick examining him as Frieda removed his socks, what was left of them. The man wouldn't lie still. He tried to get back up several times, shouting at Patrick when he tried to stop him. His shouts were joined by those of an older man who pushed Frieda out of the way as he threw himself at the bed. "Isodore! My son. My boy. You're alive!

Both men sobbed, bringing tears to Frieda's eyes.

Patrick took her arm and led her away. "They both seem relatively unscathed. Let them catch up. Someone else can check over them later. Come with me. You look like you're about to fall over."

Although grateful for his concern, she still tried to move away from him. She didn't want to become the talk of the hospital, but he stopped her by tightening his grip.

"If the events of the last twenty-four hours have taught me anything, my love, it is that life is short. We have to make the most of the time we have. I think it's about time we went public with our romance. I am sick of hiding how I feel. Aren't you?"

Did that mean he didn't see her as his sister? Or was she misreading what he was saying, again? She was so tired, her brain wasn't functioning properly.

"I don't know what you are talking about Patrick Green."

"Really? So I imagine how you blush when I catch you looking at me?" He whispered, so close his breath seemed to caress her cheek.

Her face blazed, she'd hoped he didn't notice that. Her heart thudded in her throat as she inhaled his individual scent beneath the medical smell clinging to his doctor's coat.

"So, do you mind me doing this then?" he whispered. His eyes held hers prisoner as he slowly, very slowly, bent his head. She felt the warm brush of his lips against hers

He'd kissed her. Right there in the middle of the corridor where anyone and everyone could see. It was only a slight touch of his lips on hers, but it was enough.

Her heart fluttered, as did the flurry of butterflies in her stomach. She felt dizzy and then guilty for being this happy.

"Still don't know what I am talking about?" he asked. His eyes twinkled, the expression in them making her knees weaken. "Frieda, I love you. I have for years. And I think you love me, too."

He loved her. She wanted to shout it from the rooftops. But she'd thought this before.

"You have a rather high impression of yourself, Dr. Green." She didn't know why she was protesting when she wanted to scream yes, she loved him.

He clasped her hands in his. "I love you."

Her eyes widened in astonishment but she knew from his tender expression, he meant it. He leaned into her slightly, "Did you hear me, I said I love you."

She pulled her hand free and brushed a finger across his cheek. "I love you too."

He swept her into his arms, almost lifting her from the floor and kissed her once more. This time, his lips held hers for seconds before he pulled away, breathing a little harder. "I wish we were somewhere more private. Trust me to pick the wrong location to kiss you for the first time."

Although he was whispering into her ear, she worried someone might hear him. She let him guide her to where the volunteers had set up a counter providing hot tea and coffee with sandwiches for the staff. They found a seat, squashed together, and ate their supper.

His fingers played with hers, squeezing them under the table. She looked into his face, his tender gaze causing her stomach butterflies to do cartwheels. He cleared his throat before whispering, "I love you, Frieda."

They might have been sitting in the busy hospital, but to Frieda it was as if they were alone in the world. Feeling guilty at being so happy, she glanced at him.

"I don't think I should be this happy. Not at a time like this."

"Frieda, you know more than anyone how a tragedy like this changes lives. If it wasn't for the boat accident, you wouldn't have come into my life. Something good came out of something dreadful." He picked up her hand and kissed her fingers " Maybe in time, this tragedy will change things so no other shirtwaist workers or factory employees will face such dangers daily."

She sat resting her head on his shoulder as his fingers played with her hair. Her eyes half closed as she relaxed. He loved her. Patrick loved her. A crash of crockery reminded her where they were. Looking up she saw a red faced nurse picking up pieces of broken china from the floor.

She sat up straighter putting a slight distance between them.

"Patrick, how are we going to come back from all this? What will happen to the children if Leonie doesn't survive? Have you heard how she is?"

"She's still in theater. We'll know more later or maybe tomorrow morning."

"Do you think so?" she looked in the face of the person she trusted more than anyone else in the world. Was he hiding something in an effort to protect her? "Do you think she will live?"

He closed his eyes, perhaps so she couldn't see the truth. "I hope so, Frieda. She's in the best hands. Dad asked Lawlor to assist him. He's the best surgeon in New York, next to Dad of course." Patrick stood up and held his hand out for Frieda, helping her to her feet.

"I best get back, but you, Dr Klunsberg, need to go home. Lily and Mother will be going out of their mind with worry."

"You've been working as long as I have."

"Yes, darling, but I'm a man." He winked to show he was joking. "Go on, go home. I will be fine. Come back tomorrow morning."

He leaned in to whisper he loved her as he took her empty cup. She wished he would kiss her again. Looking in his eyes, she could see he felt the same. Then he walked away, repeating his instructions to go home.

She couldn't resist. "Yes, Dr. Green."

# CHAPTER 37

*O*n her way home, she met Gustav. He seemed to be walking around in circles as she'd seen him around the hospital earlier.

"Are you all right?" she asked. He jumped as if she'd shouted. "I'm sorry Gustav I didn't mean to startle you."

"You didn't, Frieda. I was just deep in thought. I can't believe it's happened again. Just over five years later, and New York is dealing with another tragedy like the one I lost my Agatha in. You know what I mean. You lost your Vati and your brother. You understand, don't you, Frieda?"

His rambling worried her. He was usually a quiet man. When had he last had some water or food?

"Yes, Gustav, I understand. Where were you going now?"

"Just been checking in at the different hospitals, hoping to find my friends. Families I knew from Little Germany, they have girls missing."

"What about Alice? Does she know you survived?"

"Ja. I ran to the orphanage. She stayed with Emily on Friday night as I was working on Saturday. I hugged Alice. But I couldn't stay. I had to come and help other families get their girls home. I just didn't think so many had died. Why? The fire only lasted half an hour, yet so many dead. How could this happen?"

Frieda didn't have the answers for him.

"Why don't you come with me? I am going to the Sanctuary. Lily and Kathleen will be there. They can send someone to bring Alice over. She must want to be with you. You can have some food and get some rest."

"I must keep looking, so many missing." He was muttering again.

"Gustav, please walk me home. I need a friend too. Leonie is badly injured and I have to break the news to Lily and Kathleen. And the children."

His eyes widened. "How bad?"

"She's been in theater for nine hours." She kept her voice professional, afraid to show weakness. She had to stay strong, people expected that from medical staff.

"Please, Gustav, take me home."

She knew he was too much of a gentleman to refuse her request.

He offered her his arm and they headed to the streetcar. The journey passed quickly as Frieda related Celia's story, and then the story of Isadore's father turning up. Gustav knew Isodore and was pleased to know he had found his father.

He said, "I sent Mr. Wegodner to the hospital. He'd looked just about everywhere else. It's good they found each other."

Celia's story also made him smile. "Shows that girl had spirit. She was brave, Frieda. So many of those ladies were brave. Not like the bosses. They could have done so much more, but they chose not to. Put money ahead of anything else. Even people's lives."

"How do you mean?" Frieda asked. It was a way to keep him talking as they walked the rest of the way to the Sanctuary.

"I was there when the fireman came in to inspect the factory. He warned the bosses not to lock the doors on the girls, but he took no notice. Said he was afraid of thefts. As if those decent young women would be bothered with thieving."

Frieda assumed he didn't expect an answer. She couldn't agree as the hospital regularly lost property to visitors and patients. Still, she wasn't about to argue with him. He kept talking.

"The fireman and the other insurance man who came, they both recommended the bosses put in some sprinklers. I didn't fully understand what those men meant, but the boss said it was too expensive. Everything was money, money, money. All those people, they are worth more than any amount of money, aren't they, Frieda?"

Relieved they had arrived at the Sanctuary, Frieda moved to open the door, but Lily had got there first. She pulled Frieda into her arms. "Thank God you are home. We were worried sick. Gustav, how good of you to bring her home. Come in, please."

"Lily, can you send someone to fetch Alice? She knows her father is safe, but I think she'd prefer to be with him. Gustav needs water, food, and rest. He was a hero; saved Maria, her friend Conrad, and some other people from the fire."

Kathleen came out in time to hear Frieda.

"Frieda, darling, so glad you came home. Did you see my husband and son?"

"Yes, Kathleen, they were both working hard. Patrick ordered me to come home and rest. I didn't want to, but he insisted and used his position. I had no choice, but to follow his orders." Despite her own indignation, she was stunned to see Kathleen smile.

"Good, he was right. You'd never have listened otherwise, would you Frieda? You look like you are about to fall over. Come in and sit near the fire. We've been working in shifts, helping people through the night. We have had lots of visitors. People find sitting by an open fire and a pot of tea rather comforting. Don't they, Gustav?"

Frieda watched Kathleen put their visitor at ease. She was so kind. Gustav looked slightly more comfortable. He stared around him before glancing at his soot-stained clothes.

"That they do. Are you sure you want me to sit down? My clothes are rather dirty."

"Please sit down, Gustav. Lily has gone to rustle up some food."

Frieda let them talk around her as she tried to form the words to tell them about Leonie. Kathleen glanced at her and then took her hand. "Frieda, what is it? You're whiter than a sheet. Sit down."

"Leonie. It's Leonie."

Kathleen screamed bringing Lily and Cook racing. Horrified, Frieda checked the stairs but the children didn't appear.

"What's wrong? Why did you scream?" Lily put her arm around Kathleen who was sobbing quietly.

"Leonie...." Kathleen squeaked.

Lily paled as Cook grabbed Frieda's hand. "Is she dead?"

"No, but she's very seriously ill. They found her last night at the bottom of the elevator shaft. Richard has operated and we just have to wait." Frieda left out the fact Leonie was still in theater.

"What shall we tell the children?" Kathleen asked, regaining her composure.

Frieda sighed. Those children had been through so much already. "Do they know about the factory yet?"

Lily and Kathleen exchanged a glance. "We told them Leonie had probably gone to a friend's rather than come straight back here. We knew there was some confusion and we hoped the news would be good. They stayed up waiting until the early hours but finally fell asleep a while ago."

Frieda gripped her hands together. How could she destroy the children's lives? "I think you should tell them when they wake up. They need to be prepared, but it seems pointless waking them now. What do you think?"

The women nodded. Cook excused herself, her eyes watering. She reappeared with a stack of sandwiches she must have made earlier and a pot of tea. Frieda matched Gustav sandwich for sandwich. Then she had a slice of cake on top. Yawning, she thanked Cook and Lily.

Kathleen moved nearer, gave her another hug and kissed her on the cheek.

"Freida, go to bed. You need to rest, Patrick won't be happy if you don't. Gustav, if you want to rest here a while, you are very welcome, isn't he, Lily?"

Gustav stood up. "I need to go back to help."

Frieda knew he was exhausted. She had to think of a way to make him rest. If he stayed here, at least he would have some company if he wanted it. He'd be warm.

"Gustav, as a doctor, I'm telling you to rest. You can explain to Lily and Kathleen the type of help the survivors and their families will need. Those who have lost people will also need help, some girls used to send money home to Russia and other countries." Frieda saw he hesitated. "A policeman said they have run out of coffins. The city isn't ready for this scale of emergency."

"Oh my goodness," Kathleen made the sign of the cross.

"It was horrible, Kathleen. The bodies had to remain on the streets with blankets over them. They are bringing in coffins from Brooklyn. They set up a temporary morgue on the East River, just like they did with the General…" Frieda's voice broke. Kathleen rushed to her side.

"Frieda, you need to lie down."

"I will, but please look after Gustav." Frieda looked sternly at the man who looked like he would sleep on his feet. "Sit down."

Gustav sat back down.

"Lily and Kathleen will be interested to hear what you told me about the firemen and the inspectors. They have some influential friends who could make use of the information when the inquiry happens."

Gustav frowned, "Don't have much faith in inquiries."

Frieda shared Gustav's view given how little had

been achieved in wake of the General Slocum fire, but she had to believe in the system.

"Patrick - Dr. Green believes things will change now."

"I agree Frieda. Please tell us Gustav after Frieda says goodnight." Kathleen gave Frieda a look she usually reserved for Little Richie when he was misbehaving.

"I'm going." Frieda kissed them all on the cheek and left, dragging her feet up the stairs. Images of Leonie tormented her. She tried to push them away and think of something nicer. She would think about Patrick and his kiss. As soon as her head hit the pillow, she fell into a deep, dreamless sleep.

# CHAPTER 38

## SUNDAY EVENING, MARCH 26TH.

"*L*ily, what can we do? I feel so helpless sitting here." Kathleen stood and paced the room. "I can't believe they won't let us visit Leonie."

"It's safer for her to be kept in isolation. You know that. You're the one married to the doctor."

Kathleen paced more, irritating Lily who was finding it hard enough to concentrate.

"Kathleen, can you please sit down."

Kathleen ignored her.

"What are all those families going to do now? Not just the ones here in New York, but the ones in Russia, Germany, and Italy who depend on the money their girls were sending home. I can't bear to think about it."

"Kathleen, look at this. I knew we had our doubts about Mayor Gaynor being elected." Lily held up the newspaper, but Kathleen wasn't capable of reading. "We thought he was another pawn of that Tammany lot; if he got elected he would give jobs to all his friends and cronies who owed him something. We judged him badly, didn't we?"

That was an understatement. Mayor Gaynor had proved everyone wrong, and shocked New York by appointing relatively unknown civil servants to prominent positions. He based his appointments on who he felt was right for the job, not on how they voted or who they knew. Charlie had told her that more than one Tammany Hall official had cursed out both the Mayor and James Gallagher. The Mayor for not playing the politics game and Gallagher for not being successful in his assassination attempt on Gaynor. Despite shooting the Mayor at point blank range, Gallagher didn't kill him.

"Look at what he's said, 'The appalling loss of life and personal injuries call for larger measures of relief than our charitable societies can be expected to meet from their ordinary resources. I urge all citizens to give for this purpose by sending their contribution either directly to Jacob H. Schiff or me for remittance to him.'"

"Shiff? As in the Wall Street Investment banker?" Kathleen asked, coming closer to read the paper over Lily's shoulder.

"Yes. The mayor has given one hundred dollars of

his own money. This is something we can get involved with, Kathleen. The committee will need volunteers."

Inspector Griffin walked into the room just at that moment, "That they do, Lily. Forgive me for interrupting, but Cook let me in. You ladies didn't hear the front door."

Lily couldn't believe this was the policeman she had known for years. His disheveled appearance suggested he hadn't slept and he seemed to be ten years older than the last time she'd seen him.

"Inspector Griffin, sit down, you look awful."

"Thank you, Lily, for being so frank."

"Diplomacy was never her strong point, Inspector. You of all people should know that." Kathleen did better than Lily at hiding her shock. "Here, sit closer to the fire. Cook will bring you something to eat and drink. What can we do?"

"Lily, Kathleen, I don't know where to start. I'm so glad you are here. I couldn't go home to the wife. She's upset like most New Yorkers, but she doesn't comprehend just how horrible it is." Inspector Griffin stood up again. "I don't rightly remember why I came here. I had something to tell you. What I'm doing here. There's so much to do. I should get back. I just…"

Lily brushed tears from her eyes at the sight of this powerful man dissolving into a mess.

Kathleen stood up, and taking him by the arm, guided him back to a seat. "Sit down and rest for a few minutes. A cup of tea and a sandwich will make you feel a little better. Then you can remember what it was you needed to tell us. After that, you can go back and face whatever is waiting for you."

Lily waited until Kathleen had left the room. She sensed kindness or sympathy was the last thing he needed from her. She opted for a businesslike approach.

"Inspector, I can only imagine the sights you and your men have had to deal with. One of our girls, Leonie Chiver, is fighting for her life. She was found in an elevator shaft or something. Her siblings are upstairs, and God only knows what will happen to them if she dies."

"Lily, you should see them. Almost 150 dead, of which only 14 are men. The rest are women and young girls. Those poor girls had no chance. The fire department was on the scene in minutes but they couldn't help. Their ladders weren't long enough, their nets not strong enough. Nothing was good enough. Those women didn't know where the exits were, nobody thought to show them. They never did a fire drill. Heck, even the fire hoses in the building weren't connected to the water."

Lily had thought she'd heard everything, but this shocked her.

He kept muttering as if to himself, "Those people had no choice but to jump. They couldn't stand the heat behind them. Nobody warned them. When the fire broke out on the eighth floor, some guy thought he could put it out. He threw water on it, something I guess we would all try, but why didn't he send someone up to warn those girls? A few minutes and maybe they could have all got out. Or most of them. It was all over in less than thirty minutes, yet hundreds of lives are forever ruined. They came here for a new life, a chance to make something of themselves, to become an American. And what did we give them?"

"Pascal, it's not your fault."

But he didn't seem to hear her. He was looking at her, but his eyes were focused on something she couldn't see. "Why didn't we listen? When those girls were on the street back in 1909 shouting about how dangerous their working conditions were, how a fire would happen. 'Cause they said it was a question of *when* not *if*. Why didn't someone pay attention, Lily?" Inspector Griffin's tear-filled eyes stared at her, but didn't focus.

"It's not your fault," she repeated.

"Not my fault? It was policemen who hit those same girls when they went on strike for better conditions. You should see the lads today, Lily. Seasoned officers and they can't look in the mirror. They recognized some girls, the ones not burned beyond recognition. Maybe they'd seen them in the strikes or in the jails after. Or maybe just in the coffee shop or walking through Washington Square gardens. I never seen so many grown men cry like babies. Lily, how can we come back from this?"

She moved closer to take his hand and rubbed it between hers.

"I feel guilty too. I kept dreaming about a fire and knew I had to get the factory finished. But I didn't. Leonie, Maria, and other girls were going to move to work there. In safety." Lily gulped hard. "You ask how we come back from this. Same way as we come back from any other tragedy. We learn from our mistakes and move on. You can't fall apart; you're one of the good guys. Remember how you helped those strikers. I know you and your wife gave out baskets of food and you paid fines on behalf of some younger girls."

Inspector Griffin's ears turned red as Kathleen walked back in carrying a tray of food. "Cook sends her apologies, poor woman is overcome with emotion. Found her crying in the kitchen all alone, so I sent her off to see a friend." Kathleen couldn't have missed the inspector's tears but she didn't comment.

She kept talking. "Inspector, Lily has just been reading about the Mayor's collection. Do you know where his committee is meeting? We'd like to volunteer."

"Yes, that's the reason for coming to see you. The Metropolitan Life Insurance building has offered facilities to the Red Cross. Room 11, 1 Madison Avenue. Mr. Devine is in charge. The police will furnish him with a list of victims, we are still compiling it. Some bodies… have to be identified by other means."

Kathleen and Lily exchanged a glance. Taking a deep breath, Lily forced the images those words formed out of her mind.

"I will speak to the women staying here. I'm sure some will be glad to offer their services. A couple will have to remain here with the children. When Cook gets back, I'll ask her whether she wants to come, too, but I imagine she will stay with the Chivers. They aren't allowed to go to the hospital at the moment."

Inspector Griffin drank the soup but left the sandwiches untouched.

"The call is going out to all agencies, including The Society of St. Vincent de Paul, the Charity Organization Society, and the United Hebrew Charities. A lot of the families don't speak English. So they need interpreters. There will also be a police presence. These sorts of tragedies bring out the best in people, but the scumbags also appear. You have no idea how many known pickpockets we've escorted away from the temporary morgue."

"Imagine trying to steal from dead bodies."

"Kathleen, unfortunately in this job I don't need an imagination. I've seen it all." Pascal Griffin stood up. "I best be getting back."

"Sit back down and eat something." Kathleen used her mothering voice. It seemed to work on all men.

Richard said it reminded them of their mothers chivvying them along as children. It didn't fail this time. Inspector Griffin sat and ate under Kathleen's watchful eye. What he didn't finish, he took away with him wrapped up in a napkin.

"Thank you for listening and for the food."

"Inspector Griffin, Pascal," Lily moved to his side, "you are one of the good guys. Always remember that." She leaned up and kissed his cheek, his gaze catching hers before his eyes filled up once more. He turned and left without looking back.

Only once the front door closed did Kathleen let her tears fall. Lily couldn't cry as she had no tears left. She held Kathleen while her friend sobbed her heart out. Lily's heart felt like stone. Her dreams had foretold this tragedy and despite everything, she hadn't been able to stop it happening or save one of their own. Losing 145 people with more lives hanging in the balance was horrendous, but Leonie made it even more personal.

"aria, where are you going?"

Maria sighed. Her mother wouldn't let her leave the house without subjecting her to an interrogation.

"Mama, I have to go collect my pay." Rosa's too, but she didn't mention her sister. "The Triangle held back a week's wages for everyone."

"Do you have to go now?"

Maria glanced at her mother who was a shadow of the strong woman who'd held the family together after Papa died. The black shadows under her red eyes spoke of long nights crying herself to sleep. She had lost weight too, her skirt hanging off her hips.

"Mama, we need the money. We have bills to pay. I won't be long. I promise."

"Maria, I just want to keep you and my girls near

me. I want you safe. I don't trust America anymore. I want to go back to Sicily." Mama brushed the tears from her eyes. "I want to keep my family safe. This is no life."

Tears choking her throat, Maria moved to hug her mother, but Mama turned her back. Maria didn't argue. It was pointless trying to explain, yet again, that she couldn't have saved Rosa. Mama had no idea of the confusion and panic that had occurred last Saturday. Was it only a few days previously? It seemed like a lifetime.

She pulled the door of the apartment behind her, and walked down the steps onto the sidewalk. About five minutes later, she heard running steps behind her. Turning, she recognized Amita Ableson, another survivor of the fire.

"Morning, Maria. You going to collect your pay? Can I walk with you?"

"Yes of course." Maria didn't know the Jewish girl very well, not that it mattered now. The shared experience of the fire broke down any barriers that might have lay between them.

"Do you think they will give it to us, Maria? I mean it's ours, but you know what the bosses are like."

"They have to. Mama and my sisters need to eat. We have to bury Rosa. We need the money."

Amita squeezed Maria's hand. "I heard about your sister. I'm sorry. I don't know what Italians do with their dead, but in the Jewish faith, our dead should be buried within twenty-four hours of dying. Only in this case, it hasn't been possible."

Maria glanced at Amita, she wasn't sure if the girl had lost someone close and didn't know how to ask. They walked toward the University Place shop, meeting some more workers on their way. Maria was thrilled to see some old friends, but there were far too many missing faces. Bettina and Frances Miale, Jennie Poliny, Catherine Maltese and her two daughters, Rosaria and Lucia. Maria choked back tears as she remembered the Maltese girls teasing their mother about their new American names. Rosaria wanted to be called Sara and Lucia decided on Lucy.

Instead of young girls queuing for pay packets, mothers, fathers, or siblings took their place. Maria looked for Conrad, but he wasn't to be found. She assumed he was still down at the morgue where he'd been working as a volunteer.

"Your Conrad survived, didn't he?" Amita asked.

"Yes, he saved my life. He's volunteering at the mortuary."

Amita pulled a face.

"I know, I couldn't do it," Maria shuddered. "But he felt he had to. So many people were trying to get in just to gawp at the bodies. Some even stole from the dead."

Amita put a hand to her face. "Why would anyone do that? People can be so heartless."

235

"Amita, you should hear the stories. Some are heart-breaking as family members desperately try to identify the dead. But some people acted like it was a day outing. Conrad says he enjoys throwing them out."

They moved forward in the queue.

"Did you hear the bosses put in a claim to their insurance?"

Maria stopped moving, convinced she had misheard.

"I'm not joking Maria. They have already filed a claim for fire damage. My father said he wouldn't be surprised if they made a profit on this. He says that pair would make money from a dead donkey."

Maria couldn't think straight. How could anyone file a claim when the bodies hadn't been identified, never-mind given a respectable burial. She clenched her hands into fists, her nails digging into her palms as waves of anger overtook her. It was so unfair.

"There is going to be a trial. The city will charge Harris and Blanck. They have to." Maria hoped she sounded confident. She had to believe in justice other-wise what was the point in living.

"Josephine Nicolosi, you know her? I think she is Italian?" Amita asked.

Maria shook her head.

"She worked on the eight floor. She said when she came to collect her pay, Blank offered her $1000 to testify the doors weren't locked. Can you imagine what I could buy with $1000?" Amita's wistful expression worried Maria for a moment until the girl's face changed. "I hope he rots in hell, trying to make us tell lies like that. Josephine, she told the police what he was doing. She said she wasn't going to cheat her friends."

Maria's neck muscles loosened. For a moment she'd been worried. The bosses had plenty of money, and many of the survivors and the families of those who hadn't survived had next to nothing. Who knew who might be tempted to change their stories?

She shuffled forward as the queue moved, trying to close her ears to the tales she heard from the people around her. So much suffering. A man cried, asking who was going to bring his family over from Russia now. He'd lost his child and his job because of the fire. A boy came forward who'd lost his mother. His father had died some years previous.

"Do you know where I could get a job? I know I'm small, but I can be a good worker."

Maria bent down to his level. "How old are you?"

"Nine."

She stared at him, and he couldn't hold her gaze. "Six but I'm nearly seven. I have a sister at home. She's crying 'cause she misses Mutti but also 'cause she's hungry. We haven't eaten since Monday."

That was days ago.

"Here." Maria felt in her pocket for a coin. She handed it to the boy. "Go over there and buy something. I will hold your place in the queue."

His eyes lit up as he pocketed the coin.

"Will they give me a job?"

"No, we are here to collect our pay. Your mother would have been due money, too. What was her name?"

He listed out her name as if reading a grocery list. Then he ran to the nearest stall and bought two rolls, one he put straight in his pocket. The other didn't last long. He came back to stand beside her.

"Where do you live?" Maria asked him. Recognizing the street name, she made an impulsive decision.

"I will help you collect your mother's wages, and then we will go see a friend of mine. She looks after orphans like you and your sister."

The boy backed away a little.

"Please don't be scared," Maria reassured him, "Lily looks after lots of children and is very nice. Her cook makes the best cakes and cookies."

The boy's eyes widened, although he still looked suspicious.

"What's your name?" Maria asked.

"Max."

"Max, I'm Maria Mezza. Now, you need to tell the boss what your mother's name is and what floor she worked on." Maria paused for a second. Did the boy know his mother was actually dead? Who had identified the body? How could she ask him?

The queue moved forward and it was Max's turn. The boss showed no hesitation in asking questions.

"How do you know your mother was in the factory on Saturday? Maybe she just took off."

Maria wanted to slap the man in charge of the pay, but Max looked him in the eye. "I ran to the factory when I heard about the fire. A policeman let me look at some of the bodies."

Maria nearly fainted. What sights had this boy seen?

"I recognized Mutti from her necklace. I was able to tell the cop, there was a picture inside. Of Papa, me, and Nettie." Max's voice crumbled as he said his sister's name. Maria put her hand on his shoulder and squeezed.

"Your mama would be very proud of you, Max. Hand over his mother's pay or I will call in the officer standing outside keeping the queue in order." She ordered the pay clerk as Max confidently reeled off his mother's address. She felt Max stick his hand in her coat pocket, assuming he was cold or maybe just wanting the touch of another human being.

Maria collected her and Rosa's pay without argument from the pay clerk, then turned to escort Max to Lily's house. But Max had disappeared. She looked all around but she couldn't find him. In her pocket was a dime, the same amount she had given him a few minutes earlier.

Maria smiled through her tears at the boy's honesty. She'd give his details to Lily, sure her friend would check up on Max and his little sister. Meanwhile, she had to return to her family.

\* \* \*

FRIEDA PULLED the sheet over the face of Sarah Cooper, the young sixteen-year-old from the Bronx who hadn't recovered consciousness after the fire. Her family members were led away by one of the nurses. Frieda couldn't speak to them. For once, she couldn't find the words to offer her condolences. She wasn't sorry, she was angry. Why hadn't the child lived after being brave enough to jump from the building and surviving for almost five days? Frieda covered her face with her hands and wept.

She nearly jumped out of her own skin when Patrick put his arm around her shoulders. She hadn't heard him come in.

"Frieda, darling. I know. I know."

He held her as she sobbed, the tears just kept coming. It took a while for her shuddering sobs to reduce to ordinary tears.

"Why Patrick? Why? It's so unfair. Her family were so hopeful she'd make it. She shouldn't be dead. None of them should be."

He drew her closer to the door before hugging her to his chest. Nobody could come in and disturb them. Even now, he was protecting her, her reputation. She leaned against him, grateful to be held. Thankful for not having to pretend she was coping because she wasn't.

They stood like that for a while. Patrick, perhaps

sensing the worst of the storm was over, gently pushed her back from him. Holding her face gently in his hand, he forced her to look up at him.

"Frieda, you did everything you could. Nobody would even try to do anything for Sarah, she was too badly injured. It's testament to her strength she lingered so long."

"I just feel so helpless. Leonie isn't getting any better either. Every time I see Carrie, she asks me when Leonie's coming home. I have to tell her I don't know. Some doctor I'm going to be."

"Stop that now. You are going to be amazing. Frieda, you are already better than many qualified doctors. This, this...tragedy has tested us all. As you said to me a long time ago, we aren't God, just doctors. We try our best but sometimes that just isn't good enough."

Frieda blinked. "I was horrible to you over Johanna. I'm so sorry."

He kissed the top of her head. "Don't be. You lashed out in your grief, and I behaved like a sulky child. Mother would say it's because we are still learning how to be adults." He looked at her, his gaze flickering to her lips. She inched closer, lifting her face to his. His lips touched hers as he pulled her to him. The fleeting touch of his lips on hers was a comfort.

"Frieda, Sarah would thank you for your devotion to

her care, if she could. Now, we must leave her to the nurses."

Frieda glanced back at the bed. She wanted to say something but what. Patrick spoke instead.

"Sarah would tell you to fight for her friends and her family, and make sure this doesn't happen again. That's her legacy."

Frieda nodded. He took her hand and led her out of the room.

# CHAPTER 40

rieda pushed Leonie's hair back a little as she washed her friend's face. Usually a nurse would do this job, but Frieda wanted to do it. Leonie had yet to regain consciousness. Richard and Patrick had a nurse sitting by her bedside twenty-four hours a day. Patrick had confided, the longer Leonie stayed asleep, the less chance of her making a full recovery.

"A friend of yours?" the nurse asked as she straightened up the bed.

"Yes." Frieda didn't mean to be short, but she couldn't get the words out. She wanted to scream at the unfairness of it all. Leonie had lost so much already and now this.

"She's so young, isn't she? I think that's what gets me. What age is she? Thirteen?"

"Fifteen going on sixteen." Frieda couldn't chat.

The nurse looked at Frieda as her voice broke. "Can I get you something? A cup of coffee?"

"Thank you, but I'm fine." Frieda finished washing Leonie's face. Now she had to dress the stitches. The gash would leave an ugly scar across her forehead, but Leonie's hair would cover most of it. Given the extent of her injuries, Frieda doubted the girl would worry about her face.

"Nurse, do you want to get yourself a coffee? I can stay with Leonie for a while. I'd like to chat to her. I know it sounds silly, but it makes me feel a bit better."

The nurse nodded. "I do that, too. I chat about this and that. I can't bear just looking at her in the bed. She should be out dancing and making plans to meet her young man, not lying here."

Frieda closed her eyes seeing Leonie and Deleo dancing at Susie's party. Was it only a week ago?

"You can't give up hope, Dr. Klunsberg. You and the other doctors will make her better. Just believe you can do it." The nurse squeezed Frieda's arm in a rare gesture of support before leaving carrying a load of dirty bed linen.

"Leonie, can you hear me? Please squeeze my hand if you can. You have to wake up and get better. Carrie gave me this for you." Frieda reached into her pocket and took out a small drawing of two girls. "I'll leave it here, on the locker. It's a picture of you holding Carrie's hand. She wanted to come and see you, but it's not allowed. We don't want you getting an infection on top of everything else."

Frieda swallowed hard. She couldn't dissolve into tears no matter how much she wanted to. She placed the picture up against a glass by Leonie's bed side.

"Morris, Sam, and Alfred always want me to tell you they miss you. They said they wouldn't fight if it meant you got home to them quicker."

At a sound behind her, Frieda turned to see Kathleen standing there with tears running down her cheeks. Kathleen took a step forward and enveloped Frieda in a hug. It was her gentle touch that broke through the barrier Frieda had tried to erect.

"Why, Kathleen? Hasn't she gone through enough already?"

"Frieda, she's alive. We have to focus on that."

Kathleen walked over to kiss Leonie on the forehead. "Leonie, we are all here praying for you. You rest now, and take your time to get better. Carrie and the boys are fine; Cook is feeding them every five minutes. You won't recognize them when you get home. We are all planning the biggest party for when that day comes."

Kathleen squeezed Leonie's good hand before rearranging the plants and flowers on the table near the window. She adjusted the drapes, too, to allow a little sunlight to hit Leonie's face. "It's a beautiful day outside, although not as warm as it looks. Do you mind if I take Frieda home now? She finished her shift hours ago. I want to get her something to eat and some rest. She will be back tomorrow."

"Kathleen?"

"No, Frieda, you can't make yourself sick. Leonie needs you, as do all of us. Let the nurses do their job. They are excellent at looking after patients."

Frieda saw the glint in Kathleen's eyes and knew it was pointless protesting. And it was true, she *was* tired, and that could be dangerous. She could make a mistake and maybe a patient would suffer.

"Just let me say goodbye to Celia Walker." Frieda turned toward the door.

"Who?"

"Another girl from the factory who jumped into the elevator shaft."

"I'll go with you. Maybe she has a family we can help."

Frieda knew that was an excuse. Kathleen was going to shadow her now until she left the hospital.

Celia was sitting up in bed trying to read, but her bandaged hands made holding the book difficult.

"Celia, this is my friend Kathleen Green."

"Green?" Celia queried.

"Yes, she's Patrick's mother and Richard's wife."

"Thank you, Mrs. Green, for what your husband and son did for me. I don't think I would be in such good shape without their help."

Kathleen's eyes glistened as she took a seat beside Celia's bed. "I know it's not visiting time, but I don't think Matron will mind. Can I wait here with you while Frieda goes to get her stuff? I came to take her home."

"I thought she lived here," Celia said with a wink at Frieda.

"Celia, how are you faring?" Kathleen asked, pulling the seat closer to the bed. "Do you have everything you need? I can bring you in some books or some clothes, maybe a nightgown or something."

Frieda left as Kathleen fussed over Celia. She smiled as she heard the young girl tell Kathleen the story of the fur muff. No matter what these women had been through, they always found strength to laugh. That was how New Yorkers dealt with tragedy. She hoped Maria was able to find something to smile about after the devastating loss of her sister.

## CHAPTER 41

APRIL 2ND , 1911

*small* crowd had already gathered outside the Metropolitan Opera House. Maria recognized a few of the faces from her days during the strike. It was odd seeing her factory friends mixing with the fur and feathers brigade as they had once laughingly described the wealthy. She'd never been inside the Opera house and wasn't sure what to expect.

Maria had accepted Frieda's invitation with no hesitation. She hadn't seen Lily or Kathleen since before March 25th. After the tragedy, Conrad had visited the Sanctuary and returned to Maria's apartment with a basket full of food and clothing. Maria had been thankful for Lily and Kathleen's generosity, but she hadn't been able to go visit them. Mama had forbidden Maria's friends from visiting her home.

Lily gave her a hug and murmured her condolences.

Closing her eyes, Maria remembered the time she'd asked Mama and Papa if she could go work in the Sanctuary. The thought had horrified Rosa, almost more than their mother. Oh Rosa, why did you have to leave me?

Maria stumbled and would have fallen if not for Conrad's firm grip on her arm. Self-conscious, she couldn't believe she'd embarrassed herself, but Frieda's friends didn't seem to notice.

Kathleen moved closer. "Maria, I'm so sorry for your loss. How is your mother?"

She wanted to tell the truth. Tell Kathleen that Mama was furious with her for surviving. Instead, she heard herself say, "She's not doing too well."

"Would she like visitors? I thought maybe Richard and I could visit. Or would that bring back memories of your father?"

Papa! How she wished he was still alive. He'd know how to handle Mama. "Thank you, Kathleen, maybe some other time."

"You just tell us when, Maria. Have you been here before? It can be a little confusing to find your way around. The organizers are expecting about two thousand people so I suggest we find our box."

"A box?" Maria didn't know what that meant.

"A private seating area for each wealthy group. It usually has a good view of the stage," Conrad whispered as they followed Kathleen inside.

Maria looked around in awe. What would it be like

to come here to see an opera? She's seen a few open air operas when she was young and living back in Italy, but not in New York. She spotted her fellow East Siders filing into the upper galleries. Conrad pointed out the seats in front of the orchestra area, which seemed to be full of fur coats.

Everywhere was a sea of red and gold. Her shoes sank into the luxurious carpets as the glass lights draped everyone in a flattering light. Lights on the wall and along the seats shimmered like stars in a velvet night sky. She followed the others as they climbed up the stairs toward the private boxes.

"Someone said the Morgans have owned this box since the Met opened back in 1883," Conrad whispered. "Not sure that's true though, as the original opera house burned down, was taken over, and renovated. It reopened in 1903."

Maria wasn't interested in when it opened or who owned what. She was too warm, there were too many people around, and she felt out of place. She wasn't born to sit in the private boxes. Not when the other boxes were occupied by grand society dames wearing diamonds and other jewels.

Kathleen glanced around her. "If you take that seat, Conrad, and put Maria on your right. Frieda and Patrick can sit behind you when they turn up. Honestly, are doctors ever on time? I'll sit here."

Maria sat where she was told, staring around her.

She picked at her dress. Conrad grasped her hand, "You look more beautiful than anyone here."

He'd mistaken her agitation for worrying about her dress. She didn't care about looking beautiful. She was out of place, sitting up here with the rich folk. She should be with her own people.

At her continued silence, he asked, "What's wrong, Maria?"

"I should be up there with the rest of the people from the East Side. With Sarah and her friends. I don't belong up here. My people are there," she pointed to the galleries filled with factory workers and their families.

Kathleen leaned forward. "Maria, if you wish to stand with your friends, please feel free. We want you to be comfortable. Or at least as much as possible."

Conrad stood up and offered her his arm. "Come on, before it gets too crowded."

They made their way toward the hordes of factory workers and their families. They found themselves swept up in the crowds. There were so many people, Maria almost regretted leaving the box. But this was where she belonged, with people who spoke her language. Not just Italian, but those who knew what it was like to work in a factory. Conrad held her hand tightly, protecting her as always. She spotted Sarah and pulled Conrad in her friend's direction.

"Sarah, this is Conrad Schneider. You met briefly when we left the hospital, after the fire." Turning to

Conrad, she said. "Do you remember Sarah Adler? We met briefly outside the hospital on the day of the fire."

"Yes, you ladies walked the same picket lines." Conrad smiled as he held out his hand to Sarah.

Sarah shook Conrad's hand while saying, "Much good we did. Didn't save those girls, did it?"

Maria blinked back tears. Sarah gave her a hug.

"Sorry Maria, for a second I forgot. Me and my big mouth. How is your mother?"

Maria shrugged. Mama hadn't stopped crying. She blamed Maria for leaving the favorite daughter behind. She'd told Maria, more than once, she wished it was Rosa who'd survived. Maria remained silent. She'd not tell anyone what her mother had said.

The crowd fell silent as Anne Morgan, Alva Belmont, and other rich sponsors filed in. Then it seemed everyone started talking at once. The angry crowd demanded change. Maria heard the Bishop of New York comment, "This calamity causes racial lines to be forgotten, for a little while at least, and the whole community rises to one common brotherhood."

The crowd was muttering ominously until Rose Schneiderman stepped forward on the stage and started speaking.

Maria could barely hear her at first. She leaned forward to hear the soft spoken woman. Rose seemed to find her confidence as her voice grew stronger. The crowd fell silent as they got caught up in her message.

Tears fell down Maria's cheeks as Rose spoke of the issues facing the working classes.

Rose shouted, "This is not the first time girls have burned alive in this city."

Conrad grasped Maria's hand. She squeezed his back, but didn't take her eyes from Rose. When Rose finished speaking, silence filled the opera house. It took several seconds for people to realize she had finished, then they burst out in applause, cheering and roaring their approval. Maria glanced toward the private boxes and saw even there the people were clapping, although maybe slightly less enthusiastically than the people surrounding Maria.

"There must be thirty-five hundred people here," Conrad murmured as he continued to clap. The crowds filed out of the Opera House, the atmosphere brighter than before. People were still grieving, but maybe there was some hope things would change.

# CHAPTER 42

*C*onrad and Maria met up with Sarah as they pushed their way out in silence. On reaching the sidewalk, Sarah broke the silence, "Did you know there was a meeting in the Broadway Central Hotel when we were on strike back in 1909?"

Maria shook her head. Glancing at Conrad, she saw he didn't know what Sarah was talking about either.

"There were about twenty or more factory owners there, including Blanck and Harris. They were discussing ways of breaking the strike. They even talked about taking on black workers, but someone had an issue about that."

Maria could imagine. There were always problems between the Italians, Germans, and the Jews without adding in the Blacks. She couldn't understand why. Weren't they all the same people?

Sarah continued. "When one man protested 'he wasn't having blacks working in his factory,' someone else argued, 'Why not? They can work, can't they? They probably picked the very cotton you are using. They will work for lower wages than the white girls, even the new arrivals from Ellis Island. Who cares who does the work so long as we have garments to sell? The stores will not wait forever. They will buy shirtwaists from whoever produces them.'"

Maria exchanged glances with Conrad. What was the point in going over old ground? They knew what factory owners were like.

Sarah must have interpreted her expression as she pulled at Maria's arm.

"Don't you see? They really don't care. They don't see us as human beings. As one of them said, 'Workers are expendable, plenty more where they came from,' they said. Every day another ship or two arrive. Ellis Island can't keep up with the traffic."

Maria sucked in her breath. Nobody could be that heartless, but Sarah hadn't finished.

"You watch, Maria. There will be a huge funeral, plenty of people making a lot of noise about the changes they will make, and then what will happen? Nothing. Everything will go back to the same way it was. Nobody will remember all our friends. Just like they don't remember those who died in the Slocum. Why? Because we're all poor immigrants. We just don't matter."

Tears wet Maria's cheeks. She didn't want to believe what Sarah said; it made things worse. Conrad took her gently by the elbow.

"With respect, Miss Adler, I believe you are wrong. My father came to this country with only the suit he was wearing. He was lucky to escape Germany with his life. Mam came here from Ireland where her ancestors starved to death in a famine barely seventy years ago. Things are changing. The tragedy at the Triangle, losing our friends, family, our sisters," Conrad glanced at Maria, "will and do mean something. Things will change, but only if both sides work together. We must bury the dead and the hate with them. Only then we will make changes, but they start with ourselves."

Sarah looked as if she was about to argue, but Conrad cut her off.

"Maria, I think we should find our other friends. It was nice to meet you, Miss Adler. Take care of yourself."

Without another word, Conrad led Maria away from the stunned looking Sarah.

"Thank you," Maria said. "I like Sarah, but sometimes she is too…" Maria couldn't find the right word.

"Zealous? I admire people for standing up for what they believe in, but there is a time and a place for all that. We will bury our family and friends with respect and only then will we start rebuilding our lives."

They hadn't seen Kathleen walk up behind them.

"I couldn't help overhearing Conrad. I totally agree. Would you and Maria care to join us at the Sanctuary for tea?"

"Thank you, Kathleen, but I have to get home to Mama."

Kathleen tried to reply, but Anne Morgan interrupted by claiming her attention. At least, Maria thought it was the daughter of the banker as she'd seen her likeness in the newspapers. She let out a sigh of relief; she hadn't wanted to go anywhere but home.

Conrad escorted her home in silence.

"Will you come in?" Maria asked as they reached her tenement block.

"Better not. I don't want to anger your mother."

Maria didn't bother trying to persuade him. Mama seemed to blame everyone who'd survived for not saving Rosa.

Conrad kissed her, his lips grazing hers. "I would like to walk with you for the funeral march if it doesn't upset your family."

"I'd like that. Conrad, I'm scared. What if Mama never recovers?"

"She will, Maria, in time. She won't get over losing your sister, but she will learn to live with the pain. For now, we just have to be patient."

She leaned into him, raising her mouth for his kiss. Maria wanted this gentle, kind man at her side. Her family would just have to get used to him being around. She wasn't losing him.

## CHAPTER 43

rieda arrived back from the hospital to find Lily, Kathleen, and some of their friends sitting around the table discussing the meeting.

"Frieda, how's Leonie?" Lily asked.

"The same." Frieda hated seeing the light of hope die in Lily's eyes, but she couldn't pretend Leonie was improving. "How did the meeting go?"

"You should have seen it, Frieda. Over thirty-five hundred people turned up. It didn't start so well, there was so much arguing on stage, but then a young woman, Rose Schneider, started talking. You could have heard a pin drop as everyone listened to her. She had some harsh things to say, but they were the truth."

"Do you think anything will change?" Frieda asked as she reached for a cookie. Lily moved over and directed her to sit down beside her before answering, "Frieda, things are already changing. There were three women on the safety committee. You already know Anne Morgan and Mary Dreier. Frances Perkins is the third."

"All sensible ladies, but can they really make changes?" Frieda asked. She didn't want to put a damper on the evening, but she'd seen inquiries come and go before. She didn't have much faith in committees.

"The chairman is a wealthy lawyer, Henry Stimson. Charlie knows him, he says he won't stand for any nonsense. I trust my husband's judgement, so I am hopeful they can achieve a lot."

Kathleen spoke up. "Lily, most people are good at heart. Most don't know how to stop people from burning in factories. They don't want people hurt or worse. They just lack direction. What can they do?"

Frieda didn't know the lady who spoke next. "We need to keep things in perspective, ladies. Not that many people died. We're only talking about one hundred and fifty. More people die in influenza epidemics, don't they?"

Frieda bit her tongue to stop herself from replying in anger. Kathleen glanced at Frieda before replying to the woman.

"Susan, those one hundred and fifty people included

people Frieda knew personally. One of our friends is lying in a hospital in a coma. Her four orphaned siblings depend on her."

"I'm sure every story is tragic Kathleen, my point was --"

Frieda had heard enough.

"I'm tired. I've been fighting against influenza all day at the hospital. Yes ma'am, more people die from it," Frieda looked directly at Susan. "We can't see the germs, we don't understand how it spreads so quickly from person to person, and we don't have very good treatments for it. In time we will gain more under-standing and I hope a time comes when more people recover than die from influenza." Frieda took a second to stop her voice from shaking. "But it doesn't compare to the men, women, and children dying because they locked them into a factory, eight, nine, or ten floors above the sidewalk. Those people died from greed and no other cause. We can't stop the influenza, but there has to be something we can do to prevent even one person burning alive due to someone else's greed." Frieda stood up. "Please excuse me."

"Frieda, wait. I didn't mean to upset you," the lady called Susan spoke, her cheeks pink. "I meant we need to do more to help all those in need, not just the factory workers. I'm sorry I sounded so callous. My condo-lences for your losses, and I hope your friend recovers."

"Thank you." Frieda walked out and climbed the stairs to her room.   They would see how New York valued the factory workers when the funeral came.

\* \* \*

APRIL 5TH, 1911

Four days later, the whole of New York seemed to wear black. Black bunting hung from the buildings with men wearing black suits, their ladies wearing black dresses, hats and coats. Even the children were subdued, not racing around playing noisy games, but standing to attention as beautiful horses pulled the hearse carrying the empty coffin, representing the seven unidentified victims, moved past.

Thousands of people marched down the streets in silence, following the coffin. Despite the relentless rain, the crowds continued to gather as people congregated on the sidewalks, watching them.

"I don't think I've ever seen so many people in one place, Conrad."

Conrad glanced at the crowds, whose solemn expressions mirrored his own. "They feel they have to do something, but most don't know what. There must be at least a quarter of a million people here."

As Maria glanced around her, she couldn't help but wonder where these people had been when the strikers needed their support. Maybe if they had come out in support then, her sister and friends would still be alive.

"Maria, you can't change the past. Only the future." He entwined his fingers in hers as she moved closer. He was her future now.

They walked back to Maria's home, deep in thought. Eventually, Maria broke the silence.

"How will people recover from this, Conrad? Sarah told me her friend, Rose Weiner died, the sister Katie is still in hospital with her injuries. Esther's sister and brother are dead. Deleo, the boy Leonie was dancing with at the party is dead too. From what Frieda says, Leonie is still in danger. What will her brothers and sister do without her?"

"Have faith in the Greens, Maria. Richard Green has a fine reputation. If anyone can save her, they will. Frieda is at her bedside as often as possible. She couldn't get better care."

Maria didn't doubt her friends were looking after Leonie, but when they weren't sure what was keeping her asleep, how could they fix it?

"I went up to check on Mr. Maltese last night, I brought him some food. He was just sitting there, staring into an empty grate. He's aged twenty years since that night. His son said Mr. Maltese blames himself for losing his wife and daughters. He also said Rosaria was the youngest victim. So many gone.”

Conrad squeezed her hand. What could he say? Nothing would bring the dead back.

# CHAPTER 44

APRIL 1911

Maria looked at the notice in her hand. They had summoned her to give her statement about the fire. Conrad had one, too.

"Conrad, does the District Attorney really care about Rosa, the Maltese ladies, and all the other victims?"

"Charles Whitman has a reputation for seeking justice. If I was Harris or Blanck, I would be nervous. Don't fret, Maria, we know what happened that day and we just have to tell them."

"But what if they don't believe us? I heard rumors the bosses were trying to bribe some survivors to say the doors weren't locked, That the girls panicked."

Conrad's lips thinned. "You and I know the truth and no amount of money will stop us telling our story. Others feel the same way. Let's walk down there and see who else has been called to give their account."

As they walked, Maria heard the dim ringing of a fire-engine bell. Feeling weak, she grasped Conrad's arm.

"Maria, darling, it's not near here. It's another fire. You are safe." He continued whispering until she composed herself.

"When will it stop? I can't sleep. I hear fire engines and wake up in a sweat. When I fall asleep, every night, Rosa and the Maltese girls come into my dreams. I see all those I knew from the other factory. Sylvia, Mary Leventhal, all of them. They blame me for leaving them behind. I…" Maria stuttered, unable to speak properly.

Conrad led her into a park and found a bench where they both sat down. "Maria, you are not to blame. None of us are. We didn't start the fire and we didn't lock those doors. All we can do now is fight for justice for Rosa and our other friends."

Maria huddled close to him. She didn't think she could fight anyone.

"Maria, I know you've been brave,and tried to appear stronger than you are, but I'm with you every step of this journey. Together we will survive. We owe it to the others."

# CHAPTER 45

"*K*athleen, are you sure we should be doing this? It doesn't seem right to go to a party given everything that has happened." The last thing Frieda wanted was to go out celebrating. Leonie needed her.

"Richard told me you spend all your spare time at Leonie's bedside. I admire your commitment, darling, but that's not healthy. We are all here for Leonie, praying for her, visiting with her. You need to live a little. Frieda, life has to go on, and we owe it to the dead to make every day count. We missed Patrick's birthday, so let's have a good time tonight."

Frieda knew it was pointless arguing when Kathleen used that tone of voice. People thought Kathleen was softer than Lily. She was more easy going, but when it came to it, she had an inner core of steel and wouldn't let something drop until she got her way. Frieda was too tired to fight.

Kathleen helped her dress in the new clothes she had bought her. Was it only a month ago? It felt like a year or more. Only when she was fully satisfied was Frieda allowed to leave her room. She walked downstairs to where Cook and the girls were waiting for her.

"You look beautiful, Frieda. Like a Broadway star," Lily almost whispered as she held out her hand as if to touch the dress, but stopped before she reached Frieda.

"You look like a princess," Carrie added.

"Where's her crown then? All princesses wear lots of jewels. Like diamonds and all sorts," Alfred complained, bringing everyone back to reality. "Where are you going?"

Her mouth dry, Frieda whispered, "To a birthday party." She feared the children would think she was callous, but Carrie didn't blink an eye.

"Will you bring us back some cake?" Carrie asked, rubbing her stomach.

"Come on children, plenty of cake in my kitchen," Cook smiled, "Frieda, enjoy yourself."

Frieda watched the children troop after Cook before Kathleen called her to tell her the cab was waiting.

"Maria and Conrad said they would be there early so you go to meet them. I have to chase Richard. He'd only arrived home when I left to come over here. Doctors." Kathleen rolled her eyes. Then she hugged Frieda but didn't squeeze her hard like usual. "Don't want to crush your outfit. Head high now darling, you look amazing."

Frieda kissed her friend on the cheek and walked out to the cab, taking in the glance of admiration from the driver. It felt nice to be seen as a woman and not a student nurse or doctor for a change.

When the cab arrived at Charlie's , the man himself came out to greet her. "Bellissima Frieda! You look beautiful. I didn't recognize you. You look like you walked off a stage. Mama, come see Frieda, Maria's doctor friend. Isn't she beautiful?"

"The poor girl is blushing so hard, I could cook eggs on her cheeks. Stop making a fool of her and escort her to her table," Mama ordered before winking at Frieda and whispering, "All it takes is one good looking girl and every man turns into a fool."

Frieda couldn't think straight. She followed Charlie past the larger tables into the area where the smaller double booths were seated. Where were the others? She looked around, trying and failing to spot Maria or Conrad. Was she the first one there? She couldn't sit at a table on her own, that wouldn't be respectable. She looked up at a low whistle and found herself staring at Caldwell. Her spirits plummeted.

"You scrub up well, Frieda. You looking for a date?" His voice carried and some diners gasped while others laughed. Frieda's cheeks heated.

She didn't answer as Charlie directed a stream of

Italian, none of it sounding too friendly, at Caldwell. Frieda wished the ground would open up and swallow her as other diners turned to stare. She brushed a finger across her eye, she couldn't cry, not here in front of everyone, but she'd never been so humiliated in her life.

"I think this is our table."

She recognized his voice as he took her elbow and guided her to a booth for two. She glanced up at him. "Patrick?"

"I hope you weren't expecting another man?" His eyes danced with amusement.

Frieda looked around. Caldwell was on his way out the door with Charlie holding him by the shirt collar. The other diners were staring at Caldwell, not her. She didn't recognize anyone else.

"Maria, Conrad, the others?"

"The only reservation is a table for two," he said, taking a seat.

Frieda tried to focus on what he was saying. She'd never felt so shy and awkward around Patrick before. She rubbed her hands in her napkin, for fear he'd see she was sweating.

"What did Mother tell you to get you here?" he asked as he poured wine into their glasses.

"You were having a belated birthday party and everyone was coming to celebrate." Even as she said the words, she knew they sounded stupid. "Kathleen came over to the Sanctuary, helped me get ready, and told me your dad would be late home. I took her excuse at face value." She studied the cutlery on the table. "I guess I was a bit naive."

She was babbling, her nerves making her speak faster.

"You believe the best of people, Frieda. You shouldn't change. I bet Mother was very convincing."

Frieda couldn't think of Kathleen, not now. She picked up a spoon and put it down again. Folding her hands on her lap, fighting the urge to fidget, she tried to act normal.

She didn't speak as he rubbed her hand with his. "You're amazing. So beautiful and kind-hearted, so considerate of everyone else."

As he held her hand, their eyes locked, it could have been just the two of them in the restaurant.

Charlie's appearance startled both of them.

"Two of Mama's specials. You want more wine?" Charlie served their meal before taking up the wine bottle and refilling their untouched glasses. Embarrassed, she took her hand away and folded it once more in her lap. She couldn't eat, her stomach was swirling around so fast, she thought she might be ill.

"Thank you, Charlie. Please tell your wife it looks wonderful."

Charlie beamed before walking away.

"Now where were we?"

"Patrick, I…you…" she mumbled, not being able to think clearly.

"Why don't we have a toast?" He suggested.

"To your birthday," she was babbling now, but she couldn't get her mind to think straight.

"To something more important. To us."

"Us?" she repeated.

"Frieda Klunsberg, don't you know how I feel about you? I've missed you so much." He clinked his glass to hers.

"We saw each other yesterday." Why had she said that? *Talk about ruining a romantic moment.* Her heart beat faster. She moved closer to the table taking a large gulp of wine, almost choking on the unusual taste. She rarely drank and never in public.

"Easy. Have a drink of water. There's no rush. Take your time, enjoy it."

With that, he picked up his fork and ate as if he had starved the whole week. Frieda picked at her food, wondering how he could eat. Her stomach churned in protest.

"Frieda, why aren't you eating? Don't you like the food?"

"I'm just not hungry. Do you want mine?"

"Sure, I don't want to upset Charlie. He will definitely take offense if we send back full plates."

The dinner passed, he didn't seem to notice she wasn't speaking much. Charlie came to take the empty plates away. When he left, Patrick smiled at her, making her stomach turn over.

"Frieda, I've got some news. I've been offered a job in London."

Her head jerked up so fast, she hurt her neck. "What? You're leaving?"

"It's an amazing proposition. The Brompton Hospital has offered me a position. You know how much I want to specialize in heart and lung conditions. This is the best place to study, their research is second to none and I... I have accepted the position."

## CHAPTER 46

She felt winded as if someone had punched her in the stomach. "You have?" She winced at the sound of her trembling voice. *Come on Frieda, you can do better than that.* "Patrick, that's wonderful. Your dreams are coming true." She held up her glass, hoping he wouldn't notice her hand shaking. "Congratulations." Her eyes filled with tears, she couldn't help it. She sniffed hoping she wouldn't embarrass herself further.

"Frieda, I know it's a shock, but I didn't want to say anything until they said yes. With the fire and everything, it didn't seem right to be excited about something. I guess I wasn't sure I would be accepted."

"Of course you would be. You're an amazing doctor."

He reached for her hand. "Thank you. Your support

means the world to me."

She tried her best to smile and wish him well. She wanted to shout at him, and tell him not to leave. To stay in New York. With her. She looked in his face, his eyes lit up like candles on a tree, and saw the excitement he couldn't contain. This was his dream, his chance to shine away from his father's shadow.

"Are you happy for me, Frieda?"

"Yes, of course. It's wonderful news and will be brilliant for your career. The Bromptons are responsible for making a lot of progress in the treatment of respiratory infections. You won't look back. Your skills as a doctor will be in huge demand." Frieda couldn't think of anything else to say, nor could she look at him. "Patrick, would you mind if we went home? I have a headache and the noise in here is making it worse."

"Oh, of course. Just let me get the check." He left to pay Charlie for the meals. Frieda wiped her eyes with her napkin swearing she wouldn't cry until she got home to her room. She couldn't ruin his moment even if he was breaking her heart.

She forced a smile for Charlie and his wife, thanking them for the lovely meal, and promising to give Leonie and Maria a hug when she saw them next. Charlie had surprised her by visiting Leonie in hospital. He told her it was because he had a daughter the same age and couldn't bear the thought of her lying in a hospital bed without visitors.

Patrick held her coat for her. Her shoulders stiffened as his hands ran over them. He looked at her, a wary expression on his face, but he didn't comment. They walked in silence for a while as there didn't seem to be any cabs around. Finally, Frieda spotted one and nearly jumped in front of it.

"You don't have to come with me," she protested as Patrick got into the cab with her.

"I absolutely do." He seemed upset. The silence grew repressive despite the short ride. When the cab drew up to the Sanctuary, she was surprised to see Patrick pay the driver off. She thought he would take the cab back to his own house. Why was he prolonging the agony? She couldn't think of anything to say to lighten the atmosphere between them.

"You must promise to write often."

"Write?" his expression faltered.

Was he going to be too busy? Or did he want to forget about her and start a new life?

"Frieda, I don't want to write to you."

She couldn't hold the tears back as one rolled down her cheek. He muttered something under his breath and moved closer, his finger tenderly touching her cheek.

"Darling, I want you to come with me."

Frieda forced her eyes to his, wondering if she had misheard.

"You look surprised. You shouldn't be. I've told you

time and time again you are part of my family. I couldn't leave you behind."

"I thought you meant as your sister?"

He looked shocked this time. "Sister? Frieda Kluns-berg, I no more see you as my sister than I do Anne Morgan. I love you, you daft woman. I want you to marry me, share my bed, have my children, and live the rest of our lives together."

"You do?"

"Yes, I do. And I sincerely hope you do, too, or otherwise I am going to look like a right idiot."

Patrick got down on one knee despite the slightly wet ground. Taking a box out of his pocket, he said "Frieda, will you please marry me?"

"Me?"

"Yes, you."

"Yes, yes of course, Yes." She kept saying yes even as he was kissing her. He took her hand and slid a square cut emerald and diamond ring on her left ring finger.

"Do you like it? I saw it and thought of your eyes." He grinned before saying, "That sounded rather lame."

"Romantic." She stretched to kiss him, pleased at her audacity.

"I'm so happy, Frieda. You have no idea how many times I wanted to ask you, but the moment never seemed right. I don't know what I would have done if you'd said no."

"I'd never have done that."

"Really? For a while I thought you hated me."

"Not you, Patrick, but I hated the thought of being your sister."

He pulled her to him and kissed her soundly.

"Does that show you my intentions are far from brotherly?"

Feeling flirtatious, she responded. "Maybe. But you might want to do it again, just to be sure."

He pulled her into his arms once more. A light went on in a bedroom above them causing Frieda to jump away, remembering where they were.

Frieda opened the door, drawing Patrick inside. She put a finger over her mouth to tell him to be quiet, and together they tiptoed to the sitting room where Frieda hoped a fire would be lighting. It would be the perfect end to the evening to cozy up in front of the fire together. She pushed the door open only to walk in on Kathleen, Charlie, Lily, and Richard.

"Oh."

"That's all you can say, Patrick Green? After keeping us waiting this long? We thought we would have to send a search party out. So..?"

Patrick put his arm around Frieda's shoulders.

"Mother, I love you, but once in a while could you let me do something on my own?"

Everyone laughed and Kathleen flushed.

"I just want you to be happy son, and I know the two of you were meant to be and…."

"She said yes!"

Lily and Kathleen both crowded around Frieda embracing her. Charlie and Richard shook Patrick's hand. Then Richard clinked a glass.

"I'd like to raise a glass to the most perfect daughter in law any man could expect."

Frieda blushed as Richard held out his hand to her. "Frieda, thank you for taking on our son. We know you will continue his training and help him behave suitably in public."

"Gee, thanks Dad. You make me sound like a household pet." Patrick retorted. "You could at least wait until we're married before you say things like that. She may run a mile."

"That could never happen." Frieda said quietly as she moved to Patrick's side. "I've loved you far too long."

"Have you guys started on the champagne already?" Patrick asked as he looked at the glasses in their hands.

Richard clapped Patrick on the back, "Well son, you took your time and we were getting thirsty!"

Soon Frieda and Patrick had a glass in their hands as well but Frieda didn't need the alcohol. She looked around at the people closest to her. They had been her adoptive family since losing Hans and her father. She couldn't imagine life without them.

# CHAPTER 47

*L*eonie continued to lie in the bed not moving or showing any signs of coming out of the coma.

Frieda had described her ring, knowing how much of a romantic Leonie was. She watched Leonie's eyes carefully to see if there was even a flicker, but nothing.

Disappointment flooded her as she headed home. She had a charity function to go to. How was she going to plaster a smile on her face and make small talk?

Maria was sitting in the kitchen waiting for her. Cook and Carrie sat at the table as well. Carrie looked at Frieda's face but didn't ask how Leonie was. She had given up asking. Frieda walked over to the little girl and gave her a hug.

Maria jumped up and hugged Frieda.

"Frieda, congratulations. Carrie told me. Don't scold

her, she was so excited." Maria hugged her before taking her hand. "Oh my goodness, can you ask him to buy me one too?"

Frieda took off the ring to let Maria try it on. She watched as her friend twisted it around her finger three times.

"What are you doing?"

"When I was waiting for you, Cook gave me cookies and some advice. She told me to twist your ring three times around and make a wish. But I can't wish to get married as that's unlucky."

"So what did you wish for?"

"A baby. Can't have one of those unless you have a husband can you?" Maria gave the ring back.

"Thank you for coming with me. It's so good to see you smile." Frieda gave Maria another hug, knowing talk of the engagement made her think of her sister. Not that Rosa was ever far from Maria's mind.

"When you first said you needed me at a fundraising function I wanted to run a mile. But Conrad reminded me , we are doing it for the families of girls like Rosa. I owe my sister and my friends. I won't let them down."

"Of course you won't."

"Frieda, I can't wear this though and it's my best dress." Maria's cheeks flushed as she stared at the floor.

"Come this way, my friend. Lily already thought of that. Wait until you see what she picked out for you."

Maria picked up her skirt and followed Frieda up the

stairs to her bedroom. There on the bed was a rose colored gown, nothing like anything Maria had ever seen before.

"It's yours. Lily thought it would look lovely with your coloring. Hurry up and try it on. One of the women can lend you a machine if you need to do any last minute alterations, but Lily is usually a good judge."

Maria fingered the material like it would bite her.

"Maria, we have to be ready in two hours. Kathleen ordered Richard to collect us; Patrick is working. Richard doesn't like Kathleen driving at night."

Maria got dressed in silence, her eyes fastened on her reflection.

"See, it fits perfectly. Wait until Conrad sees you all dressed up like that," Frieda said with a wink.

"He won't be there tonight."

"I know, but the dress is yours. Now try these shoes, Lily wasn't sure which would go better."

Only once she was dressed did Maria revert back to her old self. "Frieda, what will you do about your exams? You had your heart set on qualifying, but if you are moving to London, what will happen? You can't give up everything, not after fighting so hard."

"I won't. Richard arranged to bring my exams forward. He believes that my extra shifts at the hospital, my exam results so far, and my experience with Lilian warrants me taking the finals early. I don't know how he got Dr. Guild to agree, but he did. So I will take my finals in December."

"Good. I like Patrick a lot and I know how much you love him, but you can't give up your career and settle down to domestic life. It wouldn't be right."

"I couldn't anyway. Patrick would starve if I had to feed him. Don't fret Maria, I aim to practice as a doctor. I've my heart set on the Women's hospital in London."

"I wish you weren't going. I shall miss you." Maria sniffed and then as if embarrassed by her weakness, she glanced out the window. "Is that Richard arriving? Come on, we can't keep him waiting."

## CHAPTER 48

*I*t was a trying evening with each girl being bombarded by endless questions about why the victims didn't leave the building sooner, why they had crowded onto the fire escape, why they had waited for their wages, and many more silly questions people deemed important.

Frieda and Maria made their way to the refreshments, both eager to escape all the questions. Furious, Maria almost exploded when they got to the less occupied side of the large room.

"I know we have to be here to help raise money for the families, but seriously, how many times do you think someone will ask if the doors were locked, or whether the girls smoked while they were sewing? Some people seem to equate not speaking fluent English with being stupid."

"Maria, I think we should get you home. Lily and Kathleen will understand. You've done enough, and you're still grieving, too."

"No, the last place I need to be is at home with Mama looking at me. She hates me for being the one who survived. She would have preferred Rosa."

"Maria, no she wouldn't. She wanted both of you to survive. She is grieving for her daughter and her husband. She leans on you because you're strong, the one she can count on. I know it's hard, but please don't think she doesn't want to be around."

Maria didn't argue. What was the point? Frieda didn't live in her house, didn't have to deal with Mama's continuous comments about what a great daughter Rosa had been, how she was never any trouble, she hadn't been on strike. By dying, her sister had turned into the perfect woman. Mama never mentioned Paulo Greco or Rosa's involvement with him. It was as if all that hadn't happened.

Frieda squeezed her hand tight as they stood in silence. Two men and a lady ventured over to the buffet table, but mustn't have seen them. They didn't speak quietly.

One of the men, well-dressed and in his early twenties, was practically shouting. "It's all about money with these people. Did you see over ten thousand visitors to the morgue in two days? Either they all had huge families, which I understand is a thing with those Catholics, or they are grifters trying to claim more money. You know the Jews hoard money. Isn't it bad enough they come over here? Why don't they stay in Russia, Germany, or wherever else they come from?"

Frieda and Maria exchanged a look. Maria was about to speak, but the lady accompanying the gentleman spoke first.

"Did you hear the Red Cross had collected almost $5,000 when it opened the doors the Monday after the fire? With that imbecile Gaynor pledging his own money and making it appear as if it was the duty of every American to contribute, I would have expected them to have more in donations. I wonder how much each family is getting? How will they prove they had someone die in the fire?" The lady surveyed the table before picking up a sandwich.

The older man put three sandwiches on his plate. "I heard all you need is an old photo. There are some boys selling pictures for that very purpose right outside the life insurance building."

"Frederick, as if these people need an excuse to beg more money. Handouts are all they were after." The woman wiped her lips delicately. "They are the same people out on strike back in 1909. Always the same. Never happy with their lot."

Frieda stepped forward, her cold tone more forceful than a scream. "Never happy with being locked inside a burning building and getting burned to death? Or never happy with being forced to jump from a window nine floors off the sidewalk because the heat got too much for them? Or..." Frieda stood with her hands on her hips, lips flaring as she faced them down.

"Now listen, lady." The man they called Frederick, took a step toward her, but retreated fast enough when Frieda moved closer to him.

"It's Doctor, not lady, and *you* need to listen. Before you go spreading your cheap gossip. Do you know how much of that $5,000 was claimed on the Monday morning by the grieving families? I'll tell you - not one cent. The first claimants didn't arrive until Tuesday, and that was four people who weren't there to claim money, but because someone told them they had to appear. The volunteers running the office went looking for the families. How did they find them? Not by photographs, as your ignorant comments suggest. They found those people who looked like they had lost their entire world. People like the Maltese family who lost all the women in their household in one afternoon. Do you think Mr. Maltese cares what money he gets when his wife and two daughters are lying in the morgue? At least, he thinks they are because he hasn't yet been able to identify them! What is more --"

The woman with the men gasped and fanned herself, as if the mention of burned victims was a surprise.

Her escort took his friend's arm before saying,

"Young lady, I think that's enough. You have forgotten yourself."

"No, Frederick, she hasn't." Anne Morgan appeared behind the man and his friends. Maria saw the man turn pale. "You and your friends stood in judgement, without knowing the facts of the manner. Frieda, a young doctor friend of mine, is correct. We had to go looking for victims. Most families do not have enough money to heat their homes or to put food on the table, never mind pay their rents, but they haven't asked for a penny. They stare at the cold hearth and wonder why their daughters came all the way to America to burn. You ask why they came here? So they could build a life. Just as my ancestors did. And yours, too, unless you claim you are related to the Indians."

Muted giggles broke out as the insult hit home. Maria watched as Frederick's neck turned red, his eyes casting around him as if looking for a way to escape.

"Miss Morgan, I never thought to…"

"You didn't think at all, did you, Freddie? You never do." Anne turned to a passing servant. "Humphrey, could you please find these guests their coats and escort them to the front door. They are leaving."

The lady huffed so much, Maria hoped her corset wasn't too tight, or she would need Freida's medical attention. She certainly recovered well from her fit of the vapors over the reference to bodies. "Well, I never!

Just wait until your father hears about this, Anne Morgan."

"I think he will be rather amused, Betty Fitzpatrick, until I mention your disparaging comments about immigrants. My father is proud of his heritage and proud of America for offering him the opportunities it has. You know your family are immigrants, too? Although perhaps Wales is more to your liking than far off Germany or Russia or Italy."

Maria wanted to clap her hands at the way Anne had dealt with those horrible people. She'd been magnificent. Anne turned her attention to Frieda.

"Frieda, I am so sorry they upset you so much. You were amazing. You are a credit to your family." Anne turned to Maria. "Maria, isn't it? Please accept my condolences for your loss. Lily told me about your sister."

"Thank you, Miss Morgan. You really put those people in their place." Maria was glad her voice sounded firm when her legs were shaking.

Anne rolled her eyes as she glanced toward her departing guests. "Unfortunately, you can't cure ignorance with money. Sometimes, I believe it only serves to make those afflicted much worse. Still, we can't worry about them. We have so much to do. As you said, Frieda, our efforts to help the victims of the tragedy aren't making much headway."

"Miss Morgan, I wasn't being critical," Frieda explained.

"I know that. I wish we could find a better way to help them. It is so frustrating."

Maria swallowed hard, "Miss Morgan, I have an idea."

"Go on."

Maria rubbed her hands on her dress, hardly daring to believe what she would suggest.

"I wonder if it would be better if you appointed local people as your representatives. I mean, people the families would know from their own neighborhoods. With all due respect to your friends, no matter how well-meaning they are, it's obvious they come from a different world. It would horrify Mama if someone like you arrived on her doorstep. Not that she wouldn't be grateful, but it would embarrass her for you to see how we live." Maria spoke quickly, hoping not to cause offense as she tried to put her thoughts into words. "She would also struggle to speak to you because her English isn't fluent."

"I think that's a wonderful idea, Maria. Perhaps you would come to our offices and help us find these people? Rose Schneider has said similar things and we all know how adamant she is about certain topics."

Maria smiled, she remembered Miss Schneider.

"Please excuse me, I hear someone calling for me. If I want to wrest some money from their wallets, I must put in an appearance. Please call, Maria. You have great insights into a world you rightly say I don't understand."

Maria stared after her.

"You found yourself a new job, Maria. You could be a political leader."

"Me?" Maria burst out laughing. "Not a chance. I have about as much patience as you do, my friend. I thought you would throw that lady's champagne into her face at one point. You really got hot under the collar."

"I got so angry. I guess if Anne hadn't come along, I just might have lost my temper. I'm sick of people judging others, especially when they don't have a clue what they are talking about. Sure, there are some who will make fraudulent claims, but if they want to look at those types of people, they should look closer to home."

Frieda glanced around the room. "How many people here have a clear conscience do you think? How many bribed an official to look the other way? How many own factories with insufficient fire escapes or have proper fire drills? How many greased the hands of those at Tammany hall?"

Maria took Frieda's drink out of her hand.

"Come on, we're leaving. Lily, Kathleen, and the rest of them can carry on the good work here. You need to get out before you upset someone."

Frieda didn't argue as she followed Maria to say

their goodbyes. She was too tired, angry, and sad to deal with anyone else asking her questions to which she had no answers. Why had so many died? Why were the doors locked, and who would pay? She glanced at the emerald ring on her finger and wondered if she had a right to so much happiness when so many had nothing.

# CHAPTER 49

"*L*ily, have you seen this? Aren't American's wonderful?" Kathleen smiled, shaking the newspaper at Lily as she walked through the door of Lily's home.

"What?" Lily groaned inwardly. She loved Kathleen, but today her friend's positivity was grating on her nerves. She hadn't slept again, worrying about Leonie and the others in need. How could she help everyone?

"Lily, so many people are raising money for the victims and their families. From newsstand owners to people like William Fox, the movie producer, they are all making pledges to help. At the Hippodrome, it says, 500 employees raffled off a gold watch–the tickets cost 50 cents and sold out. The money is pouring in, but it's not just that. People are pulling together. Some Italian families couldn't afford to bury their dead, so the

Hebrew Free Burial Society offered places in its Staten Island burial grounds. Usually only Jews are buried there. Jews helping Catholics, Lily. It goes to show most people are decent."

"Does it?"

"Lily, don't be like that. Look at this story of a little boy who sent in ten dollars to the fund. He wrote a letter to say he wanted it to be given to the family of one of the little girls who jumped out of the window. Poor child was heartbroken when his father told him about it."

Kathleen looked up, but Lily couldn't meet her gaze. She stared into the fire.

"Lily, stop moping. Believe in people. Otherwise, what's the point of getting up each morning? Now get dressed. Emily and Gustav have invited us to the children's home for lunch, or had you forgotten?"

She had. She didn't want to go anywhere, but they had rescheduled the orphanage visit so many times, she couldn't do it again. She knew Emily and Gustav wanted her opinion on the changes they had made. She screamed silently. She wanted to go back to bed.

Lily had stayed home all week, avoiding the Sanctuary. She hadn't even been to the hospital to visit Leonie. She just couldn't seem to put one foot in front of the other. But there was no way Kathleen would let her miss the lunch. She left Kathleen chatting happily to Teddy and Laurie.

When she came back downstairs, the children had disappeared.

"What did you do with them?"

"Noting. I couldn't compete with your cook's chocolate brownies. Even the older boys can't resist them."

Lily smiled. Teddy and Laurie were probably the biggest children of all when it came to Cook's snacks.

"Did Laurie bore you with talk of airplanes? The boy is obsessed." Lily shook out her scarf before wrapping it around her hair.

"He was chatting about them, but it was interesting. I get too much medical talk at home. It's nice to hear something different. He said you have agreed to him taking flying lessons."

Lily shook her head, although she was smiling. "That boy. We have not. We agreed to think about it. I can't bear the thought of him up in one of those things. But he is getting to the age where he doesn't need my permission.

"True, and it's not like it's a phase. He's been mad about airplanes forever. Let him get it out of his system would be my advice. If you were asking for my opinion."

"Kathleen Green, since when has anyone had to ask you for your opinion. You are usually happy to tell me what you think."

Kathleen shrugged, "I learned to speak up a long

time ago or I'd never get a word in edgeways, not with the way you chatter away nineteen to the dozen."

"No, I don't."

"Oh yes, you do." They squabbled like children as they made their way to Kathleen's automobile.

Lily adjusted her hat, hoping she had secured it tightly enough. "I still can't believe you drive every chance you get now."

"Lily, most people can drive an automobile, you just pretend to be a dinosaur. Charlie has had one longer than Richard."

Lily muttered something as she took her seat. She much preferred taking a cab, but she guessed Kathleen enjoyed driving. She might, too, if she didn't need glasses to see two feet in front of her. Not that she admitted that to anyone.

She looked in interest at the area surrounding the orphanage. New York was enjoying a building boom, with new homes and offices springing up all over the city. Here was no exception. She spotted a couple of large houses that wouldn't look out of place on Fifth Avenue. Next to them, the orphanage stuck out like a sore thumb.

# CHAPTER 50

*a*lice ran out to meet them as the automobile pulled up outside. Lily glanced round at her first visit to the home. It was rather unimpressive, unless they designed it to scare children into thinking it was somewhere they would be miserable. She walked up the stairs to the door where Emily and Gustav were waiting.

Emily smiled in greeting before gesturing at the home behind her, "Hideous, isn't it? I hate the outside, too."

Embarrassed at her thoughts being read so accurately, Lily couldn't think of what to say. Emily solved that . She moved forward to take her arm and draw her inside.

"Hopefully you will like what we have done with the inside. Matron loved the color gray, everything was

301

a shade of gray, including the children and staff." Emily laughed at her own joke. "So the first thing I did was paint everywhere. I couldn't afford matching pots of color, so we followed a rainbow theme. Gustav helped a lot, too. It's bright, and the children love it. The school inspectors aren't so keen."

A shadow crossed Emily's eyes at that remark, but it was soon replaced by her gentle expression once more.

There were fewer children than Lily had been expecting.

Emily continued, "Many of the children have left us. Some have been adopted, others have returned to their homes. Many have left on another orphan train. We only have six girls left."

Six was a tiny number for such a large premises, but Lily made sure her face remained unreadable. She didn't want Emily or Gustav to think she was being critical.

They walked into a huge, colorful room, each wall a different shade of blue. Girls ranging in age from four to fourteen all sat around a table drawing pictures.

"They look like angels, don't they?" Emily muttered. "It's amazing what the promise of cake will do."

Lily smiled at the scene in front of her. Kathleen complimented some girls on their pictures while Alice introduced Lily to all her friends. The young girls seemed happy and healthy. They stayed for a few minutes before the eldest, a girl called Shania, took them away for cake and cookies.

Emily watched them walk to the dining room in an orderly manner, her face like that of a proud parent. Then she glanced back at her guests. "I thought it would be easier if we had our lunch alone. The girls are wonderful, but they can get a little out of hand sometimes."

"I can imagine. Where do they play?" Kathleen asked.

"Through there." Emily pointed to the yard in the back of the school. "It's not much, but at least it gives them a safe place to run around. We'd love to have grass or a tree or something, but the city reckons it's good enough."

Lily caught the edge in Emily's voice, but when the woman didn't elaborate, Lily let it go. She sensed she would be told if she needed to know.

"This smells wonderful," Kathleen said as they took a seat in a small kitchen area.

"Gustav cooked, I'm a good baker, but with cooking meals, I think I was behind the door when that talent was given out. Thankfully, Gustav is used to producing meals for himself. The girls are relieved when he calls."

Lily tried not to look at Kathleen. They had discussed it being only a matter of time before Emily and Gustav would get married. It was obvious they cared deeply for each other, despite not knowing each other very long. But if she tried matchmaking, Kathleen was likely to laugh, and the last thing she wanted to do was offend this couple who seemed to have found love out of such a tragic story.

They ate their lunch discussing this and that. Nobody brought up the fire, and for that, Lily was grateful. Emily shared stories about her girls, as she called them. Gustav told them how Alice had decided it was time for Miss Baker and her girls to come and live with them.

"Where is everyone supposed to sleep?" Lily asked Gustav as Emily and Kathleen laughed at Alice's suggestions.

"She has it all figured out. She thinks Conrad should marry Maria and get his own house. I had to remind her we are living in Conrad's own house."

Kathleen asked Gustav, "How did Conrad react to the suggestion that he marry Maria?"

"He laughed at first, but when Alice kept asking, he muttered something about families making life difficult and went out. I should apologize. Alice finds it hard to keep out of other people's business."

"She's just a kid, she wants everyone to be as happy as she is. She sees Conrad and Maria so happy together. You would need to be blind not to see it. I can't understand why her mother is so against them being together," Lily said.

Gustav shrugged. "He's not Italian and I guess she's scared she will lose Maria."

Kathleen sniffed. "She's going to lose her faster if she chases away a good man who loves her. He helped save her life, didn't he? Emily, did you know Gustav was a real hero saving so many."

And there it was, the fire. There was no escaping from it, it had taken prisoners of all New Yorkers, just like they had imprisoned the Triangle workers in the factory.

Lily sipped her water, waiting for someone to talk, but it seemed they were all consumed by their memories. Kathleen sent her an apologetic look, but Lily ignored it.

She was thrilled when Alice came racing in and almost jumped on Gustav, "Did you ask her yet?"

Gustav turned crimson. "Alice! What did I tell you about listening to other people's conversations? Go play."

"But I want to know what she says! I think it's a wonderful idea."

"Alice," Gustav warned. Alice stared at his face as if trying to gauge how serious he was.

Emily interrupted, "Go on now, Alice, leave the adults to talk for a while."

"Yes, Emily." Alice ran out as fast as she had come in. Kathleen and Lily stared at Gustav, waiting for him to explain, but he seemed to be lost for words.

"I guess you are wondering what that was about." Emily placed a hand over Gustav's. "The City has dispensed with my services."

"It's so unfair. They accused her - us of many horrible things. They..." Gustav fell silent.

Emily stepped in. "They don't want us here, and that's the reality. They were looking for an excuse to close the place for ages. The land around here has become very expensive. I'm sure you noticed all the new buildings. Seems this part of the neighborhood has become what's called 'desirable'." Emily paused to collect her thoughts. "People want larger homes and they can't afford the streets near Fifth Avenue, so they're looking elsewhere. Someone decided, once this neighborhood was cleaned up, it would make a nice place to live. So..."

"They are throwing you out on the street. What about the girls? What will they do with them?" Kathleen asked.

"Shania has secured a live-in position as a housemaid. They are a nice family, and she will be well treated. They will send the rest of the children on the next Orphan Train, but April Lawlor will meet them in Chicago. She has found each girl a new home, and we all know it will be the best they can hope for. April has been a blessing in all of this."

Lily leaned forward in her seat, "What about you?"

# CHAPTER 51

*E*mily glanced at Gustav before admitting, "I don't know what will happen to me. I've never had a job, I mean a paid position outside of an orphanage. I only started earning a small salary when they got rid of Matron. It was barely enough to cover essentials."

Lily noticed Gustav's hand tighten over Emily's.

He spoke up, "We planned to get married, but now, we have to wait. The fire means I'm out of work. The Triangle has reopened…"

Lily and Kathleen exchanged a look of horror. Lily's voice shook with anger, "It has? But where?"

"Downtown. They called it something different, but it's the same. I just can't bring myself to go back near those fellas."

"Gustav, I promised you a job at the factory."

"I know that, Miss Lily, but the factory isn't open yet. So we were thinking, we might head to Chicago, too. Alice, me and Emily."

The man looked distinctly uncomfortable.

"Is that what you both want?" Lily persisted.

Emily shook her head, dabbing a cloth at her eyes. "Gustav doesn't want to leave New York. Alice doesn't either, says she hates the countryside. Even the thought of reuniting with Jack can't change her mind."

If Alice didn't want to live near the friend who'd saved her, it meant she really wanted to live in New York. Lily was eager to help make that happen, if she could.

"So what were Alice's suggestions? Have you asked her yet?" Lily looked straight at the couple. "Does she want you to come and live at the Sanctuary? She knows that isn't possible. We can't provide accommodation for men."

"We know that, but we were wondering, if you had room, would you be able to give my Emily a room until we find a way out of our problems? They only gave her a week's notice. We don't have much time."

"Of course you can live at the Sanctuary, Emily. We'd love to have you. The room might be small, but you are welcome to it."

"Thank you, Miss Lily. I swear we knew nothing about this until yesterday. That's when they told us. I mean we knew the girls were moving on, but we assumed a new lot would come in. I think the Orphan's Society don't really approve of the changes I've made."

"I guess they don't like bright colors or happy children," Kathleen retorted. "Sometimes I wonder what it is about the Orphan's Society that attracts those with no regard for children's feelings. Honestly, it is so frustrating."

"Tell us how you really feel, Kathleen," Lily teased her friend. Everyone laughed, which had been her intention. She could tell Emily and Gustav were uncomfortable at having to ask for help.

"Gustav, we need to get the factory open sooner. What about if I made you supervisor?" He opened his mouth to protest, but she said, "Please, just hear me out. I think the builders, plumbers, and other tradesmen would take orders better from a man. They assume I don't know what I am talking about. I guess until women get the vote, there will always be those men who don't like women calling the shots. If I was younger, I would get in and fight it out with them, but I'm tired. Charlie, Kathleen, and well, I guess everyone keeps telling me I must delegate more. So how about it?"

Gustav stared at her, a look of incredulity in his eyes. "You want me? I haven't built anything before."

"Why not you? The builders know how to build, and we have the architect. You're honest, hardworking, brave, and resourceful. You and Conrad have already been advising me on the building design. You don't need to do the building work, although you might be faster than some on that job. I might have an issue with the colors you paint rooms, but we can work on that."

Kathleen smiled at her attempt at a joke, but Emily and Gustav only had eyes for each other.

Emily threw her arms around Gustav, tears running down her face. Or was it his face? Lily beamed, especially when Kathleen came over and hugged her. "You did a great thing today, Lily Doherty."

Gustav offered his hand. "Thank you, Miss Lily, you won't regret it."

"I won't, Gustav, but you might. They are an ornery lot, those workmen."

"Men are easy to deal with. Women're the problem."

As the three women turned outraged looks at him, he burst out laughing as he stood up. "Works every time."

Lily decided payback was due. "Good joke. Now then, when's the wedding?"

Gustav sat back down again and squeaked, "The wedding?"

Kathleen and Lily exchanged a smile. No matter how much in love a man appeared to be, talk of weddings always got them flustered.

"Yes, you said you wanted to get married, but you couldn't as you don't have a job. Now if that was only an excuse, I can take Emily out to meet some of

Patrick's young friends. He'll have plenty of bachelors friends who need wives, won't he, Kathleen?"

"Don't you drag me into this, Lily." Kathleen stood up and dragged Lily to her feet. "Come on matchmaker, let's go do what we are good at and go play with the children."

They left Gustav and Emily sitting at the table staring at one another, both wearing silly grins. Lily felt lighter and happier than she had done in a long time. Maybe things would change now and start working out for all her friends. Her thoughts flew to Leonie and her siblings. What type of future was in store for them?

# CHAPTER 52

## JUNE 1ST 1911

Frieda sat by the bed, studying her notes. She should be at home resting, but she felt a pull towards Leonie. The girl hadn't moved or woken up since the fire two months ago. Her condition hadn't changed, yet Frieda felt something might happen.

"Thought I might find you here," Patrick said as he walked in and kissed her lightly on the cheek. They didn't flaunt their engagement at the hospital, and Frieda left her beautiful emerald ring at the Sanctuary.

"How is she?"

"Patrick, I can't help feeling we need to bring her out of it. What about having the family visit?"

"But you saw what happened last time. They became hysterical."

"I know, but it was soon after their mother died. I

just think we need to give Leonie a bigger reason to fight. She's just lying there."

"You think she can hear us?" he asked before he gently rearranged Leonie in the bed. The patients developed horrendous bed sores from being left lying too long in one position. The nurses were good at preventing them, but a case like Leonie was extra challenging.

"Her bones are healing. You said so yourself. The pain must have mitigated. So why is she still unconscious?"

Patrick shrugged. "Maybe you should have been a mind doc."

Frieda swatted him with her papers.

He stared at her with a gleam in his eyes.

"Frieda, we need to get married." Patrick's neck turned red before he leaned in a little closer. "Just in case she can hear me, I don't want her to hear this." He whispered something in Frieda's ear that made her cheeks heat fast.

"Patrick! You can't go around saying things like that."

"Why not? We're both adults and both doctors. Anyway, what do you say? Do you insist on waiting, or will you put me out of my misery?"

"You better check with your mother. I think she wants a society wedding."

"Then she can get married again. I'd like to elope."

"You best get out of here quick, or those types of remarks may have you needing medical care."

He blew her a kiss and left her with a silly grin on her face. Then she glanced at Leonie and the smile slid away. She couldn't stay happy when the girl in front of her had so little.

\* \* \*

When she got back to the Sanctuary later that evening, she called Sam and Alfred to come speak to her.

"I think you should come and see Leonie tomorrow."

"Has she woken up?" Sam asked, his eyes hopeful.

"No, not yet, but I think it's about time she did. She needs a reason to come back to us, and what better than her two little brothers? I think Morris and Carrie might be too young. So will you come?"

# CHAPTER 53

The next morning, Frieda sneaked the twins into the ward with Kathleen's help. Frieda knew Matron wouldn't agree with them being here, but she figured it was a risk worth taking. The boys needed to speak to Leonie in private, not at visiting time when they were likely to be recognized. Far too many people knew Leonie's story, and more than one newspaper reporter wanted to interview the siblings for the family history. Lily was concerned that this may attract Mr. Chivers, and the last thing anyone needed was that man back in the children's lives.

Frieda sent the nurse on a break, and when the coast was clear, Kathleen brought the boys into the room.

"Leonie, how can you still be asleep? Ain't you had enough yet? Mama used to say too much sleeping was bad for you. If Mama was here, she sure would be angry with you for lying around all day long doing nothing."

Alfred glared at his twin. "She can't do anything, stupid. Her legs don't work and neither does her head. That's why she just lies there. She ain't ever going to wake up again."

"Don't you say that, Alfred. You got to wake up, Leonie. Do you hear me?" Sam shook his sister's arm.

"See, stupid. She ain't doing nothing. This was a waste of time coming here. Take us home, Frieda."

Frieda wasn't listening, her eyes glued to Leonie's face. Had she imagined it, or had Leonie's eyes tried to open?

"Boys, be quiet." She whispered, still staring. "Alfred, take Leonie's good hand. Sam you hold her arm above that bandage."

Stunned, the boys did as they were told without arguing.

"Leonie, Sam and Alfred are here. Wake up, Leonie. They want to talk to you. Squeeze Alfred's hand if you can."

Frieda listened to Leonie's breathing and took her heart rate. She hadn't imagined it, Leonie's pulse was higher. She was fighting.

"Kathleen, can you find Richard or Patrick please." She didn't need to say anything else as Kathleen nodded, her eyes lit up with hope.

"Alfred, squeeze your sister's hand."

Alfred gulped before he did so. A huge smile broke through his tears. "She moved her fingers, Frieda! Leonie moved her fingers."

"Good boy. Can you move over to Sam's side while I examine her?"

Frieda took Leonie's hand. "Squeeze my hand, Leonie. Please."

Leonie squeezed, it wasn't very strong but it was definitely progress.

"She's going to get better isn't she, Frieda?"

"Yes, Alfred, I think so."

"Leonie. You came back. See, I knew she would. Now who's stupid?" Sam threw himself at the bed, making Leonie cry out in pain. Her eyes didn't open. Frieda pulled Sam back, silently berating herself for not anticipating his reaction. She hoped he hadn't hurt Leonie badly.

"Why isn't she opening her eyes, Frieda?" Sam asked, his voice trembling. "Did I hurt her too much?"

"No, darling, you didn't. Your sister's tired. After sleeping for so long, it takes a lot of effort to move her fingers. We have to go now before the nurse gets back."

As the twins lips curled, Frieda hastened to add. "I will sneak you back in tomorrow if you leave quietly now. We need to let Leonie rest, and the doctors will want to examine her."

Alfred put his arm around Sam's shoulders. "Come

on, Sam. Leonie needs us to go home. We have to listen to Frieda."

Frieda opened the door, checked there was nobody in the corridor, and whispered to the boys to wait for her at the door to the hospital as she couldn't leave Leonie alone.

She watched them from the open doorway until they were out of sight. Just two seconds later, she saw Kathleen returning with Richard. Kathleen looked around for the boys, Frieda gestured to the door hoping Kathleen wouldn't say anything to her husband. Frieda intended on keeping her promise to the boys that they could come back tomorrow.

"Kathleen told me she squeezed your hand. Did she open her eyes?"

"No. but they flickered. I'm sure they did. Her pulse was ninety so I believe she was fighting to show us she was awake, but then got too tired."

Richard examined his patient while Kathleen and Frieda watched, Kathleen holding Frieda's hand. It was hard to tell who was comforting who.

"She's breathing a little better, but her pulse has fallen again. Frieda, I don't need to tell you not to get your hopes up too much. It could have been a reflex."

Frieda didn't argue, but she instinctively knew it was Leonie battling to see her siblings.

"Kathleen, take Frieda home and keep her there. Tell Lily or Cook to lock her in her bedroom if necessary. I won't have my doctors fall ill under my care. Frieda, you are not to come back to the hospital until the morning. Leonie won't thank you for working yourself to death."

Frieda nodded.

"I mean it, Frieda. If I see you back here, I will put you on report."

Her head swung up at the threat. Did he mean it? She couldn't read his face.

"Come along Frieda, those two boys will be getting up to mischief if we leave them alone for much longer."

Frieda kissed Leonie on the forehead and whispered into her ear. "I know you are listening. I'll be back tomorrow. With the boys."

# CHAPTER 54

The boys were subdued on the streetcar back home. Nothing Frieda or Kathleen tried could make them smile. Once home, they ran to their room and wouldn't come back out, not even when Cook promised them chocolate cookies.

"Those poor children. I wish Leonie had spoken. What if Richard is right and it was just a reflex? I'll have got their hopes up for nothing."

"Stop second guessing yourself Frieda, Richard is a wonderful doctor but you know Leonie as a friend. My husband will be thrilled for you to prove him wrong. So what is your next plan? Are you taking the boys back tomorrow?"

Frieda grinned at the look of support on Kathleen's face.

"What?" Kathleen asked.

"You like doing battle with Matron don't you? Are you hoping she'll catch us?" Frieda teased.

Kathleen's neck flushed as she denied the accusation. Cook and Lily laughed while Kathleen squirmed.

"I think we should all go. We can take it in turns to sit with Leonie and the boys. They can hide under my skirts if it comes to it." Cook offered.

Everyone looked at her wide frame and burst into fits of giggles. It was exactly what they needed given the horror of the situation. Cook spread her skirts wide. "Don't you think there would be enough room?"

"Stop, you're making my sides hurt." Frieda begged as one joke after another flew around the room. Frieda thanked God for these women who helped her cope with whatever trauma came her way.

Cook dried her eyes on her apron. "Frieda, this is the best news we've had in a very long time. Now off you go to bed. I will bring you up a tray later on. "

Frieda went without argument. She was tired and emotional, and she craved the privacy of her own room. But when she got there, she found Carrie curled up in a ball on Frieda's bed with her thumb in her mouth.

"Carrie, what's wrong?"

"Is Leonie dead? Is that why the boys were crying?"

"No, darling. The boys were crying because we think Leonie might get better. They're happy tears."

"I cry when I'm sad. It's stupid to cry when you're

happy." Carrie protested. Then she wound her arms around Frieda's neck, and pulled herself onto Frieda's lap. "Will Leonie really get better? I miss her. She tells the best stories, and she chases away the monsters."

"What monsters, sweetheart?"

"The ones that come in my dream. They scare me. Leonie used to hold me until they went away. Would you hold me?"

"You want to lie down for a nap?" Frieda clarified.

Carrie nodded, her thumb back in her mouth.

Frieda gathered the child to her, and together they fell asleep. Carrie didn't cry out once. Cook had to wake them later. When she heard about Carries nightmares, she went away and came back with a ragged looking teddy bear. "This is Pugsly. He's slept with me every night since I was little. Would you like to borrow him? He stops me getting bad dreams."

Frieda couldn't speak. She watched Carrie's eyes open wider. "For me? Will he stop mine?"

"Yes, of course. He told me he thinks you are a special little girl."

"Cook, toys don't talk. I'm not a baby."

Cook covered Pugsly's ears. "Don't let him hear you say that. You'll hurt his feelings."

Carrie's eyes nearly popped out of her head. "I'm sorry. Come here Pugsly, I won't ever hurt you, I promise."

Frieda mouthed a thank you to Cook. She could only

imagine what it had cost her to give away something so precious.

# CHAPTER 55

*T*he next few days passed without any improvement in Leonie, despite the twins visiting every morning. Sam got fractious and insisted he wasn't going to the hospital again, but Alfred said they were. Frieda watched Alfred as he checked Leonie's pulse.

"Your mother said you were going to become a doctor or a scientist, Alfred. I think she was right."

"I'm going to be a doctor and cure people like Leonie. There has to be a way to make her wake up."

"You just think you're so wonderful. Leonie isn't going to get better. She just lies there and doesn't move. This is a waste of time. She should have just died when the others did." Sam burst into noisy tears.

"Sam…"

Frieda and the boys stared at Leonie who again whispered, "Sam."

Sam looked to Frieda who nodded. He moved forward and put his hands in Leonie's. "I'm sorry, I shouldn't have said you should have died. I just miss you so much. Please wake up."

Leonie opened her eyes and looked at Sam before they closed again.

"Frieda, she's squeezing my hand. She is. See?" Sam grabbed Frieda's hand and put it on top of Leonie's. Frieda felt the movement.

"Leonie, thank God. You're coming back to us. Don't do too much."

Leonie whispered, "Sam, Alfred, love you. Love Carrie, Morris."

"Why does her voice sound so weird?" Alfred asked as Sam just stared at his sister with a big grin on his face.

"She hasn't used her voice in a long time. It will come back to normal in a little while. Sit down now, and do some of the work Emily gave you. Leonie won't want you falling behind at school."

For once the boys didn't argue. They took out their paper and pencils. "I'm going to write to Leonie to tell her all she missed. That way when she wakes up I won't forget anything." Sam said.

Frieda looked over their heads at Lily who was struggling not to cry. The nurse who was now in on their secret visits went in search of Richard and Patrick.

Leonie grew stronger over the next hours and days. One morning, Sam climbed up on the bed.

"Careful Sam, your big sister has a lot of bruises from the accident. You'll hurt her legs." Frieda glanced at Leonie's face to check she wasn't in pain. Leonie looked horrified.

"He's on my legs? Why can't I feel him? I can't move my legs." Leonie raised terror-filled eyes. "They won't listen."

Frieda hoped her voice would sound more confident than she felt. "In time they might, but for now let's just concentrate on getting you stronger. You've been asleep for a long time."

"You've slept for weeks and weeks. You missed the big funeral, and Easter, and Frieda is getting married." Alfred stood straighter as he spoke. Frieda guessed he was trying to appear older than he was.

"I wanted to tell her that! It's in my letter. Why do you have to spoil things?" Sam pushed Alfred who pushed him right back.

"Boys. Stop fighting. I already knew about Frieda."

Frieda blushed at the words. "You did?"

"Yes. You can tell your doctor fiancé that people who lie in bed can still use their ears."

Frieda turned scarlet, not being able to look Leonie in the eye. She hoped she hadn't heard everything.

"Frieda, thank you for looking after my brothers. I hope they've been better behaved than they were this morning."

"They were wonderful. They get on so well together, but we figured if they started fighting you might just feel you have to intervene."

Leonie turned her head to look at her brothers, "You mean you were playacting?"

"Maybe not all of the time," Sam replied with devastating honesty.

"Sometimes brother, shut your mouth," Alfred said, grabbing Sam. His squeals brought Matron and some doctors running. Frieda wanted to disappear.

"Dr. Klunsberg, what is the meaning of this? I've told you before I won't stand for disruption on my wards. "

"Sorry Matron, but the boys got so excited because Leonie woke up."

She saw Richard push his way forward; he gave her a sly wink before turning to Matron. "Isn't this wonderful news Matron? A miracle if ever there was one! Perhaps you could rustle up a nice cup of tea and some toast for our patient. Thank you."

Matron didn't have a choice but to obey. Frieda mouthed a quick thank you to Richard. He smiled back at her before addressing his patient.

"Leonie Chiver, you nearly gave me heart failure

on more than one occasion. I hope from now on you will behave like a good patient."

Patrick came behind Frieda, putting his arms around her waist and laying his head on her shoulder. "Now can we plan our wedding?"

"Put the poor man out of his misery, Frieda, and set a date. Otherwise, find another room to do your court-ing. This one is mine."

Leonie waved them off with a big smile as Frieda flushed while Patrick laughed before pulling her out of the room.

# CHAPTER 56

*P*atrick pushed Leonie's wheelchair into the church with Frieda walking behind holding Carrie's hand. "Can I be a bridesmaid at your wedding?" Carrie asked.

"Yes, darling. Alice's father is getting married, that's why Emily picked Alice. Now why don't you sit here beside Leonie."

"Will you ever get married, Leonie?" Carrie asked with the frankness of a child. Frieda held her breath wondering how Leonie would react. Sometimes, she would smile and answer her siblings questions, other times she would tell them off.

"I have to learn to walk again first, Carrie. Now be quiet; the service will start soon."

Carrie shifted in her seat until the music started and

then she was all smiles. "She looks lovely doesn't she? Her dress is so pretty."

Frieda had to agree as Emily walked down the aisle on Charlie's arm. Gustav had asked Conrad to be his best man. Maria sat on the other side of the church with Esther and her parents. They had made an effort to come and celebrate the marriage of the man who had saved their daughter. They weren't the only ones either, as Frieda recognized many of the faces from back in the days of the strike.

She turned back to watch Father Nelson marry Gustav and Emily, her eyes filling with happy tears. Patrick squeezed her hand. "This will be us next. I can't wait."

She smiled and squeezed his hand in return. Her finals were coming up, and she didn't want the thought of exams to spoil her wedding day. The Triangle Shirt-waist Trial was set to start early December. Nobody would be able to concentrate on a party until they got the guilty verdict.

The ceremony flew past. Gustav kissed his wife despite her shyness. Frieda couldn't tell which of the couple was the happiest. Alice beamed as she followed her father down the aisle. She'd told everyone she couldn't wait to call Emily mom, and was looking forward to having brothers and sisters. Poor Emily hadn't known where to look when Alice announced this to the crowded room.

Frieda caught up with Leonie a little bit later. She saw her sitting at the edge of the dance floor.

"Would you like something to drink or eat, Leonie?"

"No, thank you."

"Leonie, I know it's hard."

"You don't know anything Frieda. You've never had to sit in a chair and have your friends and family dismiss your opinions. The fact my legs don't work doesn't stop my brain working, does it?"

Shaken, Frieda tried to be patient.

"Leonie, I didn't mean…"

"I know you didn't. I'm sorry. I just get so mad. I feel helpless sitting here not doing anything about my family. What will happen to them, Frieda?'

"They are going to go live in Riverside Springs just as we planned. They'd have gone already, but Richard feels you should be close to the hospital just in case. If the surgeons feel an operation will help you recover the use of your legs, it's best done here in New York."

"Yes, but what if it fails? Or they say they can't do it? I can't let my brothers and sister go to live with Kathleen's sister as charity cases. She's only taking them in because Lily asked her. She doesn't really want them. I was going to work to help with their keep, but who'd employ a cripple?"

At that point, Maria joined them. Leonie hadn't seen Maria walk toward them, but it was clear from Maria's expression she'd heard everything.

"Leonie Chivers, you should be ashamed of yourself, taking your bad temper out on Frieda. Do you know how long she sat by your bed willing you back to full health?"

"Maria, don't."

"No Frieda, she needs to be told. She can't go around snapping people's heads off. Sam is in tears over with Mama. Leonie told him off for something silly. I came over here to knock some sense into you. If Rosa, Mary, Surka, Esther's sister, or any of the other girls had a chance to survive, but live their lives in a chair, what choice do you think they would have made?"

Leonie didn't respond.

"I'll tell you. Rosa would have given both her legs to still be here. Anyone would. At least you get a chance to live. Now do us all a favour, and either put a smile on your face for Gustav's sake or go home. He doesn't deserve you ruining his wedding." Maria looked at Frieda. "Sorry, Frieda, but someone had to tell her." Maria marched off, past Conrad who gave Frieda a questioning look. Frieda could only shrug her shoulders. She couldn't believe Maria had spoken to Leonie like that.

"Leonie, I'm sorry."

"Don't be. She said what you are all feeling. Can you ask someone to take me home, please?" Leonie stared at some point above Frieda's head.

# CHAPTER 57

*F*rieda had to find Patrick as she couldn't maneuver the wheelchair into a cab. Patrick had driven, so he might take Leonie home himself. She quickly outlined what had happened.

Patrick wheeled Leonie out of the party without saying a word. He remained silent all the way home. With Leonie sulking, it made for a horrible trip. Frieda couldn't think of a way to make it better.

On return to the Sanctuary, Cook appeared out of the kitchen.

"What you young ones doing home? I had to rest my feet, couldn't dance another step."

"Maria told me what she thought of me. What you all think of me. It was clear I wasn't welcome, so I left." Leonie's statement left Frieda open mouthed. Cook's mouth thinned, and Frieda waited to be told off. Cook was very fond of Leonie, always making her extra special meals in an attempt to build up her strength.

"Leonie Chivers, what did you do? If I hear you ruined Gustav's and Emily's day, I will take you out of that wheelchair and put you across my knee and give you a hiding. I saw you sulking in the church, but like everyone else, I ignored it because I knew it would be a difficult day. But enough is enough. Everyone in this house has been walking on pins since you came out of that hospital. Nobody can do anything more for you. Not when you have given up. If you ever want to get out of that chair and walk, you better put your energy into your legs and stop being a nasty, ungrateful child. I know you suffered, we all do, but so did many others. Many never came home that day. What would they think of you wasting the rest of your life away in that chair when there is a good chance you could walk again if you put your mind to it? I've held my tongue too long. I don't know what Maria said, but I can guess. I tell you now, I agree with every word she said. Goodnight."

Leonie's mouth fell open as Cook slammed the kitchen door behind her. Frieda glanced at Patrick to see he agreed with Cook.

"Leonie, I can help you upstairs before I take Frieda back to the party."

"No, I will stay with Leonie. You go."

"No, Frieda. Go with Patrick. Leave me here. I need

to be alone for a bit." Leonie whispered. "Thank you, Frieda."

Patrick tugged at Frieda's arm and gestured toward the door. Torn between wanting to go back to the party and guilt over leaving Leonie alone, she stood where she was.

"Please Frieda, go."

Patrick spoke up. "Everyone will be back here in an hour or so. Leonie can manage for that time, can't you?"

Leonie nodded.

"Come on, Frieda. Gustav and Emily will worry."

As soon as they got outside, Patrick held Frieda in his arms. "Darling, Cook and Maria are right. She needs to fight back, or she will stay in the chair forever. Tough love or whatever you want to call it might work. We can't find any medical reason for her not to be able to move."

"But the operation?"

"The operation is a last resort. The surgeons told Dad they could see better if they opened her up, but Dad's written to a friend of his on the West Coast and he believes as Dad does. The trauma has stopped her walking. It isn't a physical issue, but one in her head."

Frieda didn't know enough about spinal injuries to question Richard's beliefs. She muttered, "I just want the old Leonie back."

"That's what everyone wants." He leaned over and

kissed her on the lips. "Please stop worrying about everyone else for just an hour. Let's have some fun."

She kissed him back before ordering him to drive to the wedding party, or they would both be in trouble.

* * *

When they all got home, Leonie was still in the kitchen, her face marked by her tears.

"I've been so selfish, I'm sorry. I was scared, and couldn't see I was hurting you all, too. I will do whatever it takes to get out of this chair by Christmas, I promise."

Patrick handed her his hanky. "Christmas may be pushing it, but I'm thrilled you are going to try, Leonie. Dad is convinced you will walk again."

"I am, too. But if you are, I'm still going to be Frieda's bridesmaid. She asked me first." Carrie's announcement brought a smile to everyone's faces even if they had tears in their eyes.

# CHAPTER 58

DECEMBER 4TH, 1911

*L*ily shifted in her seat as the trial began. Charlie squeezed her hand, reminding her to be quiet, or the Judge may throw her out. They were only there because of Charlie's contacts through work. Lily had to promise not to shout out, regardless of what testimony she heard or what they said.

She listened in horror as Max Steuer, Blanck and Harris' attorney, made each witness sound as if they were lying. Some of the brave women couldn't speak fluent English, and ended up tongue tied after the defense attorney had finished with them. Several times Lily wanted to scream at the Judge to stop the Lawyer attacking the witnesses, but it seemed almost as if the Judge favored Blanck and Harris.

Lily watched the faces of the men on the jury. She couldn't tell how they would vote. Some of them had real poker faces, but this wasn't a card game, they were dealing with people's lives.

When recess was announced, Lily practically jumped out of her seat.

"How can the judge let that go on? That Steuer is attacking the witnesses, making it seem they are lying. Why didn't the prosecution lawyers stop him?"

"Lily, they tried, but it appears the Judge might not be impartial."

"He's supposed to be a good judge. You don't think they paid him off, do you?"

"Lily!" Charlie looked like he wanted to throttle her. "Be quiet. You can't go around throwing accusations like that. Especially not in here."

Lily was too mad to think about being careful.

"Lily, please, for me. I have a reputation to protect. I can't be seen attacking judges in their own courtroom."

"You didn't."

"Yes, but we both know some of these people think I am responsible for everything my wife does. Now let's get out of here and find somewhere to talk, somewhere more private."

Lily fell silent, her love for her husband winning. He deserved her total support. They walked to a small restaurant two blocks away from the courthouse.

Only after they ordered a meal for Charlie and a hot tea for Lily, did Charlie speak again.

"I had my doubts about Crain being the trial judge."

"Why? I read in the papers he was good at what he does."

"He is, usually, but this case may bring back memories. There was a fire years ago in Allen Street. Twenty people died in a tenement, ten of them children."

"I remember. They found the children near a skylight, didn't they?" Lily stirred her drink. Her husband's meal sat in front of him, untouched.

"Crain was the Tenement House Commission Chairman when that happened. His office was blamed for the fact that rubbish and all sorts of material blocked the fire escapes. It cost him his job. He always protested his innocence. I'm wondering if he isn't too sympathetic to Blanck and Harris."

"No, he couldn't be. This is different. Those men locked their workers into the factory and saved themselves. They didn't go back to open doors. How is that the same?"

"I'm not saying it is, I just wonder if it might be the reason he appears to favor Steuer."

"He's another one. Why isn't he prosecuting those two? He's Jewish and he grew up on the East Side for goodness sake. He even worked in a garment factory. He should know and understand what the conditions were like and how unsafe things were."

"Lily, calm down. You won't do yourself any good. Steuer is there because he is Harris and Blancks best chance. Everything you say is true, but you forget something. Steuer had to fight harder than most to get to where he is today. He had to overcome the prejudice against Jews, the poor, his background, him being an immigrant, and all the rest. It makes him fight hard, and he's successful. I wouldn't be at all surprised if he doesn't earn every penny of his fees." Charlie took Lily's hand and caressed it. "You have to face facts, Lily. They could get off."

Lily pulled her hand away. "No. That wouldn't be justice. You heard what Bostwick said. He found the locked door, or at least his detectives did when they dug out the ruins. That's proof they locked the door."

"One door, Lily and it isn't proof the Shirtwaist Kings knew about it." Charlie pushed away his untouched meal after glancing at his watch. "I should get back. You should get home."

"No way. I'm not going anywhere."

"Lily, you --"

"I what?" Lily stared at him.

"Nothing. It doesn't matter what I say, you will do your own thing anyway. Those people mean a lot to you."

He didn't meet her eyes, but paid the check and held the door open for her. They walked back toward the courtroom in silence. But as they neared the door and saw the crowds gathered with the pictures of their loved ones, chanting for justice, she stopped.

"Charlie, you're right. I can't go back in there."

"Are you sure?"

"Yes. You were right, they mean the world to me, but you mean more. I can't promise not to get carried away. I could hurt your career, and we need your skills to help the girls. I'll get a cab to the Sanctuary; I need to be doing something, not sitting at home waiting. You can fill me in on what happens."

He kissed her, right there in the street. It was such an unusual show of affection from her husband, Lily knew she'd done the right thing. She wouldn't help the Triangle Victims by being charged with contempt of court. She could help them at home and let her husband and the Justice system do their job. She'd pray they listened.

She hailed a cab as Charlie walked into the court, the police officers paving the way for him.

*C*harlie kept them informed on the progress of the trial. It didn't sound good.

"They should have let women on the jury. Why did it have to be all men?" Leonie asked one day as they discussed the trial. From the night of Gustav's wedding, Leonie had blossomed. No matter how hard the physical exercises were, she did them without moaning. Her and Cook had grown even closer than before. Maria had been thrilled when Leonie had presented her with a new nightgown, beautifully sewn and embroidered with lace.

Conrad and Maria had forced Maria's mother's hand by eloping and getting married in a civil ceremony. Horrified, Mrs. Mezza had begged Father Nelson to marry the couple in a quiet ceremony before word leaked out Maria and Conrad were living in sin.

"Women can't be jurors, Leonie. Should you be up? You look tired." Kathleen fussed about Leonie's chair.

"I'm fine, Kathleen. I slept most of the night. I will go insane if I have to lie in bed all day." Leonie glanced at Lily. "Could I maybe do some sewing tomorrow? My hands have recovered, and I don't want to lose all my skills. Bella is expecting a trained seamstress, not an invalid."

"Don't call yourself that, and stop worrying about Bella and Riverside Springs. I said you were welcome to stay here for as long as you want, and I meant it. We both did, didn't we, Kathleen?"

Kathleen folded Leonie's blanket again. "Absolutely. You are in no fit state to go traveling all that way. Concentrate on getting better, Leonie."

Lily held her hand to her mouth so Kathleen wouldn't see her smile. She knew her friend was trying to help, but her fussing was driving Leonie up the wall.

The front door banged, announcing Charlie's arrival. He'd promised to come straight back to let them know the Jury's decision. Lily sat biting at her non-existent nails.

"They were acquitted."

Kathleen sank into her chair at Charlie's words, Leonie cried softly, but Lily just stared at her husband.

"The jury took less than two hours to deliberate before delivering their verdict. It wasn't unexpected as

Crain more or less made it impossible to deliver any other verdict."

Lily saw the vein in Charlie's neck pulsing, something that only happened when he was beyond furious. Lily couldn't move. She knew she should offer comfort, but how? What could she say? This was a travesty, and they all knew it.

"Was there a riot?" Kathleen asked. "How did those two murderers react?"

Lily winced at Kathleen's tone. The verdict wasn't Charlie's fault. He took a seat.

"Blanck seemed relieved, if somewhat bemused. He more or less fell back into his seat. Harris's reaction was more closed. Their wives cried. The rest of the courtroom was slower to react. I think everyone was so shocked. It was several seconds before the place erupted. The families of the victims screamed at the defendants and at the Judge. Harris and Blanck had to leave via the Prisoners pen. I guess the Judge didn't think they would be safe being let out the usual way."

"Charlie, this is so wrong. What can we do? Can we appeal?"

"No, Kathleen, we can't do anything. It's done."

Lily studied her husband. "What aren't you telling us?" she asked.

"David Weiner attacked their car. The police took him away, to an asylum. His sister died in the fire, and another was injured." Charlie glanced at Leonie. "Did you know them?"

"Yes, Rose died, and Katie jumped into the elevator shaft, she was in hospital for a long time."

Charlie added, "Seems David lost his mind. Or so they say."

"Did he hurt Harris or Blanck?" Kathleen asked.

"No."

Kathleen stood up. "That's a real pity."

"What else, Charlie?" Lily prompted.

"What else could there be? They got away with it." Kathleen's pacing irritated Lily.

"Kathleen, please sit down. I know my husband. He has more to say."

"I don't think this is the right time, Lily."

"It is, just tell us."

"You told me a while back they made a claim on the insurance. Harris and Blanck pocketed about $60,000—just over $400 for each victim."

Kathleen gasped. "But they only paid the victims $75, and even then, not all of them. You had to prove you were there."

Lily couldn't say anything. She listened to her husband and friends talk as if she was in a bubble and they were outside. How could New York do this to their own? This trial had the potential to show all the immigrants, the factory workers, the poor that they were valued. Instead, it had shown that money always won.

Lily stood up. "I want to go home, Charlie."

She ignored his look of surprise and Kathleen's protests. She kissed Leonie on the cheek and told her to stay strong. She accepted Kathleen's hug, and then without looking walked out of the Sanctuary and into Charlie's automobile.

He started the engine, and only when they were on the road home did he speak.

"Lily, you're worrying me. It's not like you to take news like this quietly."

"It's over, Charlie. I have to accept things will never change."

He protested, but she ignored him. When they got home, she walked past her children and straight to her bedroom. Once inside, she locked the door. She had failed them all.

rieda and Kathleen stood outside Lily's front door, with Frieda trying to calm Kathleen before they rang the bell.

"Frieda, she's been in bed for three days. Lily never stays in bed, not even when she's sick. I don't know what to say to her. I've known her almost twenty years, and I can't help her."

Frieda wished she had convinced Kathleen to stay at home. It would not do Lily any good to see her friend upset.

"Kathleen, remember you promised to stay with Charlie and the children. I need to speak to Lily alone. Doctor to patient, not friend to friend."

"Yes, but --"

"No buts. I know I'm not qualified yet, but Charlie says Lily may speak to me."

Kathleen looked hurt, making Frieda kick herself. "It's because I went through Slocum, and now this. It's not because she doesn't love you."

"I know that. I just feel I failed her."

Frieda felt better after Kathleen snapped. It meant her friend wasn't wallowing. She knocked on the door and stood back to let Kathleen greet Charlie first. She did her best to hide her shock at his appearance. Not only was he disheveled, but he looked like he hadn't slept in months.

"Thank you for coming. Frieda, do you want to go up? It's the second door at the top of the stairs. Kathleen, the children are playing up. I know they are worried, but they're driving me to distraction. Can you help me?"

Frieda knew Kathleen was in good hands, so she made her way upstairs. Hesitating for a second outside Lily's door, she knocked.

"Lily, it's Frieda. Let me in, please."

Silence greeted her. What would she do if Lily refused to open the door? She couldn't kick it down. She tried again, but no reaction. She was about to call for Charlie when she heard the lock click. The door didn't open, so Frieda turned the handle.

The room stank. Frieda wrinkled her nostrils, walking over to the window and opening them first before turning to where Lily was lying on the bed, fully dressed.

"Lily, Charlie asked me to come. He thought you might talk to me."

"Nothing to talk about." Lily turned away, her head facing the wall.

Frieda walked to the other side of the bed and sat down. "Lily Doherty, you have plenty to say, and don't deny it. I know you're hurting and feeling powerless and maybe even scared, but you have people who rely on you. You can't afford to wallow in bed. "

"I can do what I like." Lily spat back.

"No, you can't. You gave that right up when you became a mother. Your children are worried sick. Charlie looks dreadful, almost worse than you do."

Lily's lips curled. For a second Frieda was tempted to laugh and tell Lily she looked like a badly behaved child having a tantrum. Instead, she reached for her friend's hand.

"Lily, I know. More than anyone else, I guess, I know what you are feeling. I've felt it too. When Sarah Cooper died. She was the 16-year-old from the Bronx who jumped onto the street. I thought she'd make it, but she didn't. When Johanna died, I was so frustrated I took it out on Patrick. You never stopped to grieve, and your mind just gave up for a while. It forced your body to rest. But you have to come back to us. We need you."

"I can't do anything for anyone."

"Yes, you can. You can finish the factory."

"I gave that to Gustav to do."

"Then you can help your husband. It's tearing him apart to see you like this. He is hurting too. They have torn asunder his faith in the Justice system. He's quit his job."

Lily sat up a little. "What? But he loves the law. It took him forever to qualify."

"Yes, but he's quit. He says there is no point if money always wins. But it doesn't Lily. Things are changing. They will change. I don't know how many more factory fires will happen or how many will die, but they will change. But the women at the sanctuary, the poor of New York, need someone on their side. They need people like you and Charlie. You have to persuade him to come back and fight their cases. Who else will take on a case and get paid in eggs or shoes or blouses?" Frieda knew Charlie often accepted nothing in payment, but she purposely used the more unusual reimbursements to tickle Lily's sense of humor. "Do you remember when he came back to the Sanctuary covered in chicken poo, carrying that box of cranky birds? The children laughed so hard they were almost sick."

Lily smiled, not her usual wide smile, but it was a start.

"I need you, Lily."

Lily met her gaze for the first time.

"You? What's wrong?"

"It's Kathleen. I love her to bits, but she is driving me nuts with the wedding. It's in two days, Lily and everything is ready, but she isn't satisfied. She wants us to change the color of the flowers. She thinks pink would go better with Carrie's dress. You were supposed to be by my side. Patrick can have his mother." Kathleen had been nothing but kind to her, but Frieda played on her soon to be mother-in-law's reputation for fussing.

Lily blinked but looked back at the covers on the bed. "Kathleen is doing that because she loves you, Frieda."

"And you don't?"

"What?"

"You are lying here when I'm getting married. I thought you were happy for me and Patrick."

"I am, but --"

"But nothing. We aren't asking you to march or go on fundraising drives, just to come to our wedding. Is that too much? After everything we've been through together?"

Frieda hated playing on Lily's guilt, but at this point she was out of options. The next stage was admitting Lily to an asylum, something Frieda wanted to avoid at all costs. Instinctively she knew Lily was in there, she just had to be pulled out of herself. The exhaustion of pushing herself too hard, particularly after the fire had already pushed her right to the edge, but Frieda knew her friend wasn't insane. Far from it.

"Lily. Darn it anyway, I need you, and if I have to

drag you out of the bed and push you into the bath fully dressed, I'll do it."

Lily glared at her, but Frieda remained firm. "I mean it. I'll open that door and call down to Kathleen for backup. You know she won't walk away from you even if she has to move in downstairs. So what's it going to be?"

Lily let out a sob and then another one. Frieda sat on the bed and dragged her friend close. "Cry it out, Lily. You'll feel better."

"I'm just so tired, Frieda. I'm tired of being strong. I don't feel strong anymore. I feel nothing. I just want to stay in this bed and sleep."

"You need a change of scenery. A time to be Lily Doherty again. Not Lily, who runs the Sanctuary, or even mother of five children. Just Lily."

"How can that happen? I don't have a magic wand."

"No, but you have an amazing husband. Lily, Charlie wants to look after you, protect you, love you. Let him. You've always been so strong and not needed him."

"I need him. I couldn't live without him."

"So let him see that. He wants to take you away on a trip to Europe. Go with him, Kathleen will mind the children, you know she will. Not that the older boys need much minding."

"Are you kidding? If I leave, Laurie will get into the first plane he finds."

"So let him. If Laurie grew up near Maria, he would be out working. He could even be engaged, married, you could be a grandmother."

"Frieda. That's going too far even for you."

Frieda smiled, Lily was fighting back. It was a step in the right direction.

"I'm tired, Frieda. I can't explain it. Every bone in my body feels like it is one hundred years old. I just don't believe I can jump out of bed and be the old Lily."

"So invent a new one. Maybe it's time to leave the Sanctuary to Kathleen's capable hands. Leave the orphan train work to Father Nelson and his friends. Find another cause, start a new chapter of your life, but first take some time to get to know your husband, to enjoy your marriage, and to find joy in life. Go see Las Ramblas in Barcelona, the Louvre in Paris, and the green fields of Ireland. Charlie has his dream trip all planned out. He has for years, if Kathleen is right."

"Yes, he's been talking about it since we got married." Lily picked at the bedcover.

"Charlie needs to get away, too. If you can't do it for yourself, do it for him."

Frieda stood up. She'd done her bit. It was up to Lily now.

"I get married on Saturday. It would mean the world to me for you to be there. Please, Lily."

She walked over to the door. Lily hadn't answered.

When she looked back, her friend was staring ahead, deep in thought.

"Did it work?" Kathleen asked as soon as Frieda came down the stairs.

"I don't know. I told her I wanted her at the wedding. I guess we will see."

Kathleen looked like she wanted to cry. Frieda said goodbye to Charlie and dragged Kathleen out of the house. The last thing that poor man needed was Kathleen or Frieda sobbing on his shoulder.

# EPILOGUE

## THE SANCTUARY, 31ST DECEMBER 1911.

rieda paced the floor of her room, trying to even her breathing. Her heart was racing and making her dizzy. A knock on her door admitted Lily.

"You came." Frieda moved to embrace her friend, but Lily held her back.

"You'll crush your dress. You look incredible, Frieda. So beautiful. Patrick is a lucky man."

Ignoring the remark about crushing her dress, Frieda enveloped Lily in a hug. "You came. Thank you."

"No, sweetheart, thank you. You are wise beyond your years, Frieda Klunsberg. I spoke to Charlie, and we are going to London with you and Patrick."

"You are? That's wonderful!"

"Don't worry, we won't encroach on your newlywed

life. We will head to France and Ireland." Lily took up a brush. "Do you want me to do your hair?"

"Yes, please. I can't get it to sit properly."

Lily brushed Frieda's hair. "Thank you for giving me a dressing down, Frieda. I don't know what came over me, but whatever it was, it's getting better. I won't lie, I still can't sleep properly, but I can get out of bed. Last night, Laurie made me laugh, and that felt good."

Just then Maria interrupted them, "What's wrong with you two? Second thoughts?"

"I don't know, Maria. Nervous, I guess. Were you, when you married Conrad?"

Maria put a hand over her swelling stomach. "Me, no. Relieved would be the better word. Mama would have had heart failure if we hadn't got married in a church before this came out."

Frieda knew Maria's mother would have taken forever to give the young couple permission to marry. She couldn't blame them for jumping the gun, so to speak. She'd been tempted too, if she was honest, but she and Patrick had waited.

Lily stood back as Maria arranged Frieda's veil. "I'll leave you to it. Frieda, see you downstairs." Lily kissed her on the cheek before she left. Frieda didn't realize she was staring at the door until Maria poked her.

"You want to marry Patrick, don't you?"

"Yes, more than anything. I'm just not sure about living in London. I will miss New York."

"But this is an amazing opportunity for Patrick, and maybe you, too. Didn't you say you wanted to see the Women's hospital?"

"See it, not live beside it," Freida retorted before taking a seat on her bed. "Maria, what am I going to do without all of you? You are my family, and I will be on the other side of the world."

"Don't you start me off, you know what I am like. I cry at the drop of a hat. I will miss you Frieda, but you and Patrick are meant to be. This is his chance to shine, not as Richard Green's son, but as a doctor in his own right. You know he would still be in his father's shadow no matter what hospital he worked at on the East Coast. Richard's reputation as a burns specialist has only intensified since the fire. Patrick needs to be his own man. In London he can be Dr. Patrick Green. "

Frieda reached for Maria's hand. "How did you get so wise?"

"I don't know. Something about having friends like you and Lily and Kathleen. And Anne Morgan. Times are changing Frieda. Before this little one is grown, we will have the vote. Women will be equal to men in every way. You just wait and see."

"Still my revolutionary friend, aren't you?"

Maria shrugged, "Someone has to keep the fight

going here while others are off gallivanting. Will you be taking tea at the castle?"

"I don't know." Frieda replied, trying to be serious. "Lily has contacts everywhere. Wouldn't surprise me if she didn't get an invitation to court."

Frieda and Maria were giggling as they acted out being in court when Kathleen and Lily knocked and came in.

"We came up to see what the delay was. Frieda, you look wonderful. Doesn't she, Lily?"

Lily winked at Frieda. Kathleen was fussing, but that was just her way.

"She does. Fit for a princess."

Frieda and Maria exchanged a look, then the giggles hit again.

At the bemused looks on her friend's faces, Frieda tried to be mature.

"We were talking about Lily being presented at court before you two came in. That's why it's funny."

Lily and Kathleen didn't get the joke, but it no longer mattered. They heard Charlie shout up the stairs.

"Miss Klunsberg, I believe I am to escort you somewhere."

Charlie had agreed to give Frieda away as Richard was standing in as Patrick's best man. Frieda stood and let her friends fix her hair again and pull imaginary threads from her dress.

"I shall really miss you guys." She said as she hugged them all.

"You're stuck with me, darling." Lily replied.

Kathleen and Maria hugged. "We will have to keep each other company, Maria, while these two go gallivanting across the pond."

Lily threw her eyes up to heaven, "Charlie and I will be back before you know it. We are traveling back on the Titanic. Charlie told me this morning."

"On its maiden voyage. That's so sweet of Charlie. He really wants to make this a vacation you won't forget, Lily."

"More like he knows you will kill him if we don't stay in London for at least a month. Three months seems extreme though, Kathleen."

"You won't be in London for three months. Charlie wants to take you to Ireland to see where his folks came from. And you will have to tour around England, Scotland, and Wales. You won't have enough time for all the things you are going to see."

Kathleen moved to take Frieda's arm. "Most of all you will have to make sure my new daughter in law is as happy in London as she can be. I will miss you and Patrick so much, Frieda."

"Don't make Frieda cry. Come on, off you go downstairs. Carrie and Alice are waiting patiently, but Carrie won't keep her dress clean for long. Leonie will get tired. We will have to be at the church soon or Father Nelson will have a panic attack."

Kathleen held her hands up in mock surrender, "Lily, let's go. Maria, getting married made you bossier than ever."

Maria and Frieda exchanged a last hug before they two followed their friends down the stairs and out to the road where the automobiles stood waiting.

# HISTORICAL NOTE

This book would not have been possible but for so many amazing authors who have written non fiction accounts of the Triangle Shirtwaist Fire. In particular, I would recommend you read David Von Drehle's book - Triangle: The Fire That Changed America. I would also like to highlight skilled researcher, Michael Hirsch who finally, after years and years of research, in 2011 gave a name to every victim of the fire.

I have tried, where possible, to remain true to the events of the fire itself. But some details I had to change for the sake of the story and others, well they were simply too horrific to include in the book. If you ever look at old newspapers from this era, you will see that they do little to hide the horrors associated with tragedies of this type. I admit I was also conscious that discussing this fire would bring up memories of 9/11.

While the main characters in my books are fiction, they are often based on real life stories. There are real life characters too. These include, but are not limited, to the victims of the fire for example, the Maltese ladies. The meeting between Mr. Maltese and Maria's mother at the party or with Maria in the aftermath of the fire did not happen. Celia did escape with her fur muff and was in hospital after the fire. The Wegodner family, father and son met each other hours after the fire, having each believed the other was dead. I can't remember whether they were hospitalized or not.

David Weiner did try to attack Harris and Blanck, his sister Rose had died in the fire and his other sister, Katie was horribly injured.

Harris and Blanck went on to open new factories although they never attained the level of success they had previously enjoyed. Less than seventeen months after the fire, a fire inspector allegedly found locked doors at Blanck's new shirtwaist factory.

Nobody actually knows how the fire began, the suspected cause was a lit cigarette. But what people do know is that greed and the pursuit of fortune was what caused the fire. Nor were these factory owners the only ones to blame. Countless people ignored the perils attached to working conditions at that time. In fact, there is an argument that the Triangle provided better working conditions than many other similar employers.

My editor suggested I change the name Rose in my

book but so many people at that time were called Rose. Maria's sister was Rosa in a previous book before I thought about writing about this fire. It was too late to change her name and that of Leonie's sisters. I know it gets confusing but Rose Schneiderman, was a well known Trade Union activist who spoke out about the Tragedy. Lilian Wald should be better known in society for all the work she did with, and for New Yorkers. Francis Perkins went on to work with President Roosevelt and was instrumental in the creation of the New Deal. She was also the first female cabinet member. Finally, most people have heard of JP Morgan. My hope in writing about Anne Morgan and her friends was to raise their profile a little higher. I may not agree with all of their actions but the work these women did for the workers of America, and New York in particular, shouldn't be forgotten.

## Clover Springs Mail Order Brides

Katie (Book 1)

Mary (Book 2)

Sorcha (Book 3)

Emer (Book 4)

Laura (Book 5)

Ellen (Book 6)

Thanksgiving in Clover Springs (book 7)

Christmas in Clover Springs (book8)

Erin (Book 9)

Eleanor (book 10)

Cathy (book 11)

Mrs. Grey (book 12)

## Clover Springs East

New York Bound (book 1)

New York Storm (book 2)

New York Hope (book 3)

## Writing as Ellie Keaton

Women & War (World War II fiction)

Gracie

Penny

Molly

# ABOUT THE AUTHOR

Thank you so much for reading my books. Readers like you have made it possible for me to live the life of my dreams. Even now, after twenty or so books, I still have to pinch myself.

When my twelve year old son saw the new print copies of Orphan Train Escape, he said, "It's awesome people read your stories." It truly is, so thank you.

I love to hear from my readers so please do contact me at my website, Rachelwesson.com

Made in the USA
Middletown, DE
16 February 2023

24951399R00215